"You wan

Seth said knowingly.

Cassandra's chin came up. "Yes. I want the story, and so would you." Defiance glittered in her eyes. "This is news, Mr. Winter, with a capital "*N*." She rose and walked toward him. "Every reporter in Paris would give his right arm to talk to these people. If I play my cards right, I may be able to interview them. Do you know what that could mean?"

"A Pulitzer Prize for you. My, you are driven, aren't you?"

Cassandra halted in front of him, aware of, but unable to identify, the intense emotion he radiated. "What I am is a reporter," she said calmly.

"No," Seth contradicted. "That's what you do for a living. What you *are* is something else entirely."

SILHOUETTE BOOKS
300 East 42nd St., New York, N.Y. 10017

ISBN: 0-373-07290-2

First Silhouette Books printing June 1989

All the characters in this book are fictitious. Any
resemblance to actual persons, living or dead, is
purely coincidental.

®: Trademark used under license and
registered in the United States Patent and
Trademark Office and in other countries.

Printed in the U.S.A.

LYNN BARTLETT

Although Lynn is well-known in the publishing field as an author of historical fiction, writing contemporaries is a natural outgrowth of her lifelong belief in connecting literature with the politics and the society of its author. But around the Minnesota neighborhood where she lives with her husband and daughter, Lynn is known simply as "Andrea's mother, who also writes books."

Ten Years Ago

TERRORIST ATTACK CLAIMS TWO

By Henri Bruton
Dateline News Service

PARIS—The quiet suburb of Auteuil became the latest scene of terrorist activity when a bomb exploded on one of its residential streets last night. In a communiqué delivered to the authorities, a group calling itself the People's Revolutionary Committee for Freedom has claimed responsibility for the blast that took the lives of two Americans and critically injured a third.

Twenty-eight-year-old Rachel Winter and her daughter Angela, eighteen months, were sitting in the family automobile when an explosive device attached to the vehicle's undercarriage was apparently detonated by remote control. Seth Winter, thirty, husband and father of the victims, was approaching the automobile when the bomb exploded. As a precaution, the police have refused to reveal which hospital admitted Winter for treatment of his injuries. In a statement issued early this morning, however, the authorities said that Winter's condition is "grave" and that the doctors attending him have refused to comment on the chances for Winter's recovery.

The PRCF, in their communiqué, stated that Winter—a journalist for Dateline News Service—was targeted by them because of "the biased coverage he has given the People's Revolutionary Committee for Freedom, despite our repeated and continuous efforts to have him report the truth about our struggle to free our oppressed brothers everywhere."

Chapter 1

PARIS NUMBED BY ATTACKS

By C. Blake
Dateline News Service

PARIS—The crowds have thinned along the city's broad boulevards and the residents of the City of Light now avoid the sidewalk cafés that they have patronized for years. A siege mentality has taken control of Paris in the wake of the recent wave of terrorist attacks that have left seventeen people dead and sixty injured.

As of this morning, no group had claimed responsibility for the indiscriminate violence, nor had any demands been made of either the city or national governments. At a press conference today, the premier denounced the attacks and declared that he would take "any and all steps necessary" to find the suspected terrorists and bring them to justice.

This afternoon, however, a tape was delivered to a member of the press. On the tape, a man claiming to belong to a political action party called the Freedom Brigade, said the Brigade was responsible for the violence that has erupted in Paris. The attacks will continue, he said, "until the Western governments admit that we speak for those who cannot speak for themselves—for those whose voices cannot be heard beyond the borders of refugee camps and the bars of their prison cells. We are not criminals, but we will do whatever is necessary to free our brothers and sisters."

When questioned, a spokesperson for the counterterrorist community would say only that, to the best of his knowledge, no terrorist group known as the Freedom Brigade was known to exist.

The hardest part of returning to Paris was walking into the building that housed Dateline News Service. Dateline hadn't joined the exodus of business to Neuilly or Auteuil; the powers that be had preferred their Paris bureau to remain close to the heart of the city. The building had been renovated since his sojourn here, yet had managed to retain the eighteenth-century charm of its marble floors, oak wainscoting, and heavy doors with frosted glass panes. The lobby was different now. He had been stopped by the two-man team of security guards just inside the front doors. One of the guards had checked him with a hand-held metal detector while the other had scrutinized his identification. He'd apologized for setting off the metal detector, but the second guard had merely nodded, frisked him just to make certain his excuse was valid, and made a notation beside his name in the log.

The offices themselves hadn't changed. There was a large, central room that had been partitioned off. At one end was the glass-enclosed office of the bureau chief; at the other were the teleprinter room and darkroom. In between stood six desks, each with its own computer terminal, where the full-time journalists and part-time stringers worked.

There was only one person on duty this Sunday night, a stringer by the name of Armand Pommier. Because of the party, Armand had explained apologetically. No one had expected him to visit the office tonight. He had nodded, assuring the young Frenchman that he had merely stopped by on impulse.

In fact, he had spent the past three days adjusting to Paris after his prolonged, self-imposed exile. The final step in his adjustment was this visit, and his courage had nearly deserted him in the lobby.

He walked slowly into the bureau chief's office and flicked on the overhead light. His office now; Henri had packed all his belongings during the past week, leaving him with a battered wooden desk and a swivel chair on casters that, he discovered when he sat down, was definitely uncomfortable. He'd have to find a new chair.

His dark eyes roamed over the scarred desktop and came to rest on the basket containing the day's releases. His left hand trembled as he pulled the dispatches out and glanced over them. All had been transmitted to New York this evening, at six o'clock Paris time. He stopped at the dispatch written by C. Blake. The words seemed to take on a life of their own, reaching out to constrict his breathing. C. Blake was good. He gave a fair, balanced account of the day's events, which grabbed the reader's emotions even while its tone remained completely detached. "A journalist's job is to give an objective, bloodless accounting of news. If you can't do that, I suggest you write fiction." A corner of his mouth twitched in a mirthless reaction to the memory. Journalism 101. He'd been very young, very idealistic, and very hungry for success. He wasn't any of those anymore, and he had long since forgotten the professor's name.

He carefully smoothed the dispatch, which he had unknowingly crumpled in his fist, and returned it to the basket. He was going to have to keep an eye on C. Blake, particularly since he was willing to bet that Blake was the one who had received the tape.

He rose shakily to his feet and left the office. He had accepted the job in order to bury the memories, and if it wasn't as easy as he had thought it might be, he would deal with it later. Right now he had a party to attend.

"What did you get Henri?"

Kurt Leihmann grinned down at his companion. "Something perfectly in keeping with his personality."

"That's not an answer!"

"It's as much of an answer as you'll get from me. You can wait until he opens it, just like everyone else." He laughed when the woman at his side gave a disgruntled "hmph" and developed an overwhelming interest in the color of her wine. "I'll tell you if you tell me."

Brilliant aquamarine eyes rolled heavenward before glaring at him. "That's childish."

"You're the one who has an overdeveloped sense of..." He paused, searching for the correct translation. "Competition," he finished.

One finely arched brow rose. "Your English is improving."

"I wish I could say the same for your German."

"My German is progressing nicely, you said so yesterday."

Kurt nodded halfheartedly. "Quote me correctly, please. I said it was progressing nicely in comparison to your French, which is," he waited until he had her full attention, "egregious."

"Egregious? Egregious!" Cassandra couldn't help herself, she burst out laughing.

Kurt tried to look hurt, but when she buried her face in his shoulder and howled with glee he simply wrapped an arm around her waist and tried to ignore everyone's knowing looks. He and this woman were fierce competitors when it came to scooping one another, but they were also the best of friends. It was a relationship that confused all of their coworkers and drove Henri Bruton, their bureau chief, to distraction. In the past six months, he had taken to handing them their assignments and then disappearing into his office, out of harm's way.

The laughter had subsided into throaty chuckles and Kurt looked down at her. "Are you finished?"

"Almost."

Those fascinating eyes flashed up at him and he was lost. His lips curled into a smile. "The word was not correct?"

"Oh, Kurt, the word was *very* correct," she assured him. "Particularly when referring to my French accent. But egregious." She convulsed in silent laughter once more. "For a moment I thought you'd swallowed a thesaurus!" She composed herself and began rummaging through her purse.

"A wooden duck."

Cassandra paused in the act of lighting a cigarette. "I beg your pardon?"

"A wooden duck," he repeated. " I bought Henri a wooden duck. You know how he enjoys hunting."

Her brows furrowed. "You bought Henri a decoy as a retirement gift?"

"No. I bought him a wooden duck," he patiently reiterated. "You know, one that's carved and painted. For decoration."

"Oh."

"I did make one minor modification to it," he went on. "I had a friend of mine hollow it out and then we filled it with steel pellets. The damn thing must weigh twenty pounds. I hope he doesn't set it on anything fragile."

Her lips twitched. "He can always use it as a doorstop."

"True." He arched a demanding eyebrow at her and she sighed.

"Walking shorts."

"Was?" Kurt was so startled that he spoke in his native German.

"Walking shorts," she said with an air of deep satisfaction. "I had my sister get them back in the States. I couldn't find any here that were exactly the right, um, color."

He nodded in complete understanding. "Did you sign your card?"

"Are you crazy? I didn't even include a card."

"Me either." They grinned at each other with the mutual anticipation of coconspirators. "Would you like some more wine?"

"Yes, please." She handed her glass to Kurt. "And bring back some of those crunchy things. I'm starved."

Hearing that command, Clarice Bruton turned away from her conversation and stepped over to the younger woman. "Those crunchy things are canapés, you barbarian, and I spent most of the afternoon working on them," she teased. Her brown eyes narrowed in concern as she took in the other woman's expression. "What's wrong, Cassandra?"

"Nothing, Clarice." Cassandra turned away to crush out her cigarette.

"Of course. Come along, I think you need some air." She took Cassandra's arm and led her out to the balcony.

"I'm not drunk," Cassandra protested, but she allowed herself to be tugged into the mild June night. Leaning against the railing, she looked back into the apartment and the milling guests. "It's a lovely party."

"Yes, it is," Clarice agreed. "I'm enjoying this one far more than the official one Dateline gave last week." She took a tentative sip from her wineglass. "And I know you aren't drunk. Henri was very upset when he came home today. At first I thought it was because this was his last day, but I know him too well. His mood—and yours—has to do with a story, does it not?"

"Clarice, I would tell you if I could. But I can't." Cassandra gave her an apologetic smile.

The older woman nodded her understanding. "This is a bad time for Paris, but it will pass." She reached out and squeezed Cassandra's hand. "Be careful. Journalists are such opportune targets."

"I will." Clarice left her with a final smile and Cassandra hunted for another cigarette. In the stress of the past few weeks she had resumed the habit she had given up barely a year ago. Well, if I get cancer the Freedom Brigade can always claim another victim, she thought darkly. She resolutely pushed such grim thoughts aside and went back into the apartment to claim her wine and canapés from Kurt. Terrorists or not, she planned to enjoy Henri's retirement bash.

By the time Henri got around to opening his gifts, the party was in full swing. Half of Paris had to be in attendance, Cassandra thought as she wound her way through the crush of journalists to refill her glass and Kurt's. She was slightly tipsy. That realization came when Renaud Malat, a *Le Matin* reporter made a grab for her as she tried to squeeze past him and she failed to avoid his grasp.

"You look stunning," Renaud said, his voice just loud enough to be overheard by the people around them.

She was trapped, clutching an empty wineglass in each hand. There was only one thing to do. Batting her eyelashes, she managed a variation on the "What, this old thing?" routine, smiled vapidly and brought the thin heel of her pump down on his toes. She was released immediately and she scampered across the entryway and into the kitchen before Renaud could decide to pursue their meeting. While she was struggling with a corkscrew the apartment buzzer rang and she heard Henri demand that someone answer the door. Cassandra ignored the demand and resumed her battle with the corkscrew. A roar of laughter came from the living room and a few moments later the buzzer sounded again and Cassandra stuck her head out the kitchen door and glanced across the entryway. The guests, as well as Henri and Clarice, were involved with the gag gifts that were the highlight of the evening.

The buzzer sounded a third time.

With a resigned sigh, Cassandra tucked the wine bottle, corkscrew angling dangerously from its top, under her arm and retrieved her two glasses. She'd let Kurt wrestle with opening the wine. Men liked to do macho things like that, anyway. As she crossed the entryway the buzzer let out another sharp demand. She transferred the second glass to her left hand with a dexterity that she thought would have done a juggler proud, and opened the apartment door.

And stared.

Directly in front of her was a large box wrapped in brilliant silver metallic paper and topped by a stunning bow. The bow was black and wasn't really a bow at all; it was a very realistic, stuffed, furry spider and Cassandra instinctively took a step back. "What, in God's name, do you call that?"

"I call it a spider. What do you call it?"

Cassandra blinked and looked up at the masculine face partially concealed by the bow. He was very attractive, she noted absently; black, satanic brows enhanced his dark eyes and his tan had obviously been acquired through hours in the sun rather than on a tanning bed. The way he was staring at her made her uncomfortably aware that she hadn't answered his question. "Ugly, disgusting." She wrinkled her nose. "Give me another five minutes, and I'm sure I can come up with something appropriate."

"I don't doubt it. However, the box is rather heavy." When she made no move to step out of his path, he sighed inwardly. "Could I come in?"

Her gaze had fallen back to the spider. It was fascinating, in a repelling sort of way. It even had red glass eyes. "I don't think so—not if you intend to give that to Henri. You'll send him into cardiac arrest." She wondered who this man was. A friend of Henri's, obviously, she told herself acidly when she found her eyes wandering back to his face.

He had had enough. The past three days had worked on his nerves, and now this ditzy blonde in a black cocktail dress held up purely by positive thinking didn't even have the common courtesy to let him into the apartment. Impatient with the entire business, he simply started walking forward.

Cassandra fell back as the spider moved closer. She was vaguely aware of the door slamming shut behind Henri's last guest.

What is wrong with this woman, he wondered as his impatience turned into aggravation when she simply stood in his way like a rock. "Look, I don't mean to be rude, but I was invited to this party and I'd like to give Henri his gift. So, if you wouldn't mind getting out of my way..." He allowed the request to trail off and fixed her with a hard stare.

She slowly shook her head from side to side and reluctantly started toward the living room. "Okay, but Henri isn't going to like this."

In fact, Henri loved it. He laughed so hard that tears rolled down his face and he gave the spider a place of honor atop Kurt's steel pellet-filled duck. The gift the spider had been guarding turned out to be an old typewriter painted a garish purple which, the man said, would go perfectly with the purple prose Henri was planning to write during his retirement. Henri threw an arm around the taller man's shoulders and assured him that the typewriter would go wonderfully well with a pair of walking shorts another of his friends had given him. The newcomer viewed the lurid shorts done in a pink, green and lavender plaid with an expression that fell short of revulsion, but not by much.

"Those are horrible," he told Henri.

"*Oui,*" Henri agreed, and then surveyed his guests. "Cassandra. Come here, my dear."

Still clutching the wine bottle, Cassandra reluctantly joined Henri and his friend.

"Seth, I would like you to meet Cassandra Blake, one of my best reporters." Henri positively oozed Gallic charm when he delivered the final blow. "Cassandra, this is Seth Winter, your new bureau chief."

Chapter 2

Seth Winter, Cassandra decided five minutes later, was the handsomest thing she'd seen in a long time, even if his black suit did make him look like the Prince of Darkness. His black hair was clipped short in a futile effort to control its intriguing waves, and his dark eyes were positively mesmerizing. Her gaze slid to his left hand. No ring. Not that it mattered, she told herself sternly; he was going to be her boss, nothing else. A love interest was far down on her list of priorities. In a purely feminine gesture, she unconsciously lifted a hand to check that no wayward strands of hair had escaped the confines of the rhinestone clip at the back of her head. Studying Seth while he was introduced to Kurt, she became aware of the sheer physical presence of the man. He stood at least six foot three and was built like a tank, she thought whimsically. She was certain that no one in their right mind had ever tried to block his access to a phone when a story had just broken. Or if they had, she amended, a smile coming to her lips, they had only tried once.

She was still smiling when Kurt bent and whispered in her ear, "Pull yourself together, *Liebchen*; you're drooling."

As luck would have it, Seth Winter chose that exact moment to look at her, his brows coming together at the intimate picture she and Kurt made.

"You two make a good team," he said, pausing just long enough to make the remark sound insinuating before adding, "I particularly liked your pieces on the Dassault Mirage fighter jet."

"Thank you," Kurt acknowledged with a smile. He hadn't missed Seth's quick frown or Cassandra's answering blush. "I wish I could take credit for discovering the faulty arming mechanism, but Cassandra is the one with a contact inside Dassault."

"Really?" Seth turned an assessing eye on Cassandra. "You're to be congratulated. You left the competition in the dust on that story."

Cassandra smiled. "That's the name of the game, isn't it? Do it first and do it better."

Seth nodded. She wasn't terribly pretty, at least not in the conventional sense of the word. Her features were off just enough to preclude true physical beauty—her nose was just a fraction too short to suit the subtle oval of her face and her cheekbones weren't quite high enough—but her eyes compensated for such slight defects. They were large, tilted slightly upward at the corners, and their aquamarine depths dominated her face and reflected the intelligence and empathy that marked her reporting. That empathy invited confidences, assured understanding; the intelligence trapped the unsuspecting, found the truth behind the conceits. A dark premonition curled through his mind with that last thought. He had the feeling that Cassandra Blake was going to prove to be a very dangerous lady. "You're very ambitious."

Her unwavering gaze met his. Ambition was rampant in this profession; no reporter could survive, let alone prosper, without it, but he made it sound like a dread disease. "Yes, I am," she admitted bluntly. "Someday I plan to have your job."

Kurt chuckled and draped a protective arm around Cassandra's shoulders when the other man's black eyes narrowed at her reply. "She means it, you know," he said lightly, finding the interplay between his friend and their new boss amusing.

"I don't doubt it," Seth replied, feeling that curl of premonition again. He had had that same ambition once and look where it had brought him—and what it had cost him along the way.

Henri smoothly intervened. "There is, perhaps, something Cassandra should discuss with you," he told Seth.

"Oh?" Seth was aware that Cassandra's features altered slightly at Henri's statement. The light in her eyes dimmed and was replaced by stubborn determination.

"Yes, I suppose Henri is right." She took a firmer grip on her evening bag and glanced at the crowded room. "Is your office available, Henri?"

"Of course." Henri gestured to the hallway on his right. "You know where it is. Come along, Kurt, *Le Match* has just hired a new photographer who is dying to meet you." The two men turned and plunged back into the milling guests.

Cassandra took one look at the grim expression on Seth's face and fervently wished she were anyplace else. "I'm sorry; this is terribly rude of me. What I have to say can wait until tomorrow at the office."

"Henri doesn't think so or he wouldn't have brought it up." Seth placed a hand under her elbow and steered her through the crowd to the hallway. "Let's get it over with."

An odd way to phrase it, she thought, and then he was opening the door for her and they stepped into Henri's office.

"Just as I remembered it," Seth observed. Henri's office was paneled in dark wood and, in contrast to the rest of the apartment, cluttered with books. The shelving had long ago proved insufficient, so books were piled on the floor, the desk, and the two leather armchairs. The only light came from the desk lamp and the room was a study in shadows. Seth cleaned off one of the chairs and inclined his head toward it. "Sit down."

Cassandra would rather have remained standing, but there was something about the way he issued the command that made her obey. Instead of taking the other chair, as she had expected, he rested a hip against a corner of Henri's desk and stared down at her with thinly veiled hostility. "You've known Henri a long time?'' she asked politely, trying to take some of the edge off the situation.

"Yes." Seth felt a smile curl the corners of his mouth as he looked around the room. "He's still a pack rat." The smile vanished abruptly. "So, tell me about the big story that's consuming you."

"How do you know it's a story?"

He grunted and folded his arms across his chest. "I've read your stuff, Miss Blake. You're a damn good reporter on her way to becoming a damn fine reporter who will be able to write her own ticket in a few years. What else but a story would drag you away from all the shoptalk out there?"

She frowned. "You seem to have an awfully low opinion of your chosen profession."

"Not at all," he replied. "About the story..."

"This afternoon the Freedom Brigade contacted me," she said, deciding to put an end to their verbal fencing. It was a relief to have the information out in the open, but her comfort was short-lived when she saw the transformation Seth underwent. She wouldn't have believed it possible for the man's face to turn any harder, but that was exactly what happened when he assimilated her statement.

"I see." Seth had to force the words past the constriction in his throat. "How was it done?"

"By phone," she answered, leaning forward in order to see him better. "It's really quite amazing that they reached me at all. I normally don't go in to the office on Sunday, but I wanted to read through some research material that I left in my desk on Friday." She shrugged. "Anyway, I tried to tape the conversation, but he didn't stay on the line long enough for me to set up the recorder."

"Did you contact the authorities?"

She nodded. "Henri insisted. I called the Sûreté immediately, but there was nothing they could do."

"Except put a tap on the phone."

A chill crept up her spine at the lack of emotion in his voice. "What are you? Psychic?"

Seth was staring at the parquet floor. "No, Miss Blake, I'm not psychic, just experienced."

She watched the play of light across his features. "There is something else," she said hesitantly, unable to shake the feeling that she was sitting on a stack of dynamite. "The group that's been operating here didn't have a name until today, when a tape was delivered to the Dateline office. The speaker identified the group as the Freedom Brigade—"

"There's no need to continue, Miss Blake," Seth intervened. "I stopped by the office tonight and read your dispatch. I assume the tape is safely in the hands of the Sûreté?"

Cassandra nodded.

He took a deep breath. "Let me ask you a question. If Henri hadn't insisted, would you have called the Sûreté?"

His gaze shifted, pinning her to the chair. "I don't—that is, I'm not certain what you're asking," she replied.

He gave a short bark of laughter. "Please, Miss Blake, don't play that kind of game with me. It insults my intelligence and yours. Just answer my question."

Cassandra swallowed nervously. "I'm not certain what I would have done. Neither the tape nor the phone call revealed anything of any importance. The man did not make any threats, gave no clues as to where the group is hiding. . . ." Her voice trailed off at his grim expression.

"Well, that's honest, at least," he said when they had sat in silence for several moments. "Is there any reason to expect that the terrorists will try to get in touch with you again?"

"He—the man I talked to—said they wanted their side of the story told. Yes, I think he'll call again." She paused. "How do you want me to handle it?"

The question was so naive, he thought, as if she believed there was a simple answer. And maybe, for her, the answer was simple. He had thought so, once. "There is no way to *handle* this. You can kill the story, refuse to have any further communication with the Brigade."

"They'll just go somewhere else, to a different paper or agency."

"To a different reporter," he added knowingly, challengingly.

Her chin came up. "Yes."

"You want the story."

It wasn't a question, but she chose to treat it as one. "Yes, I want the story, and so would you." Defiance glittered in her eyes. "This is news, Mr. Winter—news with a capital *n*." She rose and walked toward him. "Every reporter in Paris would give his right arm to talk to these people, to get some sort of statement from them. If I play my cards right, I may be able to *interview* them. Do you know what that could mean?"

"A Pulitzer for you," he hazarded. "My, my, you are driven, aren't you?"

Cassandra had halted directly in front of him, aware of, but unable to identify, the intense emotion he radiated. "What I am is a reporter," she said calmly.

"No," Seth contradicted. "That's what you do for a living. What you are is something else entirely."

She had the feeling that he had just delivered some sort of insult, but she didn't know him well enough to force the issue. Drawing herself up to her full five feet seven inches, she said, "So you want me to kill the story?"

Seth slowly got to his feet. Only inches separated them, and he was suddenly aware of her perfume and the way the black crepe of her dress draped her curves. He was attracted to her, he realized with some distant part of his mind, and that was insanity. His life was complicated enough right now. "What I want," he said carefully, feeling as if he were balancing on a finely honed blade, "is for you to remember what you are, and that is, hopefully, a responsible journalist. I want you to report any—and I do mean any—contact with the terrorists to the Sûreté and to me. And if I think that the situation is getting out of hand, or that you've crossed that line, *I'll* kill the story."

"I understand."

One corner of his mouth kicked upward. "No you don't, Miss Blake. You couldn't possibly. Good night."

She watched him leave, puzzled. Seth Winter was a good reporter. She knew his reputation and his work—she'd been reading his byline since her college days. Until a few years ago, he'd worked for Dateline, but then he'd turned free lance. Find a hot spot in the world and you'd find Winter. He'd won his Pulitzer for his reports on the famine in Ethiopia. She lit a cigarette and perched on the corner of Henri's desk Seth had recently vacated, smoking absently.

Winter's attitude didn't make any sense. To have the inside track on a story like this was an opportunity most reporters could only dream about. This was more than an exclusive; it was a veritable coup! So why was her new bureau chief less than enthusiastic at the prospect? Not just unenthusiastic, she thought, he had been downright hostile.

He could be one of those throwbacks who believed women should be restricted to fashion news and the society page, but her reporter's instinct told her that his hostility was too deep-seated to be explained by such facile reasoning. Besides, she had encountered a few members of the "men only" club in her career—her ex-husband, for one—and Seth Winter just didn't fit the mold. Which left her with...a puzzle, and the nagging sense that she was missing something very important. Crushing out her cigarette, she twisted around and dragged the phone toward her and dialed the news agency's number.

"Hello, Armand," she said when a familiar voice answered. "This is Cassandra. I need a favor." She paused for a moment, listening. "Yes, I know. It was very noble of you to hold down the fort so the rest of us could enjoy ourselves, but I do need your help." She grinned at his lengthy, pained, assent. "Go to the morgue and pull everything we have on Seth Winter. Leave it on my desk." She shook her head when Armand questioned her. "No, no. I don't want the stuff he's written. I want anything that was written *about* him. Got it? Thanks, Armand. I owe you one." As she hung up, Cassandra felt a twinge of guilt over treating her new boss as if he were the focus of a story, but she shrugged the feeling off. If he had the right to kill her story, she had the right to know what made him tick.

The alarm clock went off the following morning with what Cassandra considered to be a particular vengeance. Wincing, she fumbled a hand free from the sheet and swatted the Off button before opening her eyes. There were very few things in life she truly hated, but mornings topped the list. Particularly mornings when she had had only five hours sleep the night before. She was definitely a night person, she decided for the thousandth time as she forced herself out of bed and into the bathroom.

The bathroom wasn't luxurious by American standards—the plumbing and fixtures could probably qualify as antiques—but at least everything worked and, truthfully, Cassandra found the claw-foot tub with its European-style shower charming. Fifteen minutes under the stream of hot water left her feeling more human, and by the time she had dressed, applied her makeup, and pinned her long, blond hair into a demure bun, she found she had time to savor a cup of instant coffee before leaving.

Seated at one of the two chairs at the dining table, Cassandra surveyed her apartment with a small flicker of appreciation. When she had arrived in Paris, she had shunned the idea of living in one of the modern apartment buildings that had sprung up all over. Instead, with Clarice's help, she had found this, a building constructed around the turn of the century. Fresh wallpaper and paint had turned the three rooms into a cozy haven that served to remind her just how far she had come since her divorce. The apartment was small—the kitchen was tiny and separated from the living room/dining area by a counter—and decorated in an eclectic fashion. A wicker sofa and chair with bright green cushions contrasted—a less charitable soul might have said warred—with brass-and-glass end tables; her dining set had been found at a flea market. Clarice had decried her choice, but when Cassandra had refinished the three pieces, the mahogany set proved to be the treasure Cassandra had thought it. Her bedroom contained a brass bed—purchased at another flea market—a nightstand, and an armoire that came with the apartment. She had tried refinishing the armoire as well, but with less success.

Still, Cassandra thought as she rinsed her cup and put it on the drain board, she was satisfied with her home. She had no pets, no plants, nothing that needed daily care. She had said goodbye to those responsibilities six years ago when she had filed for divorce. She had given Ned the house, the dog and the latest in a long string of Boston ferns she had purchased. She never acquired the knack of keeping those things alive.

The walk to the Metro was pleasant; pedestrian traffic was fairly light and the full force of summer heat had yet to descend. In addition, flowers were blooming in window boxes and flower beds. Their fragrance perfumed the air and their riotous color was like a soothing balm. In Paris, June was her favorite month, she decided. The tourists had yet to invade the city en masse, and everyone was in good spirits as they looked forward to their traditional July or August vacations. The Metro—Paris's famed subway—was running on time as usual, and within fifteen minutes, Cassandra stepped back onto the sidewalk and briskly walked the four blocks to her office.

In the building lobby she stepped into the line that had formed to go through the metal detector, and fumbled in her bag for her Dateline Press identification and her key chain. While she was waiting, she caught a flicker of movement out of the corner of her eye. Turning slightly, she saw Seth Winter enter the lobby. Instead of joining the line, however, he headed straight for the security table. Cassandra was about to call out to him, to tell him about the latest security precautions, but the words never made it past her brain. She watched as one of the security guards spoke to her boss, consulted the log, frisked him, and then admitted him to the building.

"Curiouser and curiouser," Cassandra murmured to herself when her turn came to hand over her identification, key ring and purse to one guard and then wait for the other to check her with the metal detector. Her eyes were fixed on Winter's broad-shouldered figure as he strode through the lobby to the elevator.

She was retrieving her belongings when a horrible thought occurred to her. She had told Armand to leave whatever information he could gather on her desk—in plain sight of anyone who wandered by, including Seth Winter. And if Winter saw it . . . Cassandra hurried across the lobby and was just in time to watch Seth disappear inside one of the cars. The lines at the elevators were incredible, so she all but ran to the stairway and took the steps to the fifth-floor office.

Please let me beat him there, she prayed as she yanked open the fire door to the fifth floor. Winter's impression of her had been less than grand to begin with, and if he thought she was digging into his private life just to satisfy some perverse curiosity—oh, God, there was no way she could explain this to him without making it seem like an insult. He would fire her. Who was hiring now? she wondered as she slammed through Dateline's double doors. *Associated Press? Knight-Ridder? Time?* She felt her foot catch on something and a moment later she was falling.

Straight into her boss's arms.

She shrieked in surprise and then went mute as she was hauled upright by a pair of strong arms. From somewhere behind her came the sound of applause, and Cassandra felt hot color wash into her cheeks. It had to be Kurt, of course; no one else would be so crass as to draw attention to this incident. She mentally took back every nice thing she had ever said about her friend.

"Good morning, Miss Blake."

Cassandra forced her eyes upward and met Seth's faintly amused gaze. "G-good morning, sir."

His lips twitched. "Do you normally enter a room with such . . . enthusiasm?"

"Not normally, no, sir." Kurt's laughter reached her and she glanced back to give him a venomous look. It was as she was turning back that she saw Seth's hand still rested on her shoulder. She found the sight disturbing and took a hasty step backward.

"My foot is fine. Thank you for asking," Seth offered lightly when he saw the look in her eyes.

"Oh, I'm sorry," she apologized, "I was in a hurry, and I didn't look." She shrugged helplessly. "I just didn't expect anyone to be hiding behind the door."

"Actually I was trying to find the coffeepot. Why don't you show me around and introduce me to the staff?"

Cassandra managed a sick smile and a nod and started toward her desk, Seth trailing behind.

"And feel free to call me Seth," her boss said. "I have an allergy that flares whenever people call me sir." Cassandra could only nod again, suddenly transfixed by the folder Kurt was idly waving at her.

"Armand left this for you," Kurt informed her as she put her purse in the bottom desk drawer. "Knowing how you hate a messy desk, I took the liberty of putting the material in a folder."

Wonderful. Pique the man's interest, Cassandra thought as she reached for the file. "Thanks."

Sure enough, Seth's reporter's instinct was in top form. "A story you're working on together?"

"Not exactly," she murmured, tugging on the folder until Kurt finally released it with a devilish smile. Catching Seth's puzzled frown she explained, "It's just some background material on the Brigade that I thought might come in handy." His interest abruptly vanished and she breathed a sigh of relief when she was able to slip the folder into a desk drawer. "This way to the coffee," she said brightly as she grabbed her own mug from her desk.

"I made it myself," Kurt said proudly. His announcement was greeted by prolonged groans from the teleprinter room and Cassandra made a face.

"The first thing you must learn," Cassandra explained to her boss as she led him to the large percolator, "is that all of Kurt's good taste is taken up by his writing and his wardrobe. His idea of good coffee is just this side of battery acid. It will wake you up in the morning, but you won't enjoy the process." She filled both their cups halfway and then added the same amount of cream to her mug. The color inched its way from pitch black to dark brown.

"You're joking," Seth said when she handed him the cream.

She shrugged and returned the cream to the table. "Try it."

He did, and nearly choked in the process. "My God, that's awful!"

"Precisely." She handed him the cream again.

"I know this is going to sound crazy," Seth ventured as he walked with Cassandra to the teleprinter room, "but why do you let him make this?"

"It's the rule. The first one here in the morning makes the first pot. Besides," she added with a fond glance at Kurt, "He'd be very hurt if we stopped him."

Privately, Seth thought they were all going to be seriously hurt if the German wasn't stopped, but he kept that thought to himself. He also kept to himself the niggling suspicion that Cassandra Blake might not be as cold as he had first thought her.

In the teleprinter room, she introduced him to Margot Lemay and Jules Bartheld, the other Paris stringers. Margot was busy with the weather reports while Jules was repairing one of the two teleprinters.

"There is one other stringer, Armand Pommier—"

"I met him last night," Seth interrupted Cassandra. She seemed surprised at that, but didn't comment. "Where's our photographer?" he asked. "He's gotten some of the best shots on the wires these past few years."

Margot rolled her eyes and Jules almost dived back inside the printer.

"Did I say something wrong?"

"I take it you haven't met our photographer yet?" Cassandra asked hesitantly.

Seth shook his head. "He wasn't at Henri's party last night—" Margot made a strangling sound and he looked at her sharply before continuing, "and Henri seemed rather reluctant to discuss him."

"Yes, well—" She looked around uncertainly, willing someone to come to her rescue. She was pointedly ignored. Studying her coffee, she said, "You have to understand, PJ is a little...different."

Seth grinned. "Most photographers are."

Oh, if you only knew, Cassandra thought. "We can usually find PJ in the darkroom."

He glanced in that direction. "He must not be here then. The light isn't on."

"With PJ, that's no indication." With the air of the condemned walking to the guillotine, she led the way to the darkroom and knocked on the door.

He had already decided that this photographer must really be something, but Seth wasn't prepared for the stream of profanity that answered Cassandra's knock. In fact, he actually took a step backward, as if he could avoid the abuse in that manner. Cassandra, however, merely narrowed her eyes and literally hammered at the door with her fist.

"Knock if off, PJ," she shouted through the wood. "Henri's replacement wants to meet you, *maintenant!*" This information was greeted by another string of highly inventive imprecations.

This time Seth winced, uncertain which was worse, the mysterious PJ or Cassandra's French. "Is PJ French?" he asked quietly.

"No, he's British," Cassandra replied absently. "PJ, if you don't come out, I'll come in. I swear I will. And I'll straighten up your workbench. *Comprends-tu?*" She punctuated the threat by kicking the door.

Seth was ready to retreat to his office and relinquish any thoughts he had had about meeting the photographer when Cassandra pressed an ear against the door and smiled triumphantly at him. "He's coming." She stepped away from the door and took a sip of coffee.

And that, Seth thought, was what was known as good news and bad news. "Is he always this—antisocial?"

"He blames it on his mother."

"I beg your pardon?"

Cassandra blinked. "His mother—PJ blames it on his mother."

"The swearing?"

"That in particular and his life in general," she affirmed. "You see—" The door to the darkroom opened and she smiled warmly, "Good morning, PJ."

PJ was a surprise. From the voice, Seth had expected a hulking beast to emerge from the darkroom, probably carrying a switchblade. Instead, a wiry man slightly shorter than Cassandra walked out and glared at them both. He looked to be a few years older than Seth and his hair was pale brown and thinning, but he sported an amazing handlebar mustache. "I'm PJ Piper," he said ungraciously, thrusting his hand out at Seth. At least, that was what Seth managed to understand after filtering out the verbal abuse that peppered PJ's speech.

"Seth Winter."

PJ's eyebrows rose. "Really. You've been gone a long time."

This time Seth barely noticed the profanity. PJ's casual comment about his absence overwhelmed everything else. The photographer must have been in Paris ten years ago; although he hadn't been working for Dateline then, he would know about the bombing. Perhaps PJ had already told the rest of the staff about it. Seth forced himself to nod, although his stomach had tied itself into a giant knot. "I like your stuff."

"Of course," PJ replied in a clipped, cultured tone. "Everyone does." He fixed his gaze on Cassandra. "Do you need pictures?"

"Not yet."

"Good, then kindly save your tortured French for the streets. Is there any coffee left?" Without waiting for a reply he headed for the machine.

Cassandra turned to Seth, braced for the appalled expression she was sure he would be sporting. She wasn't expecting the pallor that lay just below his tan, or the stricken look in his black eyes. All the humor drained out of her, and she laid her free hand on his arm. The muscles there were as hard as iron. "Seth?" She felt a shudder run through him and grasped him even harder. "Seth, are you all right?"

He came back to himself with a jerk. Hell, was that pity he saw in her eyes? That was the first reaction when people found out; the second was curiosity. "Yes," he said tersely. "I'm fine."

"PJ always comes as something of a shock, and there simply isn't any way to prepare a newcomer for him," Cassandra said in a quiet voice. "I was afraid to say so much as hello to him the first two months I worked here."

She didn't know. Seth relaxed slightly. "You like him."

"Guilty as charged," Cassandra sighed.

"Why?" He paused. "I mean how could you—" He broke off, unable to put the question into words.

"How could I possibly like someone who has the personality of a porcupine who just tangled with a skunk?" She finished for him. "Maybe it's because he gives the greatest impersonation of a very, very proper English lord I have ever seen."

"What?"

Cassandra smiled and shook her head. "It's a long story. Let's just say that at one point in time I desperately needed rescuing, and PJ rode in on a white steed, all flags flying." A wicked glint sparkled in her eyes. "And he's vastly enlarged my vocabulary."

"I can imagine," Seth murmured, keeping a wary eye on PJ as the photographer sauntered back toward his beloved darkroom. When the door to the darkroom had closed, he asked, "Exactly what does PJ stand for?"

This time her smile was a full-blown grin, although she cast a cautious glance at the closed door. "I'll tell you if you swear never to call him by it."

He felt himself smiling in return, and a distant part of his mind was amazed by the feelings she generated within him. Mutely he crossed his heart.

"His initials stand for Peter Jamison." She chuckled. "But if you tell him I told you, I'll deny everything." With that she went back to her desk.

It took a few seconds, but he finally realized why PJ blamed his mother for everything. Who in the hell wanted to go through life with a name like Peter Piper?

Seth was pleasantly tired by the end of the day. Since leaving Dateline, he had worked on his own and had forgotten about the rigor of meeting daily deadlines. His first day on the job had consisted of handing out assignments, viewing the photographs presented by the irascible PJ, and reading copy. His reporters were in and out most of the day, allowing little opportunity for him to become acquainted with them. They seemed like a good bunch though, he reflected now, watching Kurt read over Cassandra's shoulder as she worked at her computer. That had to be the last-minute press conference called by the Minister of Economics. He had assigned Cassandra to that, over her heated protests that it was Kurt's turn to cover the latest of the minister's fatally boring announcements. He had, in all fairness, heard her out, and then told her she had half an hour to make the conference. Someone, he had replied reasonably, had to cover the minister. Cassandra's

muttered response had been that a large rock would do well, but
she had gone.

Cassandra, Seth learned later from Kurt, had a history with
the minister, ever since she had questioned his relationship with
the president of a company that was being investigated for stock
manipulation. The minister now thoroughly detested her, and,
from what he could see, the feeling was mutual. Not the best of
all possible relationships for a reporter.

Seth's eyes narrowed. Kurt was now massaging Cassandra's
shoulders and her head was tipped back so that she could see
his face while he spoke. They made a comfortable, intimate
picture that for some reason annoyed the hell out of him. He
shuffled the newly filed stories into a neat stack on his desk and
strode out of his office.

"Have you finished the story yet?" The hostility in his
question was barely concealed and Seth winced inwardly. "I
want to get it out tonight," he added in a more conciliatory
tone.

"Almost," Cassandra replied. "I'm just trying to think up
a few adjectives for the minister."

"Keep them neutral," Seth advised. "I don't want to get hit
with a libel suit."

Cassandra chuckled. "Actually I'm trying to be nice. Our
redoubtable friend resigned this afternoon."

"Rather sudden, isn't it?" He dropped into the chair in front
of her desk.

"Oh, yes." She moved away from Kurt's hands and paged
through her notebook. "He gave the usual innocuous reasons:
getting on in years, wanting to spend time with the family, that
sort of thing." Finding the page she wanted, she continued.
"However, I have a friend inside the Ministry of Economics,
and he says that the minister is actually under investigation for
stock fraud and that the rumor is that he is about to be in-
dicted." She leaned back in her chair and smiled wickedly.

Seth grunted. "You can't print the rumor about the indictment."

"I know," she sighed. "More's the pity." She turned back
to the keyboard and began typing furiously.

"As soon as Cassandra figures out how to spell resignation—" Kurt leaned forward and tapped the screen. Cassandra groaned and made the necessary correction. "We're going to have dinner. Care to join us?" he asked offhandedly.

Seth hesitated. Watching these two only served to make him feel more alone, and yet, at this moment, he couldn't quite face going back to his hotel room.

"It should be a real adventure," Kurt urged, his eyes still on Cassandra's story. "We're going to a Bavarian restaurant so Cassandra can practice her German. God knows what we'll eat."

Cassandra punched a button, and a printer began to whir at the back of the room. "Don't listen to him," she told Seth. "My German is quite good."

Seth raised an eyebrow. "Like your French?"

"*Et tu,* chief?" She groaned theatrically. "Better than my French."

"All right," Seth decided. "Just let me read your copy first."

"PJ got some good pictures," she told Seth as he started toward the printer. "Do you want to see them all, or should I pick one?"

He glanced at the darkroom door. The red light was on and right now he didn't feel equal to the task of dealing with the photographer. "You pick one."

Half an hour later the three of them were jammed into Seth's compact car, Cassandra in the passenger seat and Kurt's long frame folded into the back.

"You drive like a native," Cassandra remarked as Seth made liberal use of his horn and edged into a lane that she was positive had been bumper-to-bumper with traffic. When he repeated the maneuver, she closed her eyes and prayed.

"It's all a matter of timing and aggression," Seth acknowledged. "Quite simple, once you have that down."

"Right." Cassandra's voice emerged a full octave higher than normal.

Seth glanced at her. "I take it you don't drive?"

"Not like this," she muttered.

In the back, Kurt laughed and told Seth how Cassandra had once been trapped in a traffic circle for an hour before she'd

managed to turn off onto a side street. Seth found the story incredibly funny and Cassandra was ready to dump them both by
the time they arrived at the restaurant.

The terrorist attacks had cut into the city's nightlife, so they
had no trouble finding an unoccupied booth. The table and
booth were of dark, scarred walnut, almost Gothic in structure, and with the waiters and waitresses in full costume, the
atmosphere was delightfully Bavarian. The men ordered beer,
which came in silver-capped steins, and Cassandra sipped a
Perrier while she studied the menu.

Kurt had been serious about letting Cassandra order, Seth
realized as the two of them went over the menu together. Cassandra had to read each item to Kurt. He would correct her if
necessary—and, to Seth's amusement, it usually was—and then
she had to translate the item into English. By the time the waiter
took their order, her German was . . . well, a lot better than her
French. At least their waiter hadn't winced, although he had
looked confused once or twice.

"How long have you been studying German?" Seth asked
when the waiter departed.

"Let's see, Kurt came to Paris about six months after I did."
Cassandra paused to light a cigarette. "I guess that means we've
been practicing for a year or so." She gave him a look that
dared him to say anything about her flair for foreign languages.

"I take it you hope to be posted to Bonn or Munich in the
near future?"

"Not Cassandra," Kurt answered. "She wants Tel Aviv or
Beirut."

"You might have a chance for Tel Aviv or Amman," Seth
said slowly. "But not Beirut. It's no place for—"

"For a woman," Cassandra interrupted acidly.

Seth fixed her with a calm gaze. "I was about to say it's no
place for a reporter, male or female. You should have learned
by now that ours is hardly a glamorous profession, regardless
of the play it gets in novels and movies. It's hard, grueling work
and sometimes it gets downright dangerous."

"I'm fully aware of that," Cassandra replied stiffly.

"Now myself, I hope to be sent to New York," Kurt said brightly, attempting to lighten the contention between his two companions. "That is such a peaceful city."

The smile he gave them was so angelic Cassandra couldn't help laughing while Seth merely shook his head. When their meal arrived, they were doing what reporters do best, talking shop, and the tension had disappeared. Conversation was abandoned in favor of the *choucroute*, a filling concocted of sauerkraut and assorted sausages, and dark bread, and when they had finished, the restaurant was beginning to fill with people. Kurt excused himself and, beer stein in hand, made his way across the room to a petite blonde who stood at the bar.

Cassandra shook her head and smiled indulgently. "It's like watching a guided missile, isn't it?"

Seth, who had been experiencing a mixture of outrage and embarrassment at Kurt's behavior was relieved by her reaction. "I was under the impression that you and Kurt were..." His voice trailed off and he gestured helplessly.

"No, not me," she said lightly. "Not again."

"From that, I assume you were once involved with a reporter?"

"You could say that." The restaurant was growing warm and Cassandra shrugged out of her suit jacket and lit a cigarette. "I was married to one."

"Oh?" Her movements had distracted him. The pale blue suit she wore was attractive enough, in a cool, professional way, but the blouse was another matter entirely. Most of it was made of cream-colored satin, but the yoke and sleeves were constructed entirely of lace that allowed tantalizing peeks at the flesh beneath. Seth leaned back in the booth and took a firmer grip on his stein.

Oblivious to where his gaze had fallen, Cassandra looked at him teasingly. "Want to trade biographies, chief?"

When she got that gleam in her eye, the woman was devastating, he decided. Absolutely positively devastating. He was responding like some helpless moth drawn closer and closer to her flame. And he didn't like in the least. "I like to know my staff."

The impish glint died a sudden death. He wasn't about to indulge in the usual, easy banter, and friendly teasing was decidedly outside his realm. She had thought, briefly, that she and Kurt had managed to breach the walls that were so tightly constructed around him. Instead, she had been put firmly in her place. Well, if that was what he wanted, that was what he would get. "I'm thirty-two years old. I graduated magna cum laude from college, after which I married, and a few years later, I was divorced. I've lived in Paris for two years; before that I was assigned to the London bureau for eighteen months. I'm very good at what I do, and it's been a number of years since a man—any man—treated me like someone's idiot child, so what exactly is it that you have against me?"

If he hadn't seen the anger flaring in her eyes, he would have laughed out loud. Put on the defensive, she counterattacked. "I don't have anything against you, Cassandra. And I certainly don't think of you as—what was your phrase?—an idiot child."

Cassandra blinked. "Oh."

"How did you end up in journalism?"

There it was: The Question. "I guess you could say I was born to it. My father is Robert Townsend." She braced herself for the inevitable reaction.

"You're Robert Townsend's daughter?"

"I thought that's what I said." She took a furious puff from her cigarette and then ground it out.

Within journalistic circles, Robert Townsend and his photos were legendary. Some of the best pictures to come out of Vietnam had been Townsend's. "That must have created some tricky situations for you."

"A few," she admitted warily. His reaction wasn't quite what she had expected. Usually she was deluged with questions regarding her famous father.

"That's why you use Blake—your married name, I assume?"

She nodded. "When I went on my first interview, I made two mistakes. The first was using my maiden name. The second was telling my father about it. My father put in a call to his old friend, the editor-in-chief. I had the job before I had even filled in the application form.''

''Needless to say, those were two mistakes you never repeated.''

''Needless to say,'' she echoed dryly. ''I am where I am because of my own work, not daddy's coattails.''

''No one's disputing that.'' Seth downed the rest of his beer. ''I've met your dad several times. You're a lot like him.''

''Not me. I don't know an f-stop from nuclear fission.''

''You're very good at that.''

''What?''

''Evasion.'' Seth leaned forward. ''The flip remarks. Your father does that, too—puts up barriers whenever something gets too painful to discuss. No one gets close to you, do they?''

''Not if I can help it,'' she answered jauntily.

The subject was obviously closed, Seth thought, but that didn't stop him from dwelling on the enigma of Cassandra Blake. When the nightmare woke him in the small hours of the morning, he thought about her, considering the brash, confident facade she assumed. Nothing frightened her; nothing stood in the way of her career; she could be as hard as nails when the occasion warranted, and yet . . . there was a vulnerability about her that crept through, like her protectiveness of Kurt's feelings regarding his coffee-making abilities. She wasn't as cold as she seemed. Not that it mattered to him, Seth assured himself. She was a reporter with a lead on the biggest story of the year, and he wanted to make sure that she would handle it without jeopardizing herself or the agency. His curiosity about her was only natural. Wasn't it?

Chapter 3

The week turned into a hectic blur of last-minute press conferences called by various government departments, a riot at a soccer game, and an international air show at the airport, which Cassandra had to cover with PJ when Margot came down with food poisoning after attending a reception for the new ambassador from Argentina. When she and PJ returned to the office, PJ had great pictures and Cassandra had good copy. She also had a bruised bottom—courtesy of an American pilot who had displayed his enthusiasm at hearing another American voice in a rather heavy-handed manner—a run in her panty hose, a blister on both feet—her high-heeled pumps hadn't been worn in anticipation of trooping across miles of tarmac—and a splitting headache. The last thing she needed was to see the edited version of her latest story, with Seth's neatly printed "constructive remarks" penciled in the margins, waiting patiently on her desk. Another rewrite. A glance showed Seth bent over his desk, hard at work, and she shook her head. He was the first one of the day crew to arrive in the mornings and the last to leave at night. The man had no life outside the office. Not that his social life was any of her concern.

Sighing, she plopped onto her chair and pulled off her shoes. Rubbing her abused feet, she studied the comments. Nearly every story she'd filed this week had been returned, and she wished she could scream discrimination; but to be honest, Kurt and the others had also received their share of rewrites. The first few times her work had been returned, she had grudgingly followed Seth's suggestions, but when she had managed the time to compare the two versions of certain stories, she understood what her boss was doing. The reworked version was crisper, tighter, conveying everything the first had, but in fewer words. Seth was paring her work to the bone and making it better in the process. She had even gone so far as to dig through her files and try the new technique on a few of her old stories and had come up with the same result. They were better. Much better.

Which didn't change the fact that she wouldn't get out of the office until late tonight, she reflected as she switched on her terminal, typed in her code key and downed three aspirin with a glass of water. Within an hour, the rewrite was chattering its way through the printer and she had begun work on the air show. When the printer was finished, she tore off the two copies and carried them both in to Seth.

"Here's the rewrite," she said after tapping on the door frame and stepping into his office.

"Just drop it in the basket," he answered, gesturing to the corner of his desk. "Were you able to shorten it?"

"As ordered."

He looked up at that, searching her face for a sign of hostility, but he found none. "I know you think I'm being hard on you—"

"Not really," she replied with a weary smile. "You're making me a better journalist. I appreciate that."

"Still after my job, right?" he teased.

"Right. One must, after all, have goals in life."

Seth watched her walk back to her desk, a smile tugging at his lips. Her usual careful bun had lost a few pins during the day and tendrils of hair were curling down her neck. There were dark smudges beneath her eyes, and she had lost her shoes somewhere along the way. She looked tired and beaten and altogether desirable. The thought sent him back to his editing until he finally realized that he had been staring at the same line in a restaurant review for ten minutes without reading a word. Oh, hell, what was the point? He tossed his pen aside, drank the last dregs of cold coffee in his mug and admitted the truth. He was attracted to Cassandra Blake; he had been since their first meeting at Henri's apartment. Even worse, he liked her, genuinely *liked* her. Physical attraction he could handle, emotional attraction was a minefield.

Ten years was a long time; long enough for him to have worked through all the guilt and horror. He'd had time to adjust, adapt. He'd picked up the pieces of his life and gone on, becoming one of the handful of free-lance correspondents who never had to worry about selling a story. Papers and agencies knew his work and respected it; there was always a news organization willing to buy whatever he was working on. For ten years he'd traveled endlessly, carrying his home in a single suitcase and a battered typewriter. He was good at his job. He got stories other reporters found impossible. He had been willing to cover anything, anywhere. As long as he didn't have to go back to France.

And where had he ended up? In Paris, running the bureau he had worked for when his life had been blown apart. The darkroom door opened and he watched PJ stroll over to Cassandra and toss a pile of photographs onto her cluttered desk. Whatever the first photo was, she obviously didn't like it because she gave a little shriek and came halfway out of her chair. PJ laughed, the first sound of that type Seth had ever heard the man make, and made a dash for his sanctuary, Cassandra hot on his heels. Seth shook his head and returned to his memories. He had been packing, preparing to go to Africa to cover a nice little rebellion there when the offer came in from Dateline. He had read the letter, chuckled mirthlessly, and picked up the phone, framing his rejection as he dialed the area code for New York City. And when Tom Burroughs had answered, Seth had been stunned to hear himself tell Tom that he'd been thinking about making a change and what kind of salary was Dateline prepared to offer?

All of which had brought him back to this office, sipping cold coffee at nine o'clock at night, sitting in an uncomfortable chair. His staff consisted of a psychotic photographer, a practical joker from West Germany, three reliable—if green—stringers, and one brash, driven American who learned and massacred foreign languages without discrimination, thanked him for his criticisms and alternately fascinated or terrified him. It was getting hard to tell who was the keeper and who were the inmates around here.

Cassandra was returning to her desk. With a sense of fatalism, he rose and made his way through the newsroom.

"Need some help?" he asked when he reached Cassandra's desk.

"Your photographer," she informed him curtly, "has a very strange sense of what constitutes news."

"Oh?" He reached for the stack of pictures.

"No!" Cassandra made a grab for the photos, but it was too late.

The first photo was of an unwilling Cassandra and an air force captain. The man had Cassandra bent backward over one arm in a ludicrous gesture of grand passion while his free hand wandered over her backside. It was, to say the least, an indelicate pose; and to have it captured on film was either revolting or hilarious, depending on your point of view. Seth found it infuriating until he saw the next few pictures. While the professional part of his mind realized that PJ had been using an electric motor on his camera in order to record the swift succession of events, he couldn't suppress the chuckles that erupted when the photos showed a highly aggravated Cassandra taking a step backward and letting the pilot have it with her shoulder bag.

"It's not funny," she said over his chuckles. She snatched the photos away and tossed the offending ones into the trash.

"No, it isn't," he agreed. "The guy was shorter than you."

Cassandra's eyes narrowed. "Very funny. You and PJ are both twisted."

Seth managed to tame his grin into a smile and rested a hip on the corner of her desk. "Want me to send him to Africa for you?"

"Which one, the pilot or PJ?"

"Either. Both." He met the angry glare of aquamarine eyes and sobered. "Did anyone else get pictures of that?"

She knew what he was asking. If another photographer had gotten the same shots, her credibility could fall to zero overnight. "One did. I didn't recognize him." She glanced at the wastebasket and shook her head.

"Okay." He sauntered to the darkroom and rapped once on the door. The question as to his identity was crudely framed, but Seth ignored it. "My office. Now." He gave Cassandra a wink as he went past.

Startled, Cassandra looked after him for a few moments. It was becoming a habit, sneaking looks at her boss. She'd never been big on physical attraction, but he was a difficult man to ignore. He had a lean, hard frame, which his tailored suits accentuated, and when he took off his jacket, as he often did, she was all too aware of the sinuous play of muscles beneath the cotton shirt.

He was much more a hands-on editor than Henri had been, but she didn't find fault with that. He was improving the entire staff, including PJ, with his criticisms. He was exacting, but never harsh, fair without being indecisive. All qualities she admired. And while he seemed to be warming to his people, there was still an almost grim reserve about him that was never completely dispelled, no matter how lighthearted the occasion. He was as much an enigma now as he had been the night of Henri's party. The file Armand had compiled on Seth at her request was still unread; there simply hadn't been time. She might find the answer there, but she really would prefer to find out by more traditional means. Say, a glass of wine in some little bistro with candlelight and soft music. . . . Cassandra blinked and turned back to her terminal. Face it, she told herself chidingly, you're developing a huge crush on the boss. Not a wise move. She didn't even notice PJ as he walked past her desk to Seth's office.

Seth was waiting when PJ walked into his office. "Close the door," he told the photographer. Before PJ could say a word, he launched his attack. "I realized something about myself tonight. I am just as chauvinistic about women in this profession as most other men are. It's not a pretty discovery." He leaned back in his chair and regarded PJ with an icy stare. "And you're every bit as bad as I am. Instead of taking pictures of that revolting little scene at the air show, you should have decked the guy. The agency would have happily paid any damages, provided the pilot had the nerve to bring a lawsuit. Whether you like Cassandra or not, whether you resent working with a woman or not, she is your colleague and in my agency, colleagues work together. Anyone who can't or won't follow that dictum doesn't work for me. Do you understand? No, don't talk. Just nod your head if you agree."

PJ nodded.

"I hope you've had the good taste to destroy the negatives."

PJ nodded again.

"Wonderful. I understand another photographer got the same shots you did. What about him?"

Leaning against the door, PJ jammed his hands into the front pockets of his jeans. When he answered, the usual abuse was missing. "I took care of it."

The tone of his voice told Seth that he probably didn't want to know exactly what PJ had done. Instead he asked, "Are we looking at any assault charges?"

"No. I very nicely explained a few things to a fellow newsman. He was very understanding and simply handed over the roll of film."

Seth studied the man for a minute before giving him a curt nod. "Fine. That's all, PJ."

"Not quite. I want you to understand something." PJ paused, bottom teeth worrying the lower edge of his mustache. "The photos were meant as a joke—a bad joke, maybe, but a joke. Cassie knows that. I may be slightly demented, but I would never, under any circumstances, do anything to damage her or her reputation. I wouldn't let anyone else hurt her either. She's my friend." With that, he left.

Seth turned his attention to one of the papers on his desk in order to conceal a sudden smile. The hard-bitten photographer had a heart of gold. Amazing. Like any other news office, this one had its own unique undercurrents and it was going to take some time to understand them all. At least, he consoled himself, it didn't appear that he would have to worry about a lot of infighting among the staff.

An hour later, Cassandra tapped on his door. "Here's the air show story and pictures."

"Thanks." He scanned the copy and photos. "It looks good. Have Armand send it tonight."

"You're kidding!" She took the story from him with a mock frown. "You can't do this to me. I was ready for an hour's rewrite. I drank four cups of coffee so that I could stay awake. Now I'll be up half the night. You've just ruined my schedule."

He couldn't help himself; he had to laugh at her furious expression, and when his laughter had abated to a grin, he realized with a start just how much emotion this office—this woman—had brought back into his life in less than a week. "Have Armand transmit the story and, since I'm directly responsible for your infusion of caffeine, the least I can do is buy you dinner."

The offer was so unexpected, his dark eyes so warm, that her heart gave a sudden lurch. "You're on," she replied in what she hoped was a normal tone. "Give me five minutes."

One of those precious minutes was chewed up with Armand; the other four she spent in the ladies' room, trying frantically to repair a day's worth of damage to her face and hair. It proved impossible to redo her neat bun with any success, so she simply brushed out the shoulder-length mass of blond waves, dusted her face with powder and blush, added a touch of coral lipstick, and pulled on the spare pair of panty hose she kept in her desk for emergencies. Her beige suite was wilted, so she opted not to wear the jacket. *This is silly,* she told herself, as her trembling fingers retied the bow of her aqua blouse into a softer look at the side of her neck and checked the simple gold hoops in her ears. *It's not as if this is a date or anything; Kurt and I have stopped for dinner a hundred times when we've worked late.* But she still dug into the voluminous depths of her shoulder bag for the bottle of her favorite perfume. When she was finished, she eyed her reflection suspiciously. *Too much? Not enough?* She brushed trembling fingertips over her cheekbones and was disgusted to find her hands were cold. *Honestly, you'd think I was getting ready for the prom.* She stuck her tongue out at her reflection and marched back into the newsroom.

Seth was waiting at her desk. "You're prompt. I like that."

A simple observation like that had no business making her smile. But it did. She sat down and wedged her protesting feet back into their pumps. *He looked good,* she thought as she called good-night to Armand. His black hair showed signs of having recently been combed—to no avail; the waves had a definite mind of their own—and, unlike hers, his suit still looked neatly pressed. The heavy shadow of his beard had not been touched during the time she had been primping in the ladies' room. He obviously thought of this dinner as all in the line of duty. Or so she had thought until he held open the door for her and she caught the unmistakable scent of his sandalwood cologne. Her nose told her it had to have been freshly applied and her spirits soared.

"Do you have a preference?" Seth asked when they reached the sidewalk.

Cassandra shook her head. "As long as it isn't a long walk. I'm game for just about anything, except snails."

He took her arm and they walked across the street to the parking lot. "We'll take my car."

Traffic was heavy, and it took a few minutes for Cassandra to realize that they were heading toward the Left Bank, Paris's famed student enclave. Taxis vied with each other for fares and parking spaces, and pedestrians ran across streets in a frenzied dash to avoid becoming a statistic. After a week of no further attacks by the terrorists, citizens and tourists alike were taking advantage of Paris's nightlife. As they skirted the area around the Sorbonne, motorized traffic slowed to a crawl along the narrow streets Seth chose and pedestrians crowded the sidewalks. Seth drove with the same daring he had displayed earlier, but this time Cassandra simply closed her eyes and kept her mouth shut.

"Aha, a parking spot." He crimped the wheel into a sharp turn that jolted Cassandra out of her lethargy.

She regarded the empty space of concrete dubiously. "I don't think so."

"Sure. Just watch." He maneuvered the car with a careless ease she envied and grinned at her. "See? Nothing to it."

"You must have been a sardine in a past life."

"How did you guess?"

"I have good instincts," she retorted teasingly. He was turned toward her, one arm resting on the back of the seat while the other was draped over the steering wheel, and the dim illumination cast by the street lamps erased the lines that usually creased his forehead. He looked younger, more at ease.

"Always?"

There was an odd glint in the depths of his eyes that made her wary. Or perhaps it was just the reflection of the headlights of a passing car. "Usually." She felt his touch against her hair, feather light. Instinct told her to turn her head, to nestle her cheek into the palm of his hand. Common sense screamed that such an action would only bring her grief. Her breath caught.

As if sensing her conflict, Seth smiled gently and withdrew his hand. "Come on, let's get you fed." The trembling was back, she realized as he helped her from the car, only now it afflicted her entire body.

The bistro was a modest establishment, catering strongly to the student crowd. Cassandra instantly fell in love with it. Judging by the strong resemblance, she guessed that the middle-aged woman behind the cash register was the mother of the two waiters, as well as the bartender. The father, she assumed, was busy at the stove in the kitchen. Along one wall ran a long zinc bar and the floor was tiled. Paper tablecloths covered the tables and the flatware was plain but sturdy. The handwritten menu from which they ordered offered a small selection of home-style dishes, but the aromas wafting from the kitchen promised an enjoyable meal. Seth asked for a carafe of house wine, which was promptly delivered, and then they were alone.

No scintillating bit of conversation came to mind, and Cassandra nervously searched her shoulder bag for her cigarettes.

"That's a very bad habit, you know," Seth said as he took the lighter from her and touched the flame to the cigarette.

"I know." She carefully exhaled. "Basically, I'm a weak-willed person."

"No, you're not." He played with the tiny gold lighter, turning it over and over in his strong fingers. "When did you start?"

"Do you want the first when or the latest when?" When he frowned at her flippant question, she shrugged, "I quit a little over a year ago. I started again three weeks ago. PJ says it's stress and that I ought to try electroshock therapy, instead."

"PJ has a very interesting outlook on life." He returned her lighter to the table. "What caused the stress?"

She waved a negligent hand. "A lot of things, including the Freedom Brigade. Could we change the subject, please?"

"All right." He leaned across the table. "What do you want to talk about?"

"You." As soon as the word was out, she could have kicked herself. Color washed into her cheeks. "I-I mean . . ."

He smiled, enjoying this softer—and, he guessed, rarely seen—side of her. "Relax, Cassandra. Or do you prefer Cassie?"

Her embarrassment faded in the face of that hated nickname. "I definitely do not prefer Cassie."

"That's what PJ calls you."

"Not to my face," she emphatically replied. After a moment's consideration she added, "And you just changed the subject."

"So I did."

Cassandra looked around the bistro. In one corner a group of students was stridently debating philosophy, while at another table a young couple held hands while they sipped their wine. "Do you come here often?"

"When I was working for Dateline several years ago, I was a frequent customer. I always liked the atmosphere—everyone is so alive, so ready to take on the world and win." He gave her a wry smile. "I once toyed with the idea of becoming a college professor. Maybe that's why I like this sort of place."

She propped her chin on her hand. "Somehow I can't see you living the quiet life of academia."

"Why not?"

She carefully considered the question before answering. "I guess because of the stories you've gotten. Look at the one you wrote about the president-for-life in that South Seas republic. You got kicked off his island with orders never to come back."

"You're saying I'm a danger junkie." He refilled their glasses.

"Not at all," she protested. "You simply know what you're good at and you've refined it into an art. There's nothing wrong with that."

He was silent for a moment before saying, "I was very lucky on that island. The president could just as easily have decided to throw me into one of his 'reeducation camps' instead of expelling me. Care to hazard what my reputation—and not coincidentally, my life—would have been worth then?"

"It obviously didn't scare you too badly," she mused. "A few weeks later you were covering a battle between Iran and Iraq. Your life wouldn't have been worth too much in the middle of a battlefield, either."

He nodded and took a healthy swallow of wine. "Parachute journalism has a great deal to recommend it," he said dryly.

"There's a certain risk on any story we file," she admitted, crushing out her cigarette. "You write an article on a senator and he doesn't like the way he came across to the public. He calls you, then your boss, and before you know it there's a big public controversy when all you said was that he frequently enjoys the nightlife in Washington."

"I think there's a slight difference," he retorted sarcastically. "A politician isn't likely to have you executed."

She arched an eyebrow at him. "Oh, really? I must be running with the wrong crowd."

In spite of himself, he chuckled. "Maybe there isn't that much difference. I think we all enjoy living close to the edge."

Cassandra laughed. "Close to the edge? Come on, Seth, the closest I've been to the edge in my career is fending off that pilot today. I was hardly in any danger. Well," she conceded when he raised an eyebrow, "not the kind of danger you mean."

"But it lent a certain spice to getting the story, didn't it?" he insisted in a tone that was half joking, half serious. "That pilot was the one you chose to interview, wasn't he? Why didn't you interview one of the others?''

"Because he was the flight commander," she answered blandly. "We—all of the reporters—were told to address our questions to him. What was I supposed to do, ignore the American part of the air show?" She snorted, "I can just imagine your reaction if I had done that!"

"I'll bet you were an overachiever in school. The harder the problem, the harder you worked to solve it. Right?"

There it was again, she thought as they stared at one another, his words hanging between them, the hint of some violent emotion buried just beneath that cool, detached exterior of his. "How *did* you guess?"

"Stop pushing so hard, Cassandra," he told her in a soft tone that wriggled into a corner of her heart and warmed her. "You don't have to be better than everyone. And you don't have to put up with morons like the flight commander."

"Spoken like a man in a man's world," she said a trifle sadly. "A woman in this profession does have to be better than her male counterparts, consistently better, unless she wants to find herself working for an advertising weekly doing the household hints column."

The underlying pain in her words hurt him. Without thinking, he trapped the hand lying on the table beneath his own. "Is that what happened to you?"

She drew a shaky breath. "I shouldn't have said that. It's all in the past."

"The past, I've discovered recently, has a nasty way of sneaking up on us." His index finger drew soothing patterns on the back of her hand, and he discovered that he liked the way her flesh felt to his touch. "Did you ever write a household hints column?"

"Oh yes," she breathed. "My husband didn't want any professional competition within our marriage. While he was making a name for himself, I was fighting crabgrass and dandelions in suburbia and writing dreadful poetry in between." To her horror, she felt tears burning behind her eyelids. "He thought it should be enough—I wanted it to be enough."

"But it wasn't?"

She shook her head. "I envied him his life, all of it. I was jealous of the deadlines, the reluctant sources. But most of all I was jealous of his stories. They were so damn good." She suddenly realized what she was doing, what he was doing. Seth had told her that he liked to know his staff, but she hadn't thought he would be so...sneaky. She pulled her hand away from his and cleared her throat. "Anyway, I'm not jealous anymore."

Cassandra's withdrawal was painful to watch. Her chin came up and her shoulders rigidly squared themselves. Seth pulled his hand back to his side of the table and fiddled with his wineglass. She had built a wall around herself that was equal to his; she allowed people in only so far before she slammed a door in their faces. Kurt and PJ might be willing to play by her rules, but he wasn't. "Who left whom?"

"I left him," she replied in a flippant tone laced with a certain amount of vindictive pleasure, "just when the crabgrass was in bloom. Any other questions?"

"Just one. Are you over him?"

"Five minutes after I walked out the door."

"Don't," he said sadly, understanding her reaction all too well. He had probed too deeply, he realized, come too close to the Cassandra who existed beneath the flip answers and breezy self-assurance and now she was withdrawing behind her wall and there wasn't a damn thing he could do about it.

Cassandra nervously lit a cigarette and looked at anything but her dinner companion. Her marriage was a subject she adamantly refused to discuss; not even her family knew all the details. They didn't know about Ned's women or the horrible truth he had hurled at her during their final argument—that her father had been one of his main reasons for marrying her. Robert Townsend's name opened a lot of doors for a young reporter. It still hurt to remember that, she thought detachedly, even after all these years. It hurt to remember that she had been that naive.

"*Mademoiselle* Blake?"

Cassandra snapped back to the present to find their waiter smiling at her. "*Oui?*"

"Telephone, mademoiselle." He gestured toward the bar.

"Merci." She gave Seth a quizzical look. "No one knows I'm here."

"Armand does. I gave him the number when we left." He smiled bleakly. "I'm on call twenty-four hours a day. Still want my job?"

She managed a smile. "You bet." Excusing herself, she rose and edged her way through the crowd to the bar. With a nod of thanks for the bartender, she brought the receiver to her ear. "Hello, Armand. What's so important it couldn't wait until morning?"

"Greetings, mademoiselle. I told you I'd be in touch, remember?"

She'd only heard the voice twice before, but it had the power to send chills up her spine. Her hands began to sweat and she tightened her grasp on the receiver. "Yes, I remember."

"Good." His English was heavily accented and she forced herself to concentrate on his words. "I'm sorry to disturb your dinner, but there is something I think you should see."

Adrenaline shot through her and she twisted so that she faced the windows and the table she shared with Seth. Their waiter was just setting their meal on the table. Trying to see out of the windows was futile; even if the man had been calling from one of the street booths, the lights inside the bistro turned the windows into a row of perfect mirrors, reflecting the interior. "How did you know I was here?"

Her question was greeted by a short, mirthless laugh. "We know all about you, *mademoiselle*. Now, to business. I think you should leave the bistro now and walk to the park two blocks away. You'll find the concert interesting."

There was a click and then the dull hum of a disconnected line. Cassandra slowly lowered the receiver.

"Finished, *mademoiselle*?"

The bartender started to replace the phone and she grabbed at his wrist. In a voice she barely recognized, she asked, "Is there a park nearby?"

"Oui." The young man smiled. "There is a concert there tonight. Just turn right when you leave. It—"

He was talking to thin air. Cassandra was hurrying back to her table. "We've got to leave," she murmured when Seth rose to seat her.

"Armand having trouble?" he asked, signaling for the check as she dropped her cigarettes into her purse.

She shook her head. "Worse, I think." When he started to question her further, she glanced around and shook her head. "Not here, Seth."

She was deathly pale, her eyes wide with alarm. He quickly paid the bill, pocketed the little gold lighter she had forgotten, and followed her outside.

"The call was from my contact with the Brigade," she explained when they were outside. Standing in a pool of light from one of the bistro windows, she told him what the man had said and watched his face harden until it looked like sculpted marble. "We've got to warn those people. The bartender said there's a concert in the park tonight. Seth, if they've planted a bomb or are planning an attack—"

"What we're going to do is call the police," he interrupted. He glanced back at the bistro. "Not from there. Too many people could overhear the conversation and I don't want to start a panic." He took her arm and pulled her into the crush of pedestrians. Midway up the block, he spotted a telephone booth on the opposite side and veered into the street, dodging cars with a hair-raising margin of safety and dragging Cassandra in his wake.

When he released her arm to dig out the necessary coins, she gave a sigh of relief and rubbed the area that his fingers had bitten into so cruelly. He began talking—his French, she noted distractedly, was far superior to her own—and she stood beside the booth like a mannequin, horribly aware of the ebb and flow of traffic all around her. The police were going to be too late to be of any help, she realized. Even if they believed Seth and acted immediately, the bomb—if there was a bomb—would likely be detonated in a matter of minutes. And if the Brigade was planning a drive-by attack . . . the thought made her sick. She held her watch up to the light. It was eleven o'clock, too late for an outdoor concert to still be in progress, surely. It had to be a scare tactic; a twisted warning to the city of Paris that the Brigade was still here, waiting for its next victims.

Seth was turned away from her, arguing with whoever was on the other end of the telephone. Without any conscious thought, she turned and started walking toward the park. By the time she had crossed the intersection, she was running, fumbling in her purse for the camera her father had given her for her twenty-first birthday and slinging it around her neck. Fear was gone— or at least pushed into some recess of her mind—and instinct was taking over. She had no doubt that a story was in the making. She almost missed the gravel path leading into the park. Her shoes skidded on loose stone, breaking off a heel. She limped along until the top of the acoustical band shell came into view to her left. She struck off across the grass, pausing only to kick off her shoes. Dodging low-hanging branches and leaping across flower beds that suddenly loomed out of no-where, it seemed to take hours to reach the area surrounding the shell. Once she did, she stumbled to a halt, panting, to find herself alone.

Stunned, she walked shakily across the lawn toward the shell, noting the crushed grass where people had been sitting not long before. She stubbed her toe against an empty wine bottle and she gave a small cry of pain, followed immediately by a laugh that was part relief, part frustration. The Brigade had tricked her; they were testing her, seeing how far she would go for a story. As she walked, she wondered idly if she'd passed their test. She smiled to herself, relieved that no one would be hurt or killed because the terrorists had decided on some kind of deranged final exam.

"Cassandra!"

She whirled toward the sound of her name, recognizing the voice at once. "Seth, it's okay!" She waved at him and started to retrace her steps.

"What the *hell* do you think you're doing?" he yelled as he strode toward her. "I told you—"

The rest of his lecture was drowned out by the explosion that destroyed the acoustical shell. The concussion from the blast knocked Cassandra flat and she felt her camera ram painfully into her breastbone. Groaning, she struggled to her knees. She had a glimpse of Seth running toward her, his face taking on a demonic cast in the light of the fire, and then something slammed into the back of her head and she sank into black, utter nothingness.

The blackness eased gradually, surrendering its grip first to the sound of sirens and a babble of excited French that made absolutely no sense until she concentrated on what was being said. The uncomfortable hardness beneath her told Cassandra she was not in her own bed. She ignored that in favor of the voices, and the concentration required for her to translate what was being said made her aware of the pain that sliced through her head. She silently uttered a few choice phrases she had learned from Kurt, the ones that definitely couldn't be printed in any foreign phrase book. The mental exercise didn't help the physical pain, but it served to reassure her that she had a firm grasp on reality.

She pried her eyelids open and, despite her blurred vision, was aware of people moving around her. Something had her left hand in a viselike grip and she reluctantly turned her head in that direction and struggled to focus on the blur beside her. Two hazy shapes slowly coalesced into one Seth and she tried to smile as she uttered a line straight out of a B-movie. "Anyone get the number of the truck that hit me?"

Seth's face was ravaged by strain and soot, the brackets around his mouth carved deeper than they had been just minutes before. His jacket was missing and when she moved her head, she could feel its material beneath her cheek; he had used it to make a pillow for her.

"No truck," he answered in a voice like ground glass. "Just a very large piece of acoustical tile. There's an ambulance on the way."

"I don't need an ambulance," she protested, trying to sit up. Pain lanced through her skull and she reluctantly subsided back onto the lawn. "Are you all right?"

He regarded her with black eyes that reflected only the flames of the fire on her other side. Whatever he was feeling was safely buried, tucked away where no one would find it. "I'm just dandy, thanks."

"You look like hell." She reached up a shaky hand and touched his cheek with her fingers. She might have seared him with a branding iron; he jerked his head back, out of her reach, as if he could not bear her touch. "Your face is dirty."

He ignored her comment. "You probably have a concussion; there's a knot on the back of your head the size of a golf ball."

"Lucky for me I have such a hard head."

He looked at her with cold, dead eyes. "Very lucky. If you'd been a few feet closer to the band shell you would have been blown to hell along with it." He looked away and caught sight of the ambulance careening to a halt on the street. Without a word he released her hand and got to his feet.

"Seth," she said hesitantly when he had taken a step away from her. "Did you call Armand? He's not as good with a camera as PJ but—"

She never had a chance to finish. Seth pivoted with a speed surprising in a man of his size and this time, his black eyes were ablaze with a fire that had nothing to do with the ruined band shell. "Don't worry, Ms. Blake, I know my responsibilities. Armand and PJ have been here for fifteen minutes. Your damn story will be on page one all over the world tomorrow." He strode off without looking back, and so he missed the tear that trickled down her soot-blackened cheek.

He found Armand behind the barrier the police had erected in order to keep the reporters out of the firefighters' way. "Well?" he barked when the smaller man smiled a greeting. Armand's smile immediately vanished at the bite in the words and Seth cursed silently. He was taking his fear for Cassandra out on the stringer, and Armand didn't deserve that. With an effort he brought his roiling emotions under control. "Are you finished?" he asked less harshly.

Armand nodded. "PJ has the pictures. The story may take a while longer. Neither the police nor the fire department is saying a word." He moved closer to Seth and motioned him toward the back of the crowd. When they had some privacy, Armand continued quietly, "The Sûreté is here as well, although they haven't announced their presence. I recognize one of their people."

Seth drew a ragged breath. "I've got the story for you. Get PJ and let's head back to the office." One of the *gendarmes* approached and informed him that Cassandra was being taken to the American Hospital. He also handed Seth his suit jacket and Cassandra's camera. Seth thanked him and went in search of his staff.

An hour later, Seth was at Cassandra's desk, composing the story while PJ worked in the darkroom. It was a simple, straightforward piece that should have taken all of fifteen minutes to write, but the words wouldn't come. The cursor on the screen winked at him, taunting, condemning. There was an invisible fist squeezing his heart, and his hands were so slick with sweat that they slipped from the keys whenever he tried to type a coherent sentence.

All he could think of was the stunned, fleeting look of understanding that had crossed Cassandra's face when the bomb had detonated. Had that same look been on Rachel's face? He hadn't considered that until now; he had drawn what comfort he could from the coroner's report that his wife and child had died instantly, spared the agony of pain. Had she known, in the brief slice of time left to her, what was happening? And Angela? What had been her last, childish thoughts? She had been too young to understand, of course, but had she been frightened? Had the explosion of sound terrified her? Sharp noises had always frightened her, he remembered now. He had been driving a nail into the wall one day and she had clung to Rachel's leg and whimpered until the sound had stopped.

The pain in his chest almost bent him double. Seth pushed away from the computer console and scrubbed his hands over his face. There was a lump in his throat threatening to cut off his breath and he coughed, fighting the sensation. The nightmares of his family's destruction were bad enough; the last thing he needed was to replay them when he was awake. He should never have returned to Paris, he knew that now. The city itself rasped across scars he had thought healed years ago, and the Brigade was rapidly opening new wounds in his soul. Cassandra, he thought, looking at the cluttered desktop. A battered plastic ashtray sat beside her phone; the lone cigarette it contained held the coral imprint of Cassandra's mouth on its

filter. She could have been killed tonight and—just as ten years
ago—he would have been helpless. He should have gone with
her in the ambulance. He knew that, but the action had been
beyond him, so he had done the next best thing. He had called
Kurt as soon as he had returned to the office, explained what
had happened and told the tall German to get over to the
American Hospital.

Shaking, he gave the center desk drawer a tentative tug and
nodded slightly when it opened. Typical of Cassandra, he reflected as he searched her desk, not to worry about security.
She'd leave her desk unlocked with the same blithe disregard
with which she ran headlong toward a possible terrorist attack. He found what he was looking for in a bottom drawer and
smiled slightly. He'd given up the habit seven years ago, but he
knew she'd have an emergency pack of cigarettes hidden away.
She was right in one respect, he concluded as he opened the
pack and shook out a cigarette. Stress could trigger a lot of old,
unwanted reactions. Cassandra's little gold lighter was still in
his shirt pocket and he used it to light his cigarette. His lungs
protested the invasion, but his nerves didn't. He smoked the
cigarette down to the filter, crushed it out and immediately lit
another.

"Here are the pictures."

Seth took the stack from PJ and sorted through it, one foot
propped on the open bottom drawer of Cassandra's desk. "I
took a quick look at Cassie's camera," PJ continued. "The
shutter mechanism is screwed up, but I'm sure I can fix it.

"And I have this," PJ added while Seth was making his selection. The Englishman set a bottle of brandy on the desk.
When Seth raised an eyebrow the smaller man smiled and
shrugged. "I keep it in the darkroom, for calming hysterical
interviewees."

"What an excellent idea," Seth murmured when PJ plunked
down the two coffee mugs he had brought along. Seth poured
a generous measure of the liquor into both cups and handed
one to PJ. "Cheers."

They both drained their cups and PJ, with a nod of agreement from Seth, poured them both another. "Has Kurt
called?"

Seth shook his head. "Not yet. I wouldn't worry, though. She's probably got a nasty concussion, but I don't think there was any other damage."

PJ sighed heavily. "This is worse than the time she disappeared for three days in Marseilles when she and Kurt were investigating the crime syndicates there." Seth jerked as if prodded by an electrical wire, but PJ, studying his brandy, missed the reaction. "Henri was frantic, of course. He called the police and the Sûreté, certain that something horrible had happened even though Kurt kept telling him that she was all right." He smiled. "She was, too. She'd been on a yacht in the Mediterranean, interviewing a drug kingpin. The only condition he'd put on the interview was that she do it alone."

"She's crazy," Seth ground out, his heart turning over when he thought of the danger in which Cassandra had willingly placed herself.

"Aren't we all?" PJ helped himself to another shot of brandy and grinned widely. "Until tonight the only really close call she's ever had was when we followed a gunrunner to Switzerland. She wasn't quite as good at trailing people then as she is now and his bodyguard caught her in a dead-end alley in Lucerne."

Listening to PJ was like worrying a sore tooth, Seth decided. The story alternately terrified and intrigued him. "You said 'we'. Where were you?"

"Sitting in a car around the corner," he answered ruefully. "We were in a red-light district, and Cassie thought a woman would be less noticeable." There was flash of some wild emotion in the black eyes regarding him so intently and PJ raised a calming hand. "I'm not stupid. I waited until she was out of sight and then followed her. When I saw the bodyguard I dumped my camera in the car, pulled on a coat and went after her." This time his grin became a laugh and he shook his head. "I became Lord Westmore, twelfth earl of Durham—I'm quite convincing you know—and Cassie launched into her rendition of a rather expensive lady of the evening."

"So that's what she meant," Seth murmured, remembering Cassandra saying that the reason she liked PJ was that he did a great impersonation of an English lord.

PJ didn't hear him. "Within three minutes we had the bodyguard convinced that I had a penchant for exhibitionism and that he had inadvertently stumbled into our rendezvous."

"Both of you need a keeper."

PJ raised his eyebrows. "Photographers are supposed to be crazy, in case you didn't know it. The incident did, however, convince Cassie that she'd better stop taking crazy chances."

Seth snorted rudely and lit another cigarette. "After what happened tonight, I rather doubt that."

"It's true," PJ protested softly. "You see, by the time I got to that alley, the bodyguard had a knife at her throat. When he left, leaving Cassie and me to conclude our 'business', she took advantage of the privacy to throw up. She's kept herself on a fairly short leash ever since."

"Not short enough," Seth growled. Snubbing out his cigarette, he glared at the computer screen and his abortive attempt at a story.

"This must be rough on you," PJ commented, following Seth's gaze. "Armand's a good writer. Why don't you tell him what happened and let him do the story?"

Seth glanced at the shorter man and saw the knowledge in his eyes. "Does anybody else in the office know?"

With his free hand, PJ thoughtfully stroked the ends of his mustache. "Not that I know of. You have a pretty young staff. I was just starting out at the time, working for the *Times* over here. That's how I know. It was my first major story." He considered the question a while longer and then shrugged. "Armand might know. Cassie had him pull a lot of clippings out of the morgue when this business with the Brigade first began. It's possible the stories on you were pulled for research, but she hasn't mentioned it."

Seth relaxed slightly. "I'd appreciate it if you wouldn't tell anyone, PJ."

"Not to worry," PJ assured him, "but it's bound to come out eventually, particularly if you react like this every time the Brigade makes news."

"And just how am I reacting?" Seth asked coldly.

PJ let loose a string of profanity that was highly inventive, even for him. "I'm no damn psychiatrist, Winter, but even I can see that this story is tearing you apart."

Seth managed a laugh. "I was wondering where your colorful speech had gone."

PJ's reply was typically profane as the photographer grabbed his bottle of brandy and disappeared into the darkroom. Seth crushed his cigarette into the battered ashtray, shoved his emotional turmoil into the back of his mind and tackled the story. This had always been his greatest strength, being able to block out his emotions in order to meet a deadline. He did that now, concentrating solely on the facts of what had taken place earlier this evening, not his emotional reaction to the bombing. Within half an hour the copy was rolling off the printer and he had selected two of PJ's photos to send to New York along with the story. When these had been entrusted to Armand, he returned to Cassandra's desk and cleaned up the mess he had made.

He'd replace her spare cigarettes tomorrow, he reminded himself. As he was closing the bottom drawer he caught sight of the sketches on the top file. They were caricatures, actually, and he pulled the folder out in order to see them better. Kurt had to have done these; he always doodled when he wasn't reading or writing a story. The younger reporter was quite good; Seth found himself smiling at the caricature of a horned PJ holding a camera in one hand and a pitchfork in the other. Seth idly flipped the folder open, wondering if he would find Kurt's version of Cassandra somewhere on the folder. It would be interesting to discover just how Kurt really felt about his ambitious co-worker.

Whatever Kurt had sketched there remained unseen. Instead of looking at the inside cover, Seth's black gaze wandered to the stack of clippings the folder contained. Leaping up at him from the first clipping was a black-and-white photo of what had once been a car but was now a twisted, burning scrap of metal. In the background stood a small house, it's windows shattered by the sound wave from the blast that had destroyed the car. The scene hit Seth with the force of a physical blow. He hadn't read the papers after the bombing ten years ago; there had been no need. The scene was forever imprinted on his memory in glorious, vicious color. His face hardening, he slowly thumbed through the clippings, hoping against hope that the file was the research on terrorism PJ had mentioned and that the article on his family was merely part of background material.

It wasn't. The file was devoted solely to him. It was a biography, pure and simple, and the tiny spark of life that had been kindled inside him during the past few days flickered and died.

His first reaction was disbelief; the next, agony; and finally, blessedly, a blinding anger that drove all other emotions out of his mind. How dare she? *How dare she!* How dare she treat him like the unknown, impersonal object of a story? And why, *why*, had she goaded him at dinner, arguing about the dangers of their profession and living close to the edge when all the time she had known the kind of pain such a conversation would cause him? And, worst of all, she had told Kurt what she was doing, had shared his private loss as if it were nothing more than yesterday's weather reports.

With great care he closed the folder, tucked it under his arm and walked the length of the room to his office. On his desk were other folders he had had Armand collate today. He dropped the one he had found in Cassandra's desk on top of the others and walked out of the Dateline offices. Thoughts of Cassandra were pushed to the back of his mind; right now he had to take some steps to protect his staff from whatever else the Brigade might be planning.

Cassandra woke to a pounding headache and a feeling that someone had used her body for a punching bag. Gentle snores emanated from somewhere on her left and she carefully turned her head until she could see Kurt, his length sprawled in an uncomfortable chair, sleeping soundly. There was no disorientation, she realized with a sense of incredulity. She remembered who she was, where she was, and why she was here. So much for the veracity of the novels she had read. She moved to her side, taking care not to disturb her IV, and stretched her free arm out to give Kurt's knee a shake.

"Wake up, sleeping beauty," she said in a voice that sounded hoarse to her own ears. When he simply gave a louder snort and burrowed further into the chair she shook him again, far less gently, and regretted her action when the sickening ache in her head increased with her movements. "Come on, Kurt. Rise and shine."

His pale blue eyes opened slowly and in spite of her aches and pains, she grinned at his moan as the effects of spending the night in a chair made themselves known. "It can't be morning already," he protested.

"I'm afraid it is," she countered, pointing to the sunlight that made its way through the drawn curtain. "You didn't have to stay, but I'm glad you did."

Kurt struggled to his feet and moved around the room in order to work out the kinks in his muscles. "I hope you appreciate the sacrifice. I was with a very charming young woman when Seth called."

"I'll make it up to you."

"No you won't," he told her, a hint of sadness creeping into his eyes. "We've had this discussion several times before, if you will remember. Your words were something about screwing up a perfectly good relationship with sex." At her hurt look he sighed, realizing his tone had been sharper than he intended.

She blinked away the tears that had instantly formed at his rebuke. "I only meant—"

"I know what you meant," he assured her in a voice that was steadier than he felt. "And I know what you want—a playmate, a friend, not a lover. I am content with the situation as it is." He flashed her a smile. "And you're probably right. Why take the chance of ruining a good thing?" Pacing back to the bed, he took one of her hands in both of his. "You scared me last night, *Liebchen*. It was worse than Marseilles. At least then you left a note."

"I'm sorry," she whispered. She was sorry for scaring him, for not being able to be more to him than just a friend.

"I know." Kurt murmured, understanding the path her thoughts had taken. He bent and kissed her gently on the lips, a friendly kiss only; he knew her well enough to realize that anything more would cause a rift between them.

When he raised his head, she was able to smile at him. "I want to go home, Kurt."

"The doctor said you would be released today, barring any complications." Still holding her hand, he made himself comfortable on the bed beside her. "I have to go to the office in a few minutes, so just call when the doctor springs you. I'll take you home."

"Thank you." Tears burned her eyes again and she fought them. "What did I ever do to deserve you?"

He brushed his lips over the hand he held. "You put a snail in my favorite pot of geraniums because I swiped one of your stories," he teased. "Lucky for you I caught the beast right after he'd had his appetizer."

She chuckled. "That was cruel of me."

"You made up for it by screaming when you found that stuffed rat in your purse." He squeezed her hand and rose. "I have to go. I have the feeling Seth will have my head if I'm late today. Don't forget to call." The order was accompanied by a wave as he disappeared into the corridor.

While Cassandra obediently took the medication brought by a nurse and waited for her doctor to arrive, Kurt negotiated the streets to the Dateline office. He was an hour late, but Seth simply acknowledged his arrival with a curt nod of his head. Margot—just barely recovered from her bout with food poisoning—greeted him anxiously, and as he answered her questions they were joined by PJ and Jules. Only Seth remained aloof, glancing at the group once from behind the glass walls of his office. Kurt thought that strange but shrugged it off. Perhaps Seth had gotten an update from the hospital that he hadn't shared with the rest of the staff. When the group's concern had been put to rest, Kurt took an electric razor from his desk and went to the men's room to make himself presentable. When he returned, he found the staff gathered around Seth's desk, obviously—judging by the brusque motion Seth made with his hand—waiting for him to join them. With a regretful look at the coffeepot, Kurt sauntered into the office.

"Now that we all know that Ms. Blake is going to survive her attack of stupidity," Seth began without preamble, leaning back in his chair, "there are a few things I'd like to make clear.

First and foremost, I want to impress on all of you the fact that we are reporters. That means that we report the news, we *do not make it*!'' He picked up a copy of today's *Le Match* and hurled it at a startled Kurt.

Kurt fumbled open the paper and read the banner with a sinking feeling in the pit of his stomach. Cassandra's name wasn't in the headline, but it was in the story beneath. In fact, she was mentioned several times, along with a good deal of supposition. Seth's name was given once. Wordlessly he refolded the paper and started to hand it back to his boss.

''Keep it,'' Seth told him shortly. ''I'm certain your absent buddy will want it for her scrapbook.'' A muscle twitched in his jaw as he brought himself under control. A moment later he continued in a cold, dangerous voice. ''Item number two—since we don't know yet precisely what the Freedom Brigade's intentions are, I want all of you to take a few precautions. Today that means that none of you leaves this office alone—Margot, this is especially true for you. Also, I don't want any of you to make appointments over the phones in this office.'' He fixed each of his staff in turn with a steely look. ''I have no idea how sophisticated the Brigade is, but we can't assume that they haven't bugged our phone lines or our offices. Therefore, anything you have to say to one another regarding where you, your family or friends will be at any given time, will be communicated on paper and then put through the paper shredder in the back room until I've had the offices and telephones swept to make certain they aren't tapped. If you find that inconvenient, then step into the corridor, go to the restroom, or use sign language, but keep your conversations in these offices completely innocuous.''

He leaned forward, picked up a stack of papers and gave them to PJ. ''Hand these out,'' he instructed the photographer and then addressed the group. ''This is my first and, I hope, only memo. Read it, shred it, and remember it.'' He'd come damn close to losing one reporter, and meant to impress upon them the fact that he didn't intend to come that close again.

The memo informed the staff that tonight they would be met by a bodyguard, women for the men in the office and, for

Margot, a man. They would be met at different locations—specified in the memo—so as to not arouse suspicion. To anyone watching, they would simply appear to be meeting a date. Armand's bodyguard would be waiting in the office when the stringer came in this evening. The bodyguards would stay with them until the next morning, when the bodyguards would drive them to an undisclosed location. Not telling the staff their destination, Seth explained, was simply another precaution taken for their safety. He registered their individual reactions with a kind of savage satisfaction; it was apparent he'd gotten his point across. "That's it," he informed them abruptly when they had read the memo and were looking at him in stunned disbelief. "Everybody back to work."

Kurt lingered as the others filed past. "I think I need to speak with you." He hesitated. "In the hall."

Seth raised an eyebrow but made no comment until the two of them were standing in the corridor. "Well?"

"Cassandra will probably be released from the hospital today," Kurt informed him in a hushed voice. "She's going to call me here so that I can pick her up."

"I'll take care of it."

"But if she calls—"

"I said I'll take care of it," Seth snapped. "Stay here and do your job. I'll make certain Ms. Blake is safe and sound."

He smiled, but the feral twist of his mouth was anything but reassuring.

Cassandra held the receiver to her ear and frowned when the call she had placed to the Dateline offices yielded the same taped message she had received the last two times she had tried to call Kurt. The pleasant female voice informed her that the number she had dialed was out of order and that no further information was available at this time. A shaft of fear twisted through her as she replaced the receiver. After last night's bombing, she could think of only one reason why Dateline's phones would be out—that the offices had been the next victim of the Brigade. There had been no news of any further bombings either on the radio or television, however, and that slender reassurance had allowed her to keep her grip on her sanity.

Sighing, she turned away from the telephone and leaned back in the chair. The untouched lunch tray caught her eye and she made a face at it. She had spent the last hour smoking, drinking coffee and trying without success to reach Kurt. At the thought of Kurt another dart of fear raced along her spine, driving her to her feet to restlessly pace the room, in spite of the dull ache in her head that the pain medication hadn't been able to eliminate. What had happened at the office, she wondered for what had to be the thousandth time? Why were the phones out of order? And if they were simply out of order, wouldn't Kurt have called her from another phone in the building? He wouldn't have forgotten his promise; Kurt never forgot anything—

The door to her room hissed open and she whirled, her hand flying nervously to her throat. "Seth!" His name escaped along with her pent-up breath. She covered the distance that separated them in a few steps and instinctively reached for his arm. "I've been trying to get through to the office, but all I get is a recording. Has anything happened?" She gave a nervous little laugh. "You can't imagine the horrible thoughts I've been having."

"Oh, I think I can," he replied smoothly, moving into the room and disengaging himself from her touch at the same time. "Are you ready to leave?"

At his cool, remote tone a wave of panic swept over her, rooting her to the floor. "Seth? What's happened?"

He regarded her silently for a moment, taking in the fact that she wore the stained beige skirt and aqua blouse she had worn yesterday and her long, golden blond hair was hanging in fascinating waves around her shoulders. "There's nothing wrong," he answered her at last, watching the bewilderment that came and went in her beautiful eyes. "The phones are temporarily out of order while the lines are being swept for wiretaps."

She frowned at him. "Why?"

"I would think it would be obvious, especially to you, that after last night we need to take some security precautions." She wasn't wearing makeup and the lack of it made it easy to watch what little color she did have wash away under the bite of his words. Ignoring her reaction, he glanced around the room. "Are you ready to leave?"

"Kurt—"

"Kurt is busy," he interrupted bluntly. "If you've taken care of the discharge papers, let's go."

Something had changed between them since last night. He had been upset then, and, from his point of view, with good reason. She had expected him to lambaste her for running off to get a story but in her wildest thoughts she hadn't anticipated his treating her with such glacial indifference. Biting her lip, she dropped her cigarettes and matches into her purse and slung the bag over her shoulder. "Yes, I'm ready, except," she hesitated before asking quietly, "You didn't, by any chance, happen to bring another pair of shoes for me, did you?"

He spared a glance at her bare feet. "Where are the ones you were wearing last night?"

She dug into her shoulder bag and produced the ruined shoe and its mate. "I broke the heel last night—" she started to explain, only to be brought up short when Seth impatiently snatched the one good shoe out of her hand.

With a quick, vicious movement he snapped the heel off the shoe and handed it back to her. "If you want my job, Ms. Blake, you're going to have to learn to improvise." He dropped the heel into the wastebasket. "Now are you ready?"

"Yes." She looked away from the contempt in his expression and slid her feet into the ruined shoes.

He let her exit the room first, and then walked beside her through the halls. In the elevator he punched the button and retreated to the opposite corner until they'd reached the appropriate level. He didn't say a word, not a single word, even when he opened the car door and helped her into the well-cushioned seat.

"Buckle your seat belt," he ordered before slamming the door on her and walking around the car.

Cassandra obeyed, a sick sensation forming in her stomach that had nothing to do with her concussion. "I'll need to stop at a pharmacy," she began, only to let the words trail off when she realized where she was sitting. "This isn't your car."

The red compact he had been driving had been replaced by a gray Mercedes, which, judging by the array of buttons and switches, contained every option offered by the manufacturer.

Seth adjusted his own seat belt before answering. "It's on loan from a friend."

"Some friend," Cassandra murmured, running a hand over the plush interior.

"Curious," he inquired scathingly. "Nothing keeps a good reporter down, does it?" He turned the key and gunned the engine. "Try to control yourself. I'm going to introduce you to the owner as soon as the Sûreté is finished with you."

"The Sûreté?" she echoed.

He didn't so much as glance at her; all his concentration was on merging with the traffic on Boulevard Victor Hugo. "They want to talk to you about last night's little episode."

"Didn't you tell them—?"

"I told them what you told me. They want to hear what your Brigade contact told you." His tone left no doubt that he, as well as the Sûreté, had considered the possibility that the two conversations could be radically different.

"I told you everything."

His black eyes sliced toward her briefly and then returned to the street. "I'm sure you did." The words were cold and distant.

Frowning, Cassandra watched their progress through Neuilly and remained silent until Seth took a corner that sent them heading west toward the Bois de Boulogne. "You're going the wrong way," she said finally when it became obvious he wasn't going to explain his actions. "The Sûreté is housed—"

"I know where Sûreté headquarters is," he interrupted. "Inspector Rocheleau and I felt it would be safer to meet elsewhere."

That irritated her. "Nice of you to consult me."

His hands tightened on the steering wheel. "We were more concerned with protecting your pretty little neck than pandering to your ego."

Cassandra held on to her temper with an effort. "Look, Seth, I realize you're upset over the way I acted last night—"

"Don't push me," he warned in a voice that was every bit as dark and dangerous as his eyes. "As a matter of fact, you'll be doing yourself a very large favor if you just sit there and keep your mouth shut."

Swallowing nervously, she subsided into the deep cushion of the passenger seat and watched the beauty of the Bois roll past the window. The vast park offered a seemingly endless vista of lawns, gardens and woodlands. She caught occasional glimpses of joggers pounding their way along carefully laid out trails and, for a time, they paralleled the route of the little train that carried children and their parents from the Porte Maillot to the Jardin d'Acclimation, the children's zoo and amusement park.

They cut through the heart of the park on Allée de Longchamp, the road that would eventually bring them to the racecourse at Longchamp, but once again Seth did the unexpected, turning north just as Longchamp came into view. When he turned off again, Cassandra realized their final destination was Bagatelle, the little château set on the edge of the park.

As Seth brought the car to a stop, Cassandra smiled involuntarily at the delightful picture the château made, nestled in grounds splendidly decorated with masses of water lilies, spring blooms and a rose garden. Without waiting for help, she exited the Mercedes and started up the path to Bagatelle. She had barely taken two steps when her arm was caught in a viselike grip.

"Rocheleau said to meet him in the rose garden." He pulled her onto a smaller, but equally well-maintained gravel path that skirted the château.

The garden was a fairly short distance from the parking lot, but the concussion had taken its toll on Cassandra's normally iron constitution, as did the uncomfortable gait caused by her mutilated footwear. By the time they entered the garden, she was more than ready to collapse onto the small bench to which Seth steered her. The garden wasn't terribly busy, in reaction to last night's bombing, and her eyes followed a young couple as they strolled through the heavily perfumed area, pausing occasionally to exclaim over a perfect bloom. Cassandra dug into her shoulder bag until she came up with a tissue with which to wipe away the film of perspiration that covered her face. She could feel Seth's presence just behind her, like some giant sentinel. A hundred questions tumbled through her brain but she didn't voice a single one. Not that she was afraid of his actions, she told herself, it was just that the questions would be better directed to the Inspector. Closing her eyes against the bright sunshine that was making her headache worsen, she breathed in the heady rose scent and forced herself to relax.

Several minutes later, Seth touched her lightly on the shoulder and her eyes flew open. "What?"

"Inspector Rocheleau."

Following his gaze, she watched a small, portly man enter the opposite side of the garden. Behind him trailed two very tall, very fit men that she judged to be in their mid-thirties. The Inspector, she estimated as he made his way along the path toward them, had to be in his late sixties. In spite of herself, she smiled as he paused to appreciate the beauty of a bloodred rose. If the look his escorts exchanged was any indication, the younger men clearly considered their boss's actions totally inappropriate.

"*Mademoiselle* Blake," the Inspector said warmly as he drew near, politely tipped his hat, and then, to Cassandra's relief, continued in English. "It was so good of you to agree to this interview when I know you are not recovered from your experience of last night. I hope you will forgive me for choosing such an unorthodox meeting place."

She inclined her head in such a regal acceptance of his apology that Seth couldn't control his snort of derision. As if he'd given her any choice in the matter, Seth thought. She'd heard his reaction, too; he could tell by the way her spine stiffened ever so slightly.

Cassandra smiled at Inspector Rocheleau as they shook hands, her bright aquamarine eyes taking in the fact that the two other men—bodyguards, she assumed—positioned themselves so they could see the various entrances to the garden. The Inspector didn't offer introductions and she didn't ask for any.

"Mr. Winter had told me what you want," she said when Rocheleau settled beside her. "I'm afraid I won't be able to add anything to what he has already told you." She shot Seth a swift look and then smiled once more at the Frenchman.

"Probably not," Inspector Rocheleau amiably agreed, reaching over to pat her hand, "but I hope you will indulge an old man."

Her smile altered subtly; instead of a sweet curving of her lips, it became harder, knowing. Mirroring his actions, she leaned closer and returned the patronizing pat on the hand. "Oh, Inspector, I think you're anything but an old man who needs to be indulged." She pulled back to her side of the bench and waited.

The genial facade faltered momentarily, allowing Cassandra to see the quick, dangerous intelligence of the man sitting beside her. The brown eyes no longer smiled; they assessed, and she returned his unwavering gaze with one of her own. And then, suddenly, the mask was back in place.

Rocheleau smiled guilelessly and looked at Seth, who hadn't moved. "*Intrépide*, monsieur." His eyes shifted back to Cassandra. "*Intrépide*."

"No, Inspector," she said quietly. "I'm not at all fearless. I just don't believe in playing games, no matter how civilized they may be, particularly when my head is threatening to split in two. So if you would just ask your questions so that I can go home, I would be eternally grateful."

Rocheleau inclined his head once in agreement and came directly to the point. "You were first contacted by the Brigade when?"

"Sunday afternoon," she replied, watching the young couple she had seen earlier. They too had taken advantage of one of the benches, and were wrapped in each other's arms, oblivious to the heat. "It was just pure chance, actually. I'd gone into the office to read through some research that I'd forgotten. If I hadn't gone in, Armand—he's one of Dateline's stringers—would have answered the phone."

"So you don't think they selected you?"

Cassandra shook her head.

"And yet the tape was addressed to you personally."

She looked at him sharply. He hadn't been the one to whom Henri had given the tape. The three men who had come to

Dateline's office had been younger, colder, harder. Drawing her wandering thoughts back to his last statement, she realized that, at the time, she hadn't given any thought to the fact that her name had been on the package containing the tape. "I assumed they used my name because they were familiar with my byline."

Rocheleau reached into an inside jacket pocket and withdrew a sealed plastic bag that contained the paper that had been used to wrap the tape recording. "Look at the address, please."

Taking the bag from him, she obediently did as he asked. It was just as she remembered; the address had been written in black ink, the handwriting crabbed. "I'm sorry, I don't understand what I'm supposed to be looking for."

From his place behind her, Seth had an excellent view of the paper. Rocheleau's statement perplexed him as well, until he remembered the first time he had seen Cassandra's byline. A cold hand reached out and squeezed his heart, freezing his blood in spite of the heat of the day. It took a moment, but he forced his voice to work even though it emerged in a lower register than was normal. "What name do you use on your byline, Cassandra?"

"My own of course," she replied with just a touch of aspersion, still studying the address. "What else—" Her breath caught as she realized what she was looking at. "Oh, God, it's addressed to Cassandra Blake, not C. Blake." She raised huge, frightened eyes to Seth.

"I am afraid," Rocheleau said gently, retrieving his one piece of evidence, "that you were not chosen by happenstance, *mademoiselle*. You were very carefully selected."

Blood thrummed in her temples; the heat made her vision blur, and the only thing that kept her upright was the fact that she refused to do something wimpishly female, such as faint. She drew a deep breath, struggling against the fear that threatened to make a shambles of her sanity. "All right," she whispered at last. "They chose me. It wouldn't be the first time. There's no law that says terrorists have to be stupid."

"Indeed not," the Inspector agreed.

Cassandra barely heard him. "The phone call last night—they knew where to find me. How?"

"Not from Armand," Seth put in before the Inspector could reply. "No one called the office last night to find out where either you or I were."

"Which means you are probably being watched," Rocheleau concluded. At her panic-stricken look, he patted her hand again, but this time his action held only reassurance. "Be at ease. We made certain you were not followed here."

"But the bomb," Cassandra protested, denying what she knew she must inevitably face as the truth. "There was no way they could have known that I was going to that bistro last night."

"You are assuming the bomb was planted before the concert," Rocheleau said in his genial voice. "In fact, it was small enough to be carried in a woman's purse. Our guess is that you were followed from the office and an appropriate site was then chosen. The bomb, you see, was not detonated by a timer, but by remote control."

The ramifications of that were almost too much to face, but Cassandra was, after all, her father's daughter. She drew herself erect and forced herself to deal with the facts in the same bloodless way she dealt with an unpleasant assignment. "Then I was right. It was some kind of sick test."

Rocheleau nodded. "I would have to agree. The Brigade followed you to the bistro and then to the park. No doubt they watched as they detonated the bomb." He transferred his gaze to the grim man behind Cassandra. "Last night was in the nature of a lesson, I suspect—to encourage the young lady to do as they ask or suffer the consequences."

A wave of nausea washed through her, whether from the concussion or the horrible feeling of violation, she wasn't sure. "Are the people I work with in any danger?"

The Inspector's Gallic shrug was eloquent. "With animals like these, who can say? But I do not think so. After all, the Brigade has chosen you to write their story."

"What if I spike the story," Seth asked roughly.

When the Inspector looked confused, Cassandra explained. "In other words, how will they react if the story is killed for one reason or another?"

Rocheleau's bow mouth pursed in thought. "They may simply go in search of another reporter—after all, they need the headlines." He studied Cassandra's pale face. "Is that what you plan to do? Kill the story?"

Cassandra shivered in the warm sunlight, permeated by a chill that went bone-deep. Covering an assignment had placed her in danger before, but she'd never gone into a story knowing that it might land her in a hospital—or a morgue. Abruptly she remembered the advice her father had given her when she had begun her career.

"You have to want the story more than anything else in this world," he'd told her over dinner her last night in New York. "You breath, eat and drink it, allowing it to consume you until it burns away everything else. Your mother never understood the way a story possesses a reporter, body and soul. That's why we divorced. She wanted a man who was home every evening at six, not one who called to say he was catching the next flight to Karachi." He'd smiled and drained his glass of whiskey. "I loved her, you know, and I loved you and your sister. That's why I agreed to the divorce. The three of you deserved more than a man who thought of home as a place to recuperate until the next time someone waved a red flag. And it costs a woman, too, Cassandra, so be sure, be very, very sure, this is the life you want."

Cassandra demurely folded her hands in her lap and returned the Inspector's direct stare. "No, Inspector Rocheleau. I have no intention of killing the story."

The Frenchman nodded, almost in relief, Seth thought, and then turned his attention to the tall American. "And you, monsieur?"

Seth fought the instinct to slug the older man. "As long as my people aren't in any jeopardy, I'll allow Ms. Blake to continue."

"Bon." Inspector Rocheleau spread his hands and gave them both a genial smile. "As far as protecting your people is concerned, I do not think you need to worry about security in that

respect. However, if it will make you feel more comfortable, I am sure that I could find a guard or two from the limited manpower of the Sûreté for your office—"

"Don't bother," Seth interrupted, reaching for Cassandra. "I've already made arrangements to keep my staff alive." He pulled Cassandra to her feet and all but dragged her back to the gray Mercedes.

Chapter 4

After sitting for over an hour in the sun, the Mercedes was stifling. Cassandra hit the switch to lower her window and discovered, to her consternation, that while the mechanism hummed obediently, the window remained firmly in place. She was hot, tired, her head ached abominably, and she was thoroughly fed up with the way Seth had been treating her since he had arrived at the hospital.

"Your friend needs to have his car looked at," she told Seth when he deposited his folded suit jacket on the back seat, slid onto the seat beside her and started the engine. "The window is broken."

"No it's not," he contradicted. "None of the windows in this car go down."

"Wonderful," she retorted waspishly. "He must be a big fan of steam baths."

"The air conditioning is already on. You'll be cool enough in a minute." He touched one of the switches and was rewarded with a muted click.

Cassandra subsided into her corner of the seat and rubbed at her temples. "What was that?"

Seth didn't reply immediately, but he felt a muscle work in his cheek at her demanding question. His eyes alternating between the traffic in front of them and the rearview mirror, he took a circuitous route out of the Bois. "I locked the doors. The seat reclines," he added when he turned onto Avenue Foch. "Why don't you lean back, close your eyes, and rest."

She would have thought he was concerned, except that he had issued the order in a cool, clipped voice that precluded such wishful thinking. Finding the switch on the side of the seat, she sank back into the luxurious upholstery and gazed out of her window. The seat had just settled at a comfortable angle when the Arc de Triomphe flashed by. "You're taking the long way to my apartment."

"I know what I'm doing."

She sighed and closed her eyes. Short of wrenching the steering wheel out of his hands, there wasn't a thing she could do. "At the risk of losing my job, do I dare ask what you're doing?"

"No."

Fine, she thought acidly. Have it your way.

A tense silence reigned for several minutes before Seth swore quietly under his breath and tightened his grip on the steering wheel. Whatever his personal feelings were for Cassandra, she had to be brought up to date on what was happening at Dateline and doing so was his responsibility. "I'm not taking you to your apartment. Now, before you start ranting," he added quickly when Cassandra's eyes popped open and her mouth started to frame a protest, "the entire staff is going to be taking additional security precautions during the next few days." His explanation was momentarily interrupted as he turned the Mercedes onto a side street without bothering to signal and then studied the rearview mirror.

"About the security arrangements," she prompted when it seemed he would not continue.

"Right now a team is sweeping the offices for bugs—and I don't mean the six-legged kind. Tonight, the employees' homes will receive the same treatment. I've also arranged to have the staff guarded, unobtrusively, of course."

"Of course," she replied dryly. "You don't think you might be overreacting just a tiny bit?"

Seth shook his head in disbelief. "I liked you better a few minutes ago—when Inspector Rocheleau told you you had been chosen by the Brigade. At least then you showed the common sense to be scared enough to pass out."

"I was not ready to pass out," she bristled.

"Of course not," he snapped. "That wouldn't fit the image of hard-boiled reporter, would it? God forbid you should be human like the rest of us."

"What, exactly, do you mean by that crack?"

"You figure it out," he snarled back.

Cassandra pressed her lips tightly shut in order to stop the flow of words that would undoubtedly cost her her job. Her temper was her worst characteristic and she had worked for years to bring it under control. But right now, temper was warring with control and threatening to win. With an effort, she closed her eyes once more and tried to relax. A shouting match right now would solve nothing.

They were stopped at a traffic signal before Seth glanced in her direction. "Cassandra," he said in a quiet voice that would not bother her if she was asleep.

Her eyes flew open and she turned so that she could look at him. "I'm awake."

"A lot of things are going to happen this weekend," he explained bluntly as the light changed and the Mercedes accelerated with the traffic flow. "In fact, a lot has happened this morning that I have to tell you about. I think a truce is in order."

"I didn't realize we were at war."

"Would it be possible for you to can the flip remarks for a while?" he asked through clenched teeth.

"Sorry," she mumbled, bringing her seat upright. "Go ahead; I'm listening."

Briefly, he ran through the precautions he had given to the rest of the staff that morning. "By Monday morning, we'll know for certain whether the office and phones are clean. If they are, then we can run the office as usual. If they aren't, we'll have to keep the precautions in place."

Cassandra puzzled over that for a few moments. "If your people find a bug, won't they simply remove it?"

Seth shook his head, his attention centered on the Paris traffic. They were crisscrossing the city in a seemingly aimless fashion before leaving for their true destination. Another precaution. "We're better off leaving any bugs that are found alone. That way we know exactly what conversations the Brigade can overhear. If we pull the bugs, we'll just have to go through the process of having the offices and homes swept again."

"Better the devil you know than the devil you don't," she said wryly. "Sorry," she apologized quickly when a muscle in his jaw flexed angrily, "force of habit." She scanned the dashboard and located the ashtray. "Do you mind if I smoke?"

"No." He pulled a pack of cigarettes from his pocket and offered it to her.

"I didn't realize you had any bad habits," she teased as she took one from the pack.

He shrugged and shook out a cigarette for himself. "Stress can defeat the best intentions. By the way, I owe you for the pack I took from your desk last night." He looked away from the traffic long enough to watch her reaction to that statement. "I hope you don't mind."

"Not at all," she assured him with a smile. "Although I do feel rather guilty."

"About what?" he asked casually, although he was silently willing her to bring up the file. He wanted to hear her explanation, wanted to rid himself of the paralyzing sensation of having been betrayed by the first woman he had been attracted to in years.

"About being the one to have participated in your downfall," she said, still smiling. "On the other hand, it's comforting to know that you have failings like the rest of us humans."

Unable to keep the disappointment out of his voice, he replied, "Oh yes, I do have failings. I seem to be a poor judge of character."

Cassandra frowned, wondering at the edge in his words, but decided not to press him. "Where exactly are you taking me?"

Seth drew a deep breath in an unsuccessful effort to suppress the bitterness washing through him. "To a little château about seventy-five miles south of the city. The rest of the staff will be joining us there tomorrow."

"You seem to be taking the long way around," she pointed out.

"This is a simple exercise to determine whether we're being followed."

She felt the blood wash out of her face. "You're not serious?"

He glanced at her and then executed another quick lane change without benefit of signal lights. "I'm very serious, and so is the man I've hired to protect the staff. He has people behind us, running interference in case we pick up a tail, and there are others watching for us at various checkpoints."

"It's his people who are also sweeping the office and guarding the rest of Dateline's staff?" When she received a curt nod in response, Cassandra sighed. "This must be costing the company a small fortune."

"It is," he agreed sharply. "But the company seems to value its employees. Do you get the message now? All you can think of is the damn story and how getting it is going to cover you in glory. This isn't just another story you've stumbled onto—these people mean business, and their business is death! They kill people with as little compunction as you or I swat a fly. Or hasn't that sunk into your thick head yet? Last night it was an empty band shell and even then someone got hurt—you—but a week ago it was a sidewalk café."

Cassandra's temper lit under the harsh indictment. "I am very much aware of what happened last night, as well as the threat the Brigade presents," she countered in a cold tone.

"Then act like it," he retorted. "Start behaving as if you have considerations other than your damn byline!"

"What would you like me to do, Seth?" she inquired sarcastically. "Burst into tears? Indulge in a fit of hysterics? What would either of those accomplish?"

"They might make you human."

That hurt more than she cared to admit, even to herself. She crushed out her cigarette, folded her arms over her chest, and glared out her window. The heavy silence hung between them for a full hour, by which time the buildings and crowded streets of Paris had been exchanged for a narrow paved road and the quiet, verdant countryside. Wanting to enjoy the setting, Cassandra touched the switch that should have lowered her window and then remembered that she was hermetically sealed in the Mercedes. "Damn," she swore peevishly, then turned on Seth. "What gives with your friend, anyway? Does he have something against fresh air?"

He didn't even bother to glance at her this time. "The windows don't work because they're bulletproof and it doesn't make sense to use bulletproof glass while at the same time allowing the people who are being protected the luxury of rolling down their windows for *fresh air*. And by the way, the Mercedes is also armor plated. Any other questions?"

The hard set of his face told her that answering questions was the last thing he wanted to do. Too bad, she decided, because she was more than a little tired of being the outlet for his hostility. "The car belongs to your friend?"

"To his company," Seth corrected tersely.

"He's a professional bodyguard?"

"A security expert. More to the point, he is an expert in keeping people and places secure."

Cassandra turned that over in her mind for several minutes. "An armored car, a hideaway in the country, a veritable army of people looking after the Dateline offices and its staff," she mused aloud. "This sounds suspiciously like a plan one of those nice Company men would come up with. You know the type—they usually work out of our embassy and have some innocuous job title like Undersecretary of Agriculture?"

"Mitch isn't CIA," he replied. "Not anymore. He retired a few years ago."

She made a small sound of disbelief. "Right. Now he's just your average small businessman."

"Something like that."

"A small businessman who, in just two years, has acquired the kind of financial base that makes possible an armor-plated Mercedes, a hideout in the country, and a sizable staff? Come on, Seth, don't be naive. He has to have backers for this kind of operation, and I don't need three guesses to tell me who—''

"Don't," Seth interrupted harshly. "Mitch is a friend of mine. I trust him and he trusts me, which is saying something when you consider the kind of life he's led. Don't even contemplate digging into Mitch's background or his company.''

"I hadn't intended to, but since you've brought it up—''

"What are you going to do, Ms. Blake? Build a file on Mitch like the one you built on me? Is that how you get your jollies?''

The accusation sent her stomach crashing to the vicinity of her knees. For the moment she didn't even wonder how Seth had found the file; what mattered was the fact that he *had* found it and was plainly furious. It explained his hostility toward her. "Seth, I—''

"I've been in this business a long time and I thought I'd seen it all," he said bitterly, enjoying the stricken look in those aquamarine eyes. "But you really take the cake. Your research was thorough, I'll say that much for you; and you're a damn good actress. All that talk about the inherent danger of our profession and how well I had survived it. What exactly were you planning? A feature about how my life had changed in ten years?''

She shook her head, horrified by the conclusions he had reached. "Seth, listen to me—''

"Ms. Blake, I'm hanging onto my temper by a thread," he ground out as he turned the Mercedes onto a narrow drive nearly concealed by a jumble of hedges and drooping tree limbs. "I am in no mood to listen to any explanations you may have to offer. Just bear in mind that Mitch is even less enthralled by having his background investigated than I am.''

Cassandra wanted to protest, but the look in Seth's eyes when he glanced at her kept her mute. The Mercedes purred along the curves of the crushed rock drive for a mile before emerging onto the beautifully landscaped horseshoe that fronted their destination. Seth brought the car to a smooth stop before a set of flagstone steps just as one of the double doors of the château opened and a man stepped into the late afternoon sunlight.

Turning to Seth, Cassandra laid a restraining hand on his arm as he touched the switch that unlocked the car doors. "You've misunderstood, Seth. If you'll just give me a chance..."

"Get out of the car, Ms. Blake," he said in a tone that matched the black ice of his eyes. He unbuckled his seat belt, opened his door and stepped out of the car.

Cassandra slowly followed suit and leaned against the car, taking in her surroundings. In front of her the graceful old château crowned a slight rise; to the château's left, and just at the bottom of the rise, stood what had once been a carriage house but now served as a garage. The lawn was beautifully landscaped and meticulously cared for. She pivoted to take in the rest of the grounds, and saw nothing but trees. They were smack in the middle of a forest, and as far as she could tell, the only entrance to the building site was the driveway they had used. The conclusion left her feeling slightly claustrophobic.

"Hello, Miss Blake." His English was pure Midwest American.

She turned to find the man who had been exiting the château just behind her. The first thing that struck her about him was that he looked rather like a rock star. The same height as Seth, he was built along sleeker lines, his body radiating lithe, supple strength. Rich gold hair brushed the collar of his shirt and framed a strong, angular face from which cold green eyes regarded the world.

The second thing that struck her was that his clothes were familiar. The shirt itself was commonplace enough, pale blue with a faint plaid, and it coordinated nicely with the darker blue summer-weight trousers he wore. It was the combination of the two that was familiar; she had seen it earlier this afternoon—at the rose garden at Bagatelle. The man who had been enjoying the delights of the rose garden with his girlfriend had had nondescript brown hair, not blond, but Cassandra was positive the two men were one and the same.

"You must be Mitch," she speculated, extending her hand and noting the controlled strength in his grasp. "Did you enjoy the rose garden at Bagatelle?"

The green gaze flickered briefly, acknowledging the truth of her deduction, before shifting to Seth. "She's quick."

"One of her less endearing qualities," Seth replied as he lifted two suitcases from the trunk and set them on the ground. "By the way, your car handles like a tank."

"That shouldn't come as a surprise." Mitch picked up one of the suitcases. "Let's get inside. Our security is excellent, but I don't like to risk long exposure when it isn't necessary. Miss Blake?" He gestured to her to precede them up the flagstone steps.

Cassandra did so, conscious of the fact that the combined state of her ruined shoes and aching head made her appear less than coordinated. At the top of the steps she heard the Mercedes's engine turn over and turned in time to see it being driven into the garage. To her relief, Seth, suitcase in hand, was climbing the steps beside Mitch. For one frightening moment, she had thought he intended to drive away and leave her here alone.

The foyer was dim and cool when she entered, a welcome relief from the afternoon sun, and she paused just inside the door, waiting for her eyes to adjust. When her vision had sharpened sufficiently to allow her to look around, she accepted with a sense of fatalism the man sitting on an elegant little chair at the foot of the curved staircase directly in front of her. She also accepted the holster slung across his shoulders and the odd-looking shotgun lying across his knees.

Footsteps sounded behind her and, realizing that she stood directly in Seth's path, Cassandra took a few tentative steps to the side. Given his present mood, he would probably walk right over her if she stood in his way.

"This is Franchot," Mitch said as he and Seth entered and put down the suitcases. "Franchot, meet Cassandra and Seth, two of our guests." He closed and locked the door behind him.

Franchot studied both of them, nodding his head as if satisfied with their appearances as he got to his feet. Cassandra swallowed nervously; not only was Franchot well armed, he was also built along the lines of the proverbial brick wall.

"Franchot, put the suitcases in the bedrooms," Mitch instructed, "and then call in the surveillance teams. When everyone is here, set the alarms and put the sentries on four-hour, rotating shifts."

Franchot nodded, handed the strangely shaped shotgun to Mitch, and took the bags upstairs. Cassandra watched the casual ease with which Mitch handled the weapon and shuddered slightly. Some primordial instinct whispered that this was a man accustomed to violence. Danger emanated from him and those green eyes held dark, unfamiliar emotions. He was as much of a threat in his own way as the terrorists were, and she had the feeling he could be even more deadly than the Brigade.

Cassandra controlled another shudder as she followed the men through the double doors into the library that opened onto the foyer. The library held three leather wing-back chairs with matching ottomans and two love seats, which flanked the marble fireplace on the outside wall. There were no paintings or mirrors of any kind on the walls—that space was taken up with bookshelves, which ran from floor to ceiling. The only exception was the bar that had been built into the bottom half of one of the bookshelves. It was to the bar Mitch went when he had closed the doors to the library, while Cassandra chose one of the love seats.

"Seth, I happen to have a bottle of twelve-year-old Scotch here if you could do with a drink."

Without a word, Seth crossed the room and poured a generous measure of the Scotch into a crystal tumbler while Mitch watched with a faint smile. "The idea is to relax," he chided when Seth took a long pull from the tumbler, "not become unconscious." He turned to Cassandra. "It's not a good idea to drink when you have a concussion, but I can offer you a glass of mineral water and one of the pills your doctor prescribed for your headache."

"How did—" Cassandra started to ask, but then thought better of it. Instead, she said, "That would be wonderful, thank you," and kicked off her shoes.

Mitch poured two glasses of mineral water and brought one to her. Digging into the breast pocket of his shirt, he brought out an envelope and handed it to her. "Your medication—at least, it's enough to last for three days. When you get back to

Paris, you can have the prescription filled." He smiled at the suspicious look she gave the tablet she had removed from the envelope, but the smile did not reach his eyes. "Trust me. This is precisely what your doctor ordered."

Curiosity won out over common sense. "How do you know?"

The smile widened. "I read your hospital chart. You'd be amazed what a white coat and engraved name tag can accomplish."

"I don't think I want to know any more," she mumbled, although she was still wary. Instinct told her not to take the pill; as she had told Seth, she was not convinced that this man was truly an independent businessman. On the other hand, even if he was CIA, he had been hired to protect Dateline and it's employees; she rather doubted even the CIA would try to poison her or slip her some sort of drug that would allow them to probe her mind with impunity. The little man with a sledgehammer was still running around inside her head; as a result, her thinking process wasn't exactly at its peak. She had the feeling she was going to need her wits about her to survive this weekend. With a little sigh of surrender, she swallowed the tablet.

"Good," Mitch said as he settled onto the love seat across from Cassandra, the shotgun resting beside him, while Seth paced the perimeter of the room. "Now, we'll wait until that kicks in and then we'll have a nice chat." He looked away from her in time to see Seth head toward the window. "Seth, stay away from there," he ordered. He was on his feet in the next instant, brushing past Seth to close the drapes.

The room was plunged into a murky twilight and Cassandra switched on the lamp that sat on the table beside her. "Is this really necessary?" she asked when Mitch resumed his seat.

"I'm afraid so," he replied unapologetically. "Until tomorrow night, I want to limit the number of people who know where you are. I can't do that if either you or Seth show yourselves. That's rule number one around here—stay away from the windows and the outside doors."

"I'm starting to feel like a prisoner," she murmured, digging through her purse for her cigarettes.

"For all intents and purposes, that is exactly what you are,"
Mitch agreed. "My people didn't see anyone follow you here,
but there is always the chance that they missed something. Until we can sanction the environment you will be returning to, I
want you to simply disappear for a few days."

"Why did I have to disappear today? Why couldn't I have
come with the rest of the staff?" Seth demanded. "She's the
one the Brigade has talked to."

"But if they've been watching her—and the evidence we have
up to this point says they have—then they saw you with Cassandra last night. My guess is that they've decided that your
relationship is more than reporter and editor. If Cassandra
drops out of sight, they'll follow you, hoping that you will lead
them to her."

The glare Seth directed at her spoke volumes and Cassandra
shifted uneasily. "I'm sorry, Seth."

For an answer he muttered a curse and stalked back to the
bar to refill his glass.

With hands that shook slightly, Cassandra lit a cigarette and
curled into the corner of the love seat. "What exactly is that?"
she asked Mitch, pointing to the shotgun.

"This?" He lightly stroked the barrel. "This is a twelve-
gauge, ten-shot Jackhammer. It's very efficient."

"I don't doubt it." She took a sip of water and then, her
heart in her throat, asked, "Do you think you'll need to use
it?"

An ominous silence descended on the library while Mitch
considered her question. At last he replied, "In my profession, nothing is certain. Experience has taught me to prepare
for the worst."

"You haven't answered my question."

Mitch sighed. "The odds are seventy-five to twenty-five that
the Jackhammer won't be used. That's as close to a definitive
answer as I can come."

"Thank you," Cassandra said in a quiet voice. "I appreciate your honesty." She dredged up a smile. "I guess this is
pretty standard stuff for your security firm."

For a moment, she saw a flash of emotion in Mitch's eyes,
but it was gone too quickly for her to be certain. "Security

firm," he repeated, turning to look at Seth, a sardonic twist to his features. "What a lovely euphemism."

Seth bared his teeth in a less than friendly smile. "It encompasses everything you do."

Mitch laughed and raised his glass in salute to the other man. "Now, let me tell you what I've discovered about your Freedom Brigade."

An hour and six cigarettes later, the faint tremor in Cassandra's hands had extended through her body to the point where she wasn't certain she could walk out of the room under her own power. Inspector Rocheleau had managed to strike fear in her; Mitch managed to terrify her with his calm, bloodless recital.

Seth's "lovely euphemism", Cassandra decided, was precisely that. Mitch might be a security consultant, but his expertise lay in the area of counterterrorism. And his expertise was impressive. In less than twelve hours, he had managed to penetrate from the top layers of the Brigade all the way down to its roots. In point of fact, she was certain he knew as many people in the terrorist community as he did in the law-abiding world.

The Freedom Brigade, Mitch told them, was a new organization; until a few months ago, no one had heard of it.

From what he had been able to find out, the nucleus of the Brigade had been formed by the more radical members of the old People's Revolutionary Committee for Freedom—known in the trade as the PRCF—that had surfaced eleven years ago. The PRCF still existed, but it was generally agreed within both the terrorist and counterterrorist communities that it was more or less ineffectual these days. Its power base had eroded several years ago when the more radical members began arguing with the newer, conservative members. Then the split had occurred. These days, the PRCF was limited to cranking out pamphlets and scrounging support for their cause. They seemed to have neither the money nor inclination for bombings or assassinations.

The Freedom Brigade, on the other hand, had it all. Support money rolled into its coffers from laundered sources, leaving the members enough free time to indulge in their pas-

sion for political statement through violence. The group was
wealthy and unhindered by anything as plebeian as a conscience. And Mitch's shadowy sources all agreed on another
point—the Brigade was planning something big. No one knew
what they were planning or when it would be executed—
Mitch's choice of words sent a chill up Cassandra's spine—but
whatever it was, they wanted a lot of publicity for it. That was
why they needed Cassandra.

"They set off the bomb to impress you," Mitch concluded.
"They want to be certain you know—and report—exactly how
powerful they are and what lengths they are willing to go to in
order to achieve their brand of justice."

The pill she had swallowed had taken away her headache, but
Cassandra almost wished it hadn't. It would be pleasant to have
something as mundane as a headache to distract her thoughts
from the current conversation. "They nearly killed me in the
process of impressing me."

Mitch nodded. "A mistake on their part, I think. My guess
is that one of the members got a little overanxious and set off
the bomb too early. They don't want you dead, Cassandra.
They want you alive and well, able to write their version of the
truth."

"How comforting." She nervously lit another cigarette.
"What about the people I work with, my friends? Do you think
they are in any danger?" Although she had asked Inspector
Rocheleau the same question, she wanted Mitch's opinion. His
expertise impressed her, even if his personality did not, and she
felt she could trust his judgment.

Mitch knew what she was doing, as evidenced by his mock-
ing smile. "For the present, I agree with the Sûreté's opinion.
That's also the reason for our little get-together this weekend.
We're going to do our best to insure your friends' continued
good health. With our help, your friends should be just fine."

"As long as I don't back away from the story," she added
darkly.

"It's impossible to call which way this bunch will jump."
Mitch shrugged. "But from what I've been able to gather, I'd
say your opinion is right on the money. Look," he added when
he saw the fear darkening her eyes, "whatever the Brigade is

planning is going to go down in the next week to ten days. So we get you through that time frame and everyone is home free. In the meantime, we'll take some extra security precautions around everyone's home and the office—little things, common-sense things that most people don't even think about. Nothing that will make you feel like a prisoner. I guarantee it.''

"I don't suppose it has occurred to either one of you that the simplest course of action might be to just put Cassandra on the next plane for the States,'' Seth asked coldly.

"I wasn't aware that was an option,'' Mitch said before Cassandra had a chance to voice the same thought.

"Escape is always an option,'' Seth replied, then drained the last of the Scotch from his tumbler.

Mitch considered that for some time before saying, "There are one or two drawbacks to that course of action. One, since the primary threat is directed against Cassandra, if she leaves now, the Brigade just may decide to make an example of her before she leaves Paris—it's called cooperation through intimidation—show everybody what happens when they don't cooperate with the Brigade. Not a very likely possibility, since they would have little time to plan such an action, but something that must be taken into consideration, anyway. Two, with the primary target out of the way, the Brigade may decide it's been betrayed by the press. I'll let you figure out the ramifications of that on your own.

"Three, the Sûreté is involved, and from what Rocheleau said—or rather, didn't say—I think he's planning something. And his plan involves Cassandra.''

Cassandra frowned, shifting under Mitch's stare. "I can't see how I could possibly be of any help—''

Seth ground out a curse that would have shocked Cassandra if she hadn't had a long association with PJ to fall back upon. "I hope to hell you're not thinking what I think you are,'' he told Mitch threateningly.

"Thinking what?'' Cassandra interrupted. "I don't understand what has you so upset!''

Seth's dark eyes pinned her to the cushions. "Does the term 'live bait' clarify matters?''

* * *

The bedroom assigned to her was obviously designed with solitude in mind. Aside from the bed and armoire, the room contained two comfortable chairs and an entertainment unit, which held a stereo, a color television set and a small refrigerator stocked with soft drinks. She had been shown to the bedroom by another of Mitch's employees, a slender, dark-haired man who wore a perpetual smile and did not speak English or French. Or so it seemed. In desperation she tried out her German, but that only seemed to confuse him, so she shook her head and gave up. She didn't even try to introduce herself or learn his name. He showed her the amenities and went his merry way. On one wall, a door led to a bathroom of sybaritic proportion; on the opposite wall there was a connecting door to the adjoining bedroom.

Curiosity compelled her to try the door, and she did so only to find it locked. Shrugging, she helped herself to a soft drink and settled onto the bed to survey her gilded cage. That was exactly what the bedroom was, she thought as she propped the pillows against the headboard and snuggled into them. The bedroom was, by any standard, luxurious.

It was also bugged. A camera was mounted on an upper inside corner. In view of the little red light that glowed just below the lens, Cassandra guessed it was in working order; and if Mitch and his cronies had no qualms about the camera, it stood to reason they weren't above a little eavesdropping as well.

Feeling emotionally and physically battered, Cassandra curled up on the bed, and went to sleep, hoping that when she awoke she would be able to sort out everything that had happened within the past twenty-four hours.

In the adjoining room, Seth sat in a wing chair and stared at the curtains which blocked his view of the garden below. Not that it mattered; the view was indelibly imprinted on his brain. His room and Cassandra's were at the rear of the house, similarly decorated, and offered a beautiful view. Beyond the garden, with its lush carpet of grass, neatly trimmed box hedges, and riotous flower beds, was a thick, primeval forest, and beyond that was the blue ribbon of the stream that threaded its way along the eastern edge of the property. The forest should have abounded with wildlife, but it did not. The forest had been painstakingly cleared of deer, rabbits and the like before the booby traps had been laid.

Only the birds inhabited the area, and not in the numbers that could be expected in a forest of this size. Animals were smarter than people, he theorized; they avoided areas they knew to be dangerous. So here he was, back at the château that had served as a CIA safehouse ten years ago. This was where he had been taken to recuperate and to allow various law enforcement agencies to pick his brain about his contact within the PRCF. He momentarily indulged in speculating about this very tangible link between Mitch and the CIA. Mitch had burned a lot more than bridges when he had 'retired.' His insistence that there was a Russian mole within the Agency had made a few people nervous and a lot more people extremely defensive. Apparently he still had a few friends in high places though, Seth mused, unless the CIA no longer operated the château.

His head resting against the back of the chair, he closed his eyes and allowed himself the luxury of relaxing for the first time in nearly twenty-four hours. In the time that had passed since the explosion he had not slept or eaten. Not that he had had much desire—or time—to do either, he thought grimly.

He had contacted Mitch in the early morning hours and contracted protection for his staff. By four o'clock in the morning Mitch and another man had entered his hotel room and proceeded to explain exactly what would be required of him and his staff. When they had left, he had called Tom Burroughs and explained the situation and Mitch's cash-and-carry accounting system. By eight o'clock, Dateline's Paris bank account had received a very large deposit; by eight-thirty, that same account balance had been cut in half.

The withdrawn funds Seth brought to his meeting with Mitch at a small café a block from the Dateline offices. Mitch had taken possession of the attaché case and, in exchange, had given Seth the keys to the gray Mercedes and instructions on how to get to the château. By nine o'clock, Seth was at his desk, trying to act as if this were simply another working day. Inspector Rocheleau had nearly thrown a monkey wrench into their plans but Mitch, as usual, was unflappable. He told Seth to arrange the meeting to be held at Bagatelle and not to worry; his people would be covering them the moment Cassandra stepped foot outside the hospital.

He opened his eyes and glared at the connecting door to Cassandra's bedroom. She was a younger, feminine version of himself; perhaps that was why he was reacting so strongly to her involvement with the Brigade. She was undoubtedly heading down the same road he had taken years ago, and the harder he tried to get her to change direction, the more she insisted on going her own way. Her persistence frustrated him. He didn't want to see her hurt, either physically or emotionally. He wanted her to live out her life without a gaping hole in her chest where her heart should be. That she was an attractive, desirable woman had nothing whatsoever to do with his motives.

Like hell it didn't. He gave a stifled groan and scrubbed his hands over his face. He had been attracted to her that first night, when she'd sat in the shadows of Henri's library and calmly set forth her reasons for doing the story on the Freedom Brigade. As they worked together this week, he had grown to respect her professionalism and had been even more attracted to the woman beneath the journalist.

If only he hadn't found that damn file. That was what really ate at him, knowing that she had dispassionately researched his life. He didn't know why she had done it, and he didn't want to know.

Of course he did; otherwise he wouldn't insist on worrying the question of the file. His gaze fell on his attaché case. He had inadvertently left it in the Mercedes and Franchot, after searching it to make certain nothing had been added to the contents during the few minutes it had been out of Seth's sight at the offices, had delivered it to his room just a few minutes ago. Seth had removed seven folders from it and handed them to Franchot, with instructions to give them to Mitch. The folders were copies of the personnel files of the current employees of Dateline's Paris bureau.

He was tired, Seth suddenly realized, both physically and emotionally. Tired of existing with constant pain rather than living. Tired of the hollow ring in his laugh—and of the fact that he rarely laughed anymore. He had thought the past ten years had healed him; it had taken being thrown back into the same situation to bring him to the realization that he was far from whole.

Rising, he picked up the attaché case, laid it on the bed and switched on the lamp on the nightstand. The locks opened with a metallic click that seemed to echo in the silent room. Dimly aware that the camera suspended from the ceiling tracked his every move, he withdrew the five folders he had put in the case early that morning. Four of the files dealt with the war-crimes trial that would begin next week; they were research material that he wanted Cassandra to study so that she could do the background pieces while Kurt covered the trial. Those he returned to the attaché case. The fifth he stared at, the caricature on the front of the folder swimming dizzyingly in his vision.

Like a blind man, he groped behind him for the chair and sank weakly onto the cushion. Drawing a deep breath, he opened the folder and began to read the first clipping. He read the clipping from beginning to end, unaware of the sweat that beaded on his forehead and soaked his shirt down the length of his spine and under the arms. When he was finished, he carefully turned the clipping over and read the next.

It took a little more than an hour for him to read the contents of the folder, an hour in which Seth was alternately assaulted by blinding rage and overwhelming sorrow. There was a moment, when he saw the grainy photographs of himself and his family reprinted in one of the clippings, when he questioned tearing open the old scars; the process could very easily drive him insane. He kept on, however, knowing that he had not been a whole man since the bombing. He could not live the next ten years the way he had the last ten. When he was finished, he returned the folder to the attaché case and went into the bathroom.

The camera's range did not extend to the bathroom, since it contained no windows or doors that led to the outside. Seth turned on the shower and stripped off his clothes. As he was stepping under the spray, he caught sight of himself in the full-

length mirror on the opposite wall and paused, staring at the
ridged, crazy-quilt pattern of scars that deformed his chest and
abdomen. He had become so inured to them that until now he
had been able to ignore their existence, unless some of the
shrapnel the doctors hadn't been able to remove shifted and
caused him pain.

Turning away from his reflection, he stepped into the tiled
shower stall and directly under the spray of hot water. He
worked the soap into a lather and washed away the trails of
sweat, scrubbing until his flesh felt raw. He rinsed away the
soap, turning his face into the heated spray; then bracing his
hands against the wall, he hung his head and let the water work
on the knotted muscles of his neck. A vision of his wife and
daughter flashed through his mind, and tears merged with the
water that rolled over his cheeks.

The mirrors were steamed over when he finally emerged from
the stall and dried himself with one of the thick bath towels that
hung on the heated bar. When he was dry, he cleared a space on
the mirror behind the double sinks and studied his reflection.
He barely recognized the man staring back at him. He looked
drained, empty; the old wounds had been ruthlessly opened and
cauterized but the process had left him numb. Too numb to feel
anything, even the pain of Cassandra's betrayal.

Out of deference to the camera—he knew Mitch was an equal
opportunity employer, and whoever was monitoring the screens
was just as likely to be a woman as a man—he wrapped a dry
towel around his hips and padded back into the bedroom.

Not knowing or caring what time it was, he turned down the
bed and crawled between the fresh sheets. He snapped off the
lamp, closed his eyes, and was instantly asleep. This time he did
not dream.

Cassandra woke to darkness and silence so complete that she
was disoriented for several moments before remembering where
she was and how she had arrived. Rolling to her side, she
stretched an arm out to the nightstand and fumbled for the
lamp switch. She found it, and the darkness in the room retreated from the light to the corners of the room. Yawning, she
sat upright and stretched, feeling the soreness in her muscles.

This minor inconvenience she shrugged off; at least her head was feeling better. A glance at her wristwatch showed that it was ten o'clock—her weariness combined with the pain medication had allowed her to sleep almost six hours, which, her rumbling stomach reminded her, meant that she had missed dinner. Her gaze wandered around the room before coming to rest on the suspended camera, and she wondered idly if whoever was monitoring the camera had been able to see the room before she had turned on the lamp. Perhaps the camera utilized infrared equipment that could be used during the night. The thought of being spied on while she slept was rather upsetting—not that she was exactly thrilled with being watched while she was wide awake.

She pushed those thoughts aside and made her way to the bathroom. At least in here she had a bit of privacy. When she had dealt with her most pressing need, she took advantage of the items provided and washed her face and brushed her teeth. She felt better, but when she studied herself in the mirror she groaned. She had seen pictures of war refugees who looked better than she did.

Without makeup she looked every day of her thirty-two years, and her hair was little more than a mass of tangles. Looking at her reflection in the full-length mirror she groaned again. Her skirt and blouse were beyond redemption, stained as they were with grass and dirt. She went back into the bedroom and opened the armoire. Her guide, through hand signals and smiles had made clear that the clothes inside were for her use. At the time she hadn't been interested, but right now she wanted a shower and clean clothes.

Frowning, Cassandra sorted through the clothes on the hangars, the lingerie neatly folded in the drawers, and the three pairs of shoes available. Everything was her size, or close to it, and obviously new. That led to some rather interesting questions regarding Mitch's operation and the suitcases Seth had taken from the car that afternoon.

Questions, she reminded herself, that could be answered anytime. She selected a pair of jeans, a long-sleeved, oversize white shirt, sneakers, and underwear from the armoire and headed back to the bathroom. "Sorry, guys," she muttered as she passed the camera.

Twenty minutes later, she was curled up on one of the chairs, working the tangles out of her hair. Mitch had obviously slipped up, she thought with the first twinge of amusement she had felt in nearly twenty-four hours, because she hadn't been able to find hairpins or binders in either the bathroom or the armoire. Not that it mattered—the knot on the back of her head was still too tender to even consider putting her hair up in a bun—but it was nice to know that Mr. We-Think-of-Everything was capable of making a mistake now and then.

Finished with her hair, she tossed the brush onto the bed, and set out in search of the kitchen. The upstairs hallway was dimly lit, utterly silent, but not deserted. It ran the width of the château and was bisected by the central, curved staircase. Two men—dressed in dark colors and well armed—were positioned at the landing; another four guards—identically dressed and similarly armed—were paired at both ends of the hallway. One of the guards, she was surprised to see, was a woman. The sight reminded Cassandra exactly why she was here. Aware of the six sets of eyes watching her, she took a deep breath, stepped out of her bedroom and quietly closed the door behind her.

Immediately one of the guards at the landing stood and walked toward her while his partner spoke into a hand radio. The man coming toward her was carrying what appeared to be an Uzi, but Cassandra couldn't swear to it. Until now she'd never had the need to become familiar with assault-type weapons. "Is something wrong?" he asked, coming to a stop a few feet away.

His English was good, but with a strong accent she did not recognize. "No, nothing is wrong." She offered him a small smile but he did not return the gesture. Civility was apparently not a requisite in this line of work. "I thought I'd raid the refrigerator, if that's not against the rules."

The look he gave her said more clearly than words that no "guest" at the château had ever made such an outlandish request before. "I can have a meal brought up to your room."

"That won't be necessary," she countered sweetly. "I don't want to disturb anyone. Just point me toward the kitchen."

"Wait here." He walked back to his partner and spoke into the radio. Cassandra entertained herself during the wait by noting the position of the camera in the hallway. Big Brother— or at least Mitch—was definitely watching. The guard returned. "Go ahead. When you reach the bottom of the staircase, wait and you'll be met and escorted to the kitchen."

"Look, all this really isn't necessary," she tried to assure him, feeling her patience erode beneath his bland assumption that she would simply do as she was told. "I'm perfectly capable of making a sandwich without supervision."

His expression did not waver. "You will be escorted because several alarms must be turned off in order for you to reach the kitchen. Once you're there, the alarms will be reactivated. Of course, when you are ready to leave, the same process must be repeated."

"Of course," Cassandra replied, pretending that the security precautions had slipped her mind when, in truth, she had not even considered the possibility of alarms. Feeling foolish, she did as she was told.

The guard on the first floor was less garrulous than the one upstairs; he nodded and preceded her through the lower level. She followed silently, trying without success to find some evidence of the alarm system in the rooms and short hallway they passed through. She did, however, spy the ubiquitous cameras silently keeping their vigil throughout the château. When they reached the kitchen at the back of the château, Cassandra opened the refrigerator, while her guard spoke into his radio and took up a position by the door that she assumed led to the outside world, his weapon slung over his shoulder.

After considering the contents of the refrigerator, Cassandra decided against a sandwich and instead pulled out the makings for an omelet and set them on the butcher-block island. "Have any idea where they hide the pots and pans?" she asked her impassive companion.

"The cabinets beside the stove," he answered.

Which was a feat in itself, she thought, since she could have sworn he spoke without opening his mouth. And then her mind registered the fact that his accent was American and she couldn't help but smile. "Thanks." She found a frying pan without any trouble and a brief search yielded mixing bowls, dishes and silverware. Knives and a cutting board were stored in the island and she was soon merrily dicing and cubing ingredients. "Would you like one?" she asked her guard. "My cooking abilities aren't exactly *cordon bleu*, but I do make a mean omelet."

"No thank you, ma'am."

"Ma'am," she echoed, her eyes widening. "I don't know whether to be flattered or insulted."

His impassive expression slipped ever so slightly. "You can take it as a compliment, ma'am."

"Okay." She broke two eggs into a bowl, beat them and added cheese, onion, and ham. "Do you mind if we talk? I mean, is it allowed or do you have to take some kind of oath to keep quiet around whoever you're protecting at the moment?"

"No oath," he told her, watching as she dropped butter into the pan. "But it's not a good idea to get too friendly."

Cassandra frowned at the pan, readjusted the height of the flame and, when she judged the melted butter to be the right temperature, added the makings. "Why is that?" she asked, glancing between her companion and the pan.

"Because you lose your edge, and in this business that can be fatal."

"I see. I suppose introducing ourselves falls into the category of losing one's edge?"

"Afraid so. Besides, there is no reason for you to know my name and I already know yours."

She smiled, not deterred in the least by his oblique refusal to be drawn into conversation. "Have you been doing this long?"

A faint flicker of amusement shone in his eyes at her tenacity. "Long enough to know what I'm doing."

"That is comforting. No, I mean that sincerely," she continued when he frowned at her. "If I have to place my life in someone's hands, I certainly hope he or she knows what to do." She turned back to the stove to check on the progress of her omelet. "I suppose you and Mitch are old friends?"

"What would make you think that?"

"You're both American, and close to the same age." She slid the omelet onto her plate and took it to the table that occupied one corner of the kitchen. "It's a logical assumption."

He watched as she crossed back to the refrigerator and removed a pitcher of orange juice from it. "It would be logical," he agreed as she located a glass and filled it.

Cassandra paused. "But not correct."

"I didn't say that." He smiled. "I think it would be best if we pursued another topic, ma'am."

"Meaning you aren't about to answer any of my questions," she guessed ruefully.

"No offense, ma'am, but none of us make a habit of talking to reporters."

"How did—" She stopped herself before she could voice the question. "Never mind; I imagine that information was part of Mitch's briefing."

His slight smile told her she was right. Digging into her food, she thought about the events that had led to her somewhat melodramatic exit from Paris.

It was when she speculated about the information Mitch had imparted to his staff that she experienced an odd—almost violated—feeling, realizing that at some point she had been dispassionately discussed by a group of strangers. She wasn't certain how closely her life could have been examined in the limited time Mitch had had, but the simple knowledge that she *had* been scrutinized—particularly by someone who didn't care about any redeeming qualities she may have—sent a wave of disquiet through her.

"Something wrong, ma'am?"

Her guard's voice broke through her musings and Cassandra discovered she had paused with the fork suspended between the plate and her mouth. Her appetite had suddenly disappeared. "No," she answered in a small voice. Dazed, she went about the task of clearing the table.

"Leave the dishes," her guard said when she started to fill the sink.

She did not have the energy to argue with him. When he used the radio to inform whoever was in charge of the alarms that they were leaving the kitchen, her only thought was, "So this is how Seth felt when he found the file in my desk." Quiescent now, she followed the guard through the first floor to the stairs.

When he would have turned and walked away, she laid a hand on his arm. "Thank you," she said softly. "I'm sorry if I caused any problems for you."

"You didn't," he assured her. "Good night, ma'am."

"Good night." She slowly climbed the stairs and halted in front of the two guards on the second floor landing. "Do you know where Mr. Winter is staying?"

The question sounded brazen, but neither of the men so much as blinked. The guard with whom she had spoken earlier answered. "As he requested, he is in the room that adjoins yours."

Hiding her surprise, Cassandra nodded and continued on to her bedroom. Half expecting to find Seth waiting in her bedroom, she was relieved to find the room empty.

Ignoring the headache that was making itself known once again, she sank onto one of the chairs, lit a cigarette and stared at the blank television screen, knowing what she had to do, but unable to decide how to go about it. Apologies came hard to her; during her disastrous, short-lived marriage, it seemed she had apologized for nearly everything that had gone wrong. When she had been free of Ned and his uncanny ability to make her feel guilty, she had resolved to take responsibility only for her actions, not those of the world—and people—around her.

Which was why now she knew without a shadow of a doubt that she had been wrong to create a file on Seth Winter. He had nicked her pride at their first meeting, when he had questioned her professionalism, and his skepticism had angered her, driving her to investigate him the way she would a story. It had been a stupid, shallow thing to do, Cassandra admitted now, but at the time she had seen him only as a challenge, not a flesh and blood human being. She only hoped she had not so alienated him that he would refuse to listen to her apology.

Crushing out her cigarette, she went to the connecting door and knocked softly. There was no answer, and she pressed her ear to the door, listening for any sound of movement. No sound came from the other side, and the doorknob didn't move when she tested it. The door was still locked. She rapped again, louder this time and waited. Nothing. If Seth was there he was either sleeping or else he wanted nothing whatsoever to do with her. At this point, Cassandra couldn't blame him for wanting to wash his hands of her and all the trouble she had managed to cause.

Feeling miserable and thoroughly ashamed of herself, she found a nightgown in the armoire and went into the bathroom to change. She brushed her teeth and downed another pain pill before crawling into bed. A glance at the illuminated face of the alarm clock showed that it was just after midnight. It was amazing how much damage could be done in a little over twenty-four hours.

Chapter 5

Saturday morning began with someone pounding on Cassandra's door with enough force to wake the dead. Dragging herself out of bed, she didn't bother to locate a robe to put over her long cotton nightgown before opening the door.

"What?" she managed to ask through a yawn as she struggled to focus on the source of the disturbance. When her vision cleared, the blood drained from her face as she saw the pistol aimed squarely at her chest. "Mitch! What are—"

"Lesson number one," Mitch informed her in a bland voice, "is that you never answer your door without knowing who is waiting for you on the other side. Understood?"

"Y-yes." She curled a trembling hand around the doorknob for support. "This is a lousy trick to play."

"I don't play tricks," he said in a tone that was every bit as hard as the green flint of his eyes. "What I do is teach people like you to stay alive."

Cassandra swallowed nervously. "Is that thing loaded?"

In answer, Mitch opened the cylinder of the revolver, exposing six empty chambers. "I also try to never place my clients in any more danger than they are in already." The cylinder gave a muted click when he closed it and replaced the revolver in his shoulder holster. "It is now nine o'clock. The first of the Dateline employees should start arriving within an hour." Reaching to the side, he pulled a covered breakfast cart into the doorway. "I'll expect you in the parlor at ten." With a curt nod, he turned and walked away.

Mitch had disappeared by the time Cassandra recovered enough from the shock of having a gun pointed at her to roll the cart into her room and close the door. With the cart in tow, she crossed the room and sank onto one of the chairs before her legs completely turned to jelly. Whatever appetite she might have had had evaporated, and she noted with a professional's detachment that she was trembling from head to foot.

Tears pricked her eyelids and Cassandra huddled into the depths of the chair, her arms wrapped protectively around her body. Fear rolled through her, leaving in its wake the sensation of being trapped. The Brigade had trapped her as surely as she was trapped in this château until Mitch and his people decided it was safe for her to return to Paris.

Paris. She had been so excited when she had been transferred here from London. Paris had felt like home and she had fallen in love with the city and its inhabitants. Until a few weeks ago, she had taken pleasure in the fact that her street lacked the harsh, modern lighting of some of the streets in Paris. Now, she knew, the walk from the Metro would no longer be enjoyable, nor would she take her usual walks around the neighborhood as she had in the past. The Brigade had deprived her of such simple pleasures, for now she knew that the shadows could come alive with a malignancy that threatened the innocent. Wiping at her wet cheeks with a cold, shaking hand, she considered what returning to the city and her job would mean. If Mitch was correct, the terrorists were watching her. Which meant she could expect the Brigade to get in touch with her again. She shook her head in despair. How could she have known that the story she had been so anxious to get would ultimately invade every corner of her life?

She was drawn from her dark introspection by the quiet, insistent tapping from the other side of the connecting door. It did not take a genius to figure out who was knocking, and Cassandra suddenly lacked the strength to rise. Not only had she complicated her life by involving herself with the Brigade, she had ruined the budding relationship between Seth and herself. It was probably just as well, she tried to convince herself; the last thing she needed was to be accused of sleeping her way to the top. The tapping continued and she gave a heavy sigh.

"It's locked, Seth," she called wearily. "And there's no key on this side."

After a slight hesitation, Seth's voice carried softly from the other side of the door. "There is on mine. May I come in?"

He probably wanted to pick up where they had left off yesterday. Which, she admitted to herself, was no more than she deserved. "Yes." Quickly Cassandra wiped away the telltale dampness that remained on her cheeks. When she saw the doorknob turn, she busied herself by pouring coffee into one of the two fragile china cups on the cart.

"Good morning."

Bracing herself for whatever was going to happen, she managed to compose her features and say calmly, "Good morning. Mitch brought me breakfast. Would you like some coffee?"

"Thank you, that would be nice. Black, please."

The cup rattled on the saucer when she dared a quick glance at Seth as she offered him the coffee. Dressed in gray cotton pants and a striped, short-sleeved shirt, he looked rested and, to her, incredibly attractive. He was also carrying a buff-colored folder under one arm.

Before accepting the coffee, Seth laid the folder on top of the covered plates on the breakfast cart. "You left this at the restaurant the other night," he said, fishing her gold lighter from his shirt pocket.

"Thank you." She carefully took the lighter, avoiding contact with his hand. The metal carried with it the warmth of his body.

Seth rescued the cup and saucer from Cassandra's precarious grip and took the chair opposite her. "About yesterday—"

"Don't," she interrupted softly, steadily, her eyes fixed on the lighter. "I owe you an apology. I treated you like a story and I shouldn't have. I'm sorry, Seth." She put the lighter with her cigarettes on the table by her chair and poured coffee for herself. A heavy silence grew between them as they sipped their coffee.

"Why did you do it?" he asked at last.

Sighing, she set her cup aside and nervously lit a cigarette. "Does it matter?"

"I think so," he replied.

She risked looking at him, expecting to find resentment hardening his features, but found instead a sad curiosity. "I did it because of the way you acted at Henri's party," she answered honestly. "Any editor would have been thrilled at the possibility of an exclusive interview with the Brigade. You were—I don't know—angry, indignant. Your reaction was confusing, given your own accomplishments. So, lacking any explanation for your behavior, I decided that the answer must be somewhere in your past." She shrugged helplessly. "I called Armand and had him put the file together."

"You could have asked me," he said, his eyes haunted.

"No, I could not," she contradicted, looking away. "We'd only just met; it was hardly the time to begin asking personal questions."

"So instead you did background research."

The bleak note in his voice brought fresh tears to her eyes. "Whatever you may think, I didn't do it maliciously. I only wanted to understand why you acted the way you did." She crushed out the cigarette in the crystal ashtray on the table.

Seth nodded. "I can accept that, I guess. What I find hard to swallow is, knowing what you did, how you could have deliberately led me into a conversation about the danger a journalist sometimes encounters when he's after a story. Even by your standards, that has to rank as cruel."

Cassandra pressed her lips together in order to control the cry rising in her throat. "That's the point, Seth," she said when she could trust her voice not to break. "I *don't* know. I never had the chance to read that file."

"Then why accept my dinner invitation?"

The breath caught in her throat. "You can't think that I accepted in order to...interview you?" He said nothing, a clear indication that her assumption was correct, and her heart constricted. "Oh, no. That is exactly what you think." She pressed her fingers over her lips and shook her head, experiencing a sense of loss that chilled her to the bone.

The silence that fell over the room this time was far more ominous than the first.

Seth watched her, aware of the way she held herself unnaturally still, as if she would shatter at the smallest movement. Her head was averted now, but he had seen the telltale redness in those magnificent aquamarine eyes that proved she had been crying. Over what? Seth wondered. The threat posed by the Brigade? Or his discovery of the file? He thought back over the past week. Their acquaintance was short, but in that time he had learned a great deal about her. Cassandra Blake was many things—ambitious, aggressive, intense. But, to the best of his knowledge, she was also honest.

He returned his cup to the cart. "God help you if you are lying to me," he said in a hushed voice that promised a merciless retribution if she was deceiving him.

Slowly Cassandra turned her head to look at him. Unknowingly echoing his thoughts she avowed, "I've been called a lot of things—and most of the time I've deserved the appellations—but I have never been accused of being a liar."

Her gaze locked with his, and after several moments Seth nodded. "Maybe the reason I've been so hard on you is that you're very much like I once was."

Some of her uneasiness faded and Cassandra watched him curiously. "Am I?"

He nodded again and leaned forward to tap the file. "Ten years ago you were fresh out of college. I was a reporter for Dateline, based here in Paris. I had it all. My wife, Rachel, adored me, my daughter, Angela, was a delight . . . but my job obsessed me to the point where I often forgot about them." He paused, feeling the ever-present pain twist dully in his heart. "Terrorism was just coming into its own then. A great many people truly saw the different bands that emerged in the seventies as freedom fighters. Some thought—as some do today—that terrorists were heroes. The world was just starting to learn the difference between terrorists and legitimate political factions the hard way. Do you remember?"

She nodded, a sense of foreboding enfolding her like a shroud.

"There was a group active in Paris then that called itself the People's Revolutionary Committee for Freedom. Mitch mentioned them yesterday. The Freedom Brigade was formed by the radicals of the old PRCF." He had to swallow the lump that rose in his throat before he could go on. "I was doing a series of six articles on world terrorism that was less than flattering to the different terrorist bands working in Europe. After the third article, I was contacted by one of the PRCF members. He wanted to meet with me in order to 'enlighten me' about his organization.

"I was young enough to find the offer exciting, and ambitious enough to find any danger a meeting with the PRCF might hold a challenge. I had, after all, survived twelve months in Vietnam. So I met with the man, listened to the case he made. The interview ran four hours, and I taped it—with his permission. I promised the contact nothing beyond accurate quotes and we parted on amicable terms. I wrote the story the next morning and Dateline used it as the fourth article of the series.

"The story was honest, but not exactly what the PRCF had expected. My contact called the office to tell me he wanted a retraction as well as a rewrite. I refused. The first threat arrived that afternoon. It was innocuous enough, I suppose, just a letter with no postmark or return address that threatened my life. Henri was the bureau chief then and he called in the Sûreté. The Sûreté immediately put taps on my office and home phones and set up round-the-clock surveillance on my family and myself."

Cassandra sat absolutely still, some dark instinct whispering that she should be able to guess what had happened ten years ago. She wanted to tell Seth to stop, that she didn't need to hear any more, but she could not bring herself to interrupt.

"The Sûreté did everything it could, and one afternoon a couple of weeks later, they intercepted a letter bomb addressed to me in care of the Dateline office. At that point, the Sûreté contacted the CIA and it was decided that the wisest course was to move my family and me to a CIA safehouse.

"We were living in Auteuil and I normally drove to work. The CIA assigned me a bodyguard—Mitch, as it happens—and he checked my car thoroughly before we made the drive back to Auteuil. The Sûreté was guarding my house, so Mitch came inside with me to help get Rachel and Angela ready to leave."

Each word he spoke was a nail in her heart. Cassandra locked her jaws together and waited, unaware of the tears sparkling her eyes.

"The authorities were never certain what methods the PRCF used to penetrate the security around my home, but that's what they managed to do. The guards were eliminated and the terrorists assumed their posts so that everything appeared normal. Mitch and I put the luggage in the trunk while Rachel settled herself and Angela in the car. At the last minute, Rachel realized that she had forgotten the stuffed elephant that Angela slept with. I started back to the house and Mitch crossed the street to tell the guards their job was finished.

"One of the terrorists must have panicked. Mitch was shot before he made it across the street." A fine tremor assailed Seth. He closed his eyes, lost in the past, oblivious to the present. "If the sound of the shot hadn't warned me, Mitch's yell would have. I turned around just in time to see the bomb the PRCF had planted under my car detonate. In less time than it takes to blink, they were gone. My wife and daughter were the price I paid for my ambition."

"Oh, Seth," was all Cassandra could say. Rising, she knelt in front of him and wrapped her arms around his stiff frame, conscious of the shudders that racked him. She clung fiercely to him, seeking to erase the demons torturing his soul. After several agonizing minutes, she felt Seth's arms go around her in an embrace that nearly drove the breath out of her.

"I'm so very sorry," she whispered when he was finally still. "I had no idea—" She broke off as his hands wove through her hair to cup the back of her head.

Seth pulled her head back just far enough to look into her eyes. "You really didn't know, did you," he asked in a hoarse voice. "You didn't read the file."

Any hurt she might have felt at his distrust was pushed aside. Given the past, he was entitled to a measure of suspicion. Her lips quivering with sympathy, Cassandra shook her head.

They stared at each other for several moments, each struggling with a past that had left deep scars of fear and doubt in its wake.

It was Seth who broke the silence. "Now you know why the thought of you doing a story on the Brigade leaves me cold."

"I understand," she replied. "Seeing that bomb go off the other night must have been horrible for you."

His fingers tightened in her hair. "I sense a 'but' at the end of that sentence."

"But the situation is different now. For one thing, no threats have been directed at me. For another, I don't have a family here that the Brigade could go after." She offered him a trembling smile. "You are afraid of history repeating itself. But it can't happen, Seth, not again."

"Never say never," he growled.

She laid a gentle hand against his cheek before she had time to wonder at the intimacy of the gesture. "Look at where we are. We're safe, protected, and Mitch is going to teach us all kinds of little tricks to make sure we stay that way. You've done your job; you've taken care of your people, Seth."

His dark eyes burned into hers as he pulled Cassandra upward. "If you think I called on Mitch solely to ensure the security of Dateline and its employees, you're not as smart as I thought you were. The Sûreté could have done that; so could the CIA. I brought in Mitch because of you, because after ten years of desolation you've made me feel alive again." Not giving her a chance to reply, he bent and captured her lips with his.

Startled, Cassandra stared into his dark eyes for an instant before her lids closed and she gave herself up to his kiss. His lips brushed back and forth across her mouth until she mindlessly followed his every movement. With a low groan he stopped the teasing motion and gathered her against his chest while his tongue explored the outline of her mouth and the line where her lips met.

Cassandra shuddered at the sensual request and opened her mouth to him. He invaded her with a slow, erotic deliberateness that heated her blood and brought her arms around his neck. One of Seth's hands disentangled itself from the wild mass of her hair and kneaded a path down her back. His tongue sparred with hers, seeking and withdrawing until she followed his line of retreat and found herself exploring the moist cavern of his mouth.

An explosion of heat burst through Seth. He eased back in the chair, his strong arms pulling Cassandra onto his lap. Instinct and the hand he pressed between her shoulder blades drove her closer, until her breasts were crushed against the solid wall of his chest.

He should have known that kissing Cassandra would be unlike anything he had experienced before, he thought as he tore his mouth from hers to explore the line of her throat. Desire, pure and sweet, shot like wildfire through his veins, causing his breath to come in short, rasping gasps that seemed to echo in the room. When he touched the tip of his tongue to the hollow of her throat, Cassandra gave a soft moan and sank her nails into his shoulders. His eyes opened lazily to watch his hand insinuate itself between their bodies to toy with the scooped neckline of her nightgown.

Cassandra felt the back of his hand brush across her collarbone, felt the scrape of new lace against her flesh as he pushed at the elasticized neckline. "S-Seth." Was that her voice, she wondered, sounding so eager, so... yielding. His breath fluttered hot and provocative over the tops of her breasts, and then his mouth was nudging familiarly against the lace.

Nothing in her life had prepared her for the sweet ache sweeping through her. Her ex-husband had considered himself an excellent lover, but he had never brought forth the rush of desire she felt for Seth. His mouth opened over her, his teeth scraped her nipple with an exquisite eroticism that drained the strength from her and left her clinging helplessly to his broad shoulders when he took her into his mouth and suckled gently.

She brought out the primitive in him, Seth thought, suddenly remembering the fact that this room also contained a security camera. The knowledge did little to dampen his ardor, particularly when Cassandra locked his head between her hands and urged him to repeat his attentions to her other breast.

He nuzzled the cleft between her breasts before reluctantly lifting his head and folding her against his body. At least he seemed to have had the same effect on her that she had on him, he noted, silently echoing the small sound of disappointment she made at his withdrawal.

"My God," Cassandra whispered, shaken by the intensity of what had just passed between them. His hand cupped the back of her head, pressing her cheek into the hollow of his shoulder.

"Exactly," he told her in a voice left raw with desire. Reluctantly he tugged the bodice back into place. "I wish we were any place but here. I want to lay you down…" His voice trailed off as a wave of anticipation lifted her head away from his shoulder, her lips blindly seeking. This kiss was the essence of carnality, born of frustration, and before he could remind himself why they had to stop, he lifted himself against her.

This time when they broke apart, Seth kept his hands on her shoulders, holding her motionless against his aching body. Her eyes slowly opened, and he caught his breath at the naked emotion in their jewellike depths. "If you continue to look at me like that, we're going to give Mitch and his cameras quite a show," he warned. Her eyes darkened; her fingers dug into his forearms and he bit back a groan. His body wanted her; his mind wanted her. And neither one cared that this just was not the time or the place.

"Stop it," he ordered, chagrined at his own lack of control. If she didn't help, they were going to end up on her bed and to hell with the camera. "Cassandra…"

She watched the dark fire in his eyes, admitting that his judgment was better than hers. "This is not the wisest thing we could do right now. In the past two days both of us have been through a lot."

"Meaning?" he asked, rubbing a knuckle along her jaw-line.

Her gaze slid away from his. "Meaning that getting involved right now—you and I—we can't be sure this… involvement isn't the result of being caught in an emotional pressure cooker."

Placing a finger under her chin, he forced her gaze back to his. "Is that what you think is happening?"

"Given our present, um, state, I think it's a distinct possibility," Cassandra told him dryly.

Seth's mouth curled slightly in response to her humor. "Why does that upset you?"

"Because I don't indulge in one-night stands," she answered with a blush. "And I don't want to be accused of sleeping with my boss in order to advance my career."

"I'm glad you don't indulge," he admitted, a vaguely satisfied gleam in his dark eyes. "Neither do I, as it happens."

"How comforting."

Seth smiled, choosing to overlook her sarcasm. The Cassandra he knew liked a neat, tidy life free of emotional entanglements; the realization of what had just happened between them set her world on its ear. He stroked her back soothingly. "Yes, it is comforting . . . for both of us. It means that we happen to believe in some form of commitment." Cornered, she started to argue but the fierce look in his eyes stopped her. "And as far as sleeping with your boss is concerned, no one at the office—including me—would believe that about you."

"Dateline isn't the only news organization in Paris," she argued. "My reputation—"

He gave her an impatient little shake. "Whatever happens between us is going to develop openly and honestly. Does the thought of that frighten you?"

Her life seemed to be filled with traps these days, Cassandra reflected, staring into his dark velvet eyes. "Yes," she whispered, nestling her head against his shoulder once again. She was less afraid of the damage to her reputation an affair would cause than she was of the damage done to her heart if she fell in love with Seth. And that was the problem. She knew herself very well; her attraction to him was more than physical. It would be all too easy to fall in love with Seth, and, given the tragedy in his past, she was very much afraid that he would never allow himself to be that emotionally vulnerable again. The wisest course would be to stop the affair before it began.

Seth held her close, his cheek resting against the top of her head. "If you're worrying about work, don't. I won't allow our relationship to intrude at the office." He dropped a kiss onto her hair. "I need you, Cassandra."

And that admission, Cassandra discovered, knocked any thought of fighting the attraction between them right out of her. Feeling the strong, steady rhythm of his heart under her cheek, she sighed, surrendering to the inevitable. "Yes, Seth."

When the black-and-white images of Seth and Cassandra melted into one another, Mitch turned off the video and audio feeds from the bedroom. Looking away from the bank of camera monitors to the young man standing beside him, he asked, "Satisfied, Greg?"

A grin lit the boyish face. "I would have accepted your word that the Blake woman was safe. This makes me feel a little like a voyeur."

"Just a little," Mitch asked, a hint of laughter in his eyes.

Greg shrugged, an action that seemed to detail every muscle of his wrestler's body. "Okay, a lot."

Mitch nodded. "Which is why I'm giving them some privacy. They seem to have forgotten they're constantly watched. I do have a few scruples left." He rose. "I'll walk you to your car."

Greg followed Mitch out of the room that—with its surveillance and communication equipment—was the nerve center of the operations carried out at the château.

The walk through the basement only served to strengthen Greg's suspicion that it was to serve as the last line of defense if the occasion arose. In the area they were leaving, the walls and ceiling had been lined with concrete that had been reinforced by prestressed steel. An emergency generator, cunningly vented nearly a mile away in the surrounding forest, squatted in one corner, unused as of yet, but conscientiously maintained. To Greg's knowledge only one entrance to the basement existed—the stairway they were using that opened into the butler's pantry. This entrance seemed to Greg the one flaw in Mitch's otherwise perfect line of defense.

As they passed through the door, Mitch caught the disparaging glance Greg cast at the frame and smiled inwardly. There was no point in enlightening his friend that the pantry was

wired for detonation from any place in the château. Or that the
same electronic signal would trigger the descent of a concrete-
and-steel slab to seal off the entrance. Or the fact that the
detonation would set off a series of secondary explosions
throughout the rest of the château, guaranteed to leave the
structure an inferno.

Those in the specially enhanced basement would survive the
blaze; the generator would provide minimal light and heat and
emergency food stores were maintained there as well. A second generator, which Greg had not seen, would recirculate the
air. Mitch had designed this ultimate defense when, through a
series of dummy companies, he had acquired the former CIA
safehouse. Anyone not in "the business" might either laud the
system or abhor it. Mitch did neither—he viewed this Götter-
dämmerung dispassionately, as a tool to be used if the exi-
gency arose.

He walked to the driveway with Greg, smiling faintly at the
black sedan the younger man used for transportation. "You
people have no imagination," he mocked, opening the door
with an elaborate show of courtesy.

Greg grinned, but made no move to get into the car. Instead, he propped an arm against the roof and considered his
former mentor. "I appreciate the call. The Embassy went crazy
yesterday."

Mitch shrugged. "When the CIA puts out the word that they
are looking for a certain journalist, it sets off all sorts of
alarms." Cupping a hand around the flame of the battered
lighter he carried, he lit a cigarette. "The last thing I need is the
Agency blundering around in its usual heavy-handed manner
and jeopardizing the lives of my clients."

Greg straightened, his grin fading. "Come on, Mitch. We're
not that bad."

"Kid," Mitch sighed, exhaling a plume of smoke, "you had
so many tails when you left the embassy this morning, it looked
like you were leading a goddamned parade."

"A fact your people took great delight in telling me," Greg
interjected, looking harassed.

"Once they'd pulled the tails," Mitch reminded him. "At least you were clean once you left the city."

"I'm so grateful, teach," Greg shot back. "I didn't ask to be dragged out here, remember. You were the one who insisted on this little jaunt. Talk about paranoid."

"Paranoia is the reason I'm still alive. If you value your hide, you'll develop a bit of it yourself." The gravel crunched underfoot as he turned back to the château. Greg's voice stopped him.

"Since you seem to think the Agency is run and staffed by a bunch of morons, why'd you call?"

Mitch considered that for several minutes without looking at the CIA man. At last he nodded and turned to face his questioner. "I know you're not a moron. I trained you. And, like I said, I didn't want you or anyone else from the Firm running around Paris, screaming that Cassandra Blake had disappeared and implicating the Freedom Brigade. The lady's got enough trouble."

Greg frowned. "I don't understand. She's safe enough here."

"Right, only she's not going to stay here. I've got another twenty-four hours and then she's back in the city."

"That's crazy," Greg argued. "Keep her here until the French get the Brigade."

Mitch gave him a cynical look. "I thought I knocked all that naiveté out of you before I left. This is the big, bad world, kid. The Sûreté doesn't have a snowball's chance of rounding up all the Brigade. And if just one of them is free, that means my client is still in danger."

"Then this entire operation is futile," Greg concluded, waving a hand at the château. "Either give her to us or send her home. The government doesn't intend to lose another citizen."

"Translated, that means the current administration doesn't want another black eye," Mitch surmised.

A dull flush rose in Greg's face, but he didn't back down. "There's something wrong with this whole business. I can feel it and so can you," he stated when the older man was about to argue. "There's something so out of kilter about this situation that it makes my blood run cold."

"I know," Mitch admitted, watching the curl of smoke from his cigarette. "And that's why I'm not about to hand her over to either the Agency or the Sûreté. The pattern emerging here is identical to another."

"And?" Greg prompted, his curiosity aroused.

Mitch dragged his thoughts back to the matter at hand. "Ancient history, kid. Forget I mentioned it."

Dissatisfied, knowing that Mitch would not say any more, Greg climbed into the sedan and slammed the door. Gunning the engine in spite of Mitch's long-suffering look, he poked his head out the open window. "If you need help, you know how to find me."

Mitch gave a grunt of bitter amusement. "I'd rather not have the Firm's heavy footprint over my operation, thank you very much."

"I was offering my help," Greg corrected in a wounded tone. "Not the Agency's."

"In that case, I'll keep your offer in mind." Mitch dropped his cigarette to the driveway, crushing it beneath his foot. "I appreciate everything you've done. If you ever want to change careers . . ." He smiled grudgingly and offered his hand.

"Keep your job, teach," Greg retorted, grinning. "Your pension plan sucks."

Greg took off with a spray of gravel that made Mitch wince. Sighing, Mitch strolled back to the château. Seth's call had set off all kinds of alarms, none of which had been assuaged when he had listened to the journalist's story. Was the Brigade intentionally creating the same situation the PRCF had ten years ago? He found that almost impossible to believe. Terrorists might not be mental giants, but they wouldn't be stupid enough to repeat their mistakes.

No, there was something else, something he and his people were missing. He shook his head as he entered the château. He had scheduled a meeting of the Dateline bodyguards after dinner this evening. Maybe listening to them would enable him to discover what there was about Miss Blake's predicament that made him feel that he had walked into a trap.

The château's parlor was as richly decorated as the rest of the house, Cassandra noted when she followed Seth into the room. Heavy velvet drapes of royal blue were drawn over the parlor's windows, leaving the task of illumination to the handsome crystal lamps scattered throughout the room. Couches and chairs with delicately turned legs were upholstered in brocade and satin. Furnished with antiques, its devotion to modern technology discreetly concealed from the casual observer, the château was a constant dichotomy; it was easy to believe the facade it presented to the uninitiated.

Mitch and several members of his staff were waiting, Cassandra saw, as were the Dateline employees. Her scrutiny ended abruptly when Kurt saw her and swooped across the room to gather her into an embrace that lifted her off the floor and threatened her rib cage.

"Where have you been?" Kurt demanded, putting her down and giving her a furious shake. "I called the hospital and they said you had left. I tried your apartment all afternoon." With a killing look tossed over his shoulder at someone who was out of Cassandra's sight, he added, "I would have called last night, but Frau Rambo there would not allow me to use the telephone."

Cassandra peered around Kurt and the rest of the Dateline staff, who had crossed the room to greet her and Seth. She wanted to get a look at the subject in question. As she was expecting to see an eighties' version of an Amazon, the petite woman with long, raven-black hair standing in front of the fireplace came as quite a shock. Looking up at Kurt, suppressing the laughter that bubbled up, Cassandra asked, "*She* kept you from using the phone?"

Kurt grimaced. "She's mean."

"I'll bet."

"She carries a gun," Kurt said in a pained tone. "And she swore she would shoot me if I tried to use the telephone."

The image his words conjured up was too much for Cassandra's good intentions. She started laughing and not even Kurt's hurt expression could stop the torrent. In the end, recognizing the faintly hysterical note in her laughter, Kurt pulled her against his chest and stroked the cascade of her hair. "I was worried about you."

"I'm sorry," Cassandra said, regaining her self-control.

"Are you all right?"

Cassandra nodded and pulled away. "Just scared. It's been an upsetting couple of days."

"At least you were nice and cozy here." PJ interrupted, pushing Kurt aside to give Cassandra a quick hug. "You should see the one they gave me," he went on, giving Kurt's bodyguard a quick once over. "Mine is taller than me and has the worst mouth I've ever heard," he finished in disgust.

"That," Cassandra declared, "is impossible."

"Just wait," PJ advised darkly, his mustache fairly bristling with indignation. "I'll introduce you at lunch. The experience will be enough to ruin your appetite."

Ignoring PJ, Kurt turned his attention to Seth. "You might have told me what was going to happen with Cassandra."

A lesser man might have been enraged by the sight of the woman he had nearly made love to in the embrace of two other men, Seth thought as he turned away from Margot, Jules and Armand and met Kurt's challenging look. Fortunately he was above that kind of petty jealousy, knowing as he did the relationships that existed between Cassandra and the two men. Thus the picture they presented and Kurt's attack were not enraging, only annoying. "The point of all of this is security," he told the younger man, unaware of the snarl beneath the surface civility of his tone. "Or haven't you realized yet the danger Cassandra is in? Whether or not you would worry wasn't high on my list of priorities."

"Seth." Recognizing the escalating tension in him, Cassandra laid a hand on his arm, anxious to defuse the situation. "Everyone is on edge."

Seeing the distress in her eyes, Seth relented. Taking her hand in his, he smiled at Kurt. "If there had been any way to let you know what was going to happen, I would have done so, but my first concern had to be Cassandra's safety."

Seeing their laced hands, Kurt's features contorted briefly. What he had feared had come to pass; that glimmer of awareness that had sparked between Cassandra and Seth from their first meeting was now in full flower. He recovered quickly enough, but his smile seemed a trifle forced as he accepted Seth's apology. "I understand." He glanced at Cassandra. "Cassandra's safety is, naturally, of utmost importance."

"Ladies and gentlemen," Mitch said in a voice that carried commandingly through the room. "If you would be so good as to sit down, I'd like to tell you all how to protect yourselves."

Obediently, like wayward school children, Cassandra thought, everyone found a seat and gazed expectantly at Mitch.

Mitch seemed to think the same thing, given the wry twist of his mouth as he took a place in front of a pair of closed drapes. "First of all, this isn't a lecture, so you don't need to take notes." He raised an eyebrow at a flustered Margot, who immediately flipped her notepad closed and returned it and the pen to her purse. "Also, since I had better not end up as a story for any of you, there is no need to make certain you quote me accurately." This time his gaze rested on Armand. The young Frenchman mumbled an apology and switched off the tape recorder he had placed on an end table. At a nod from Mitch, one of his men ejected the tape cassette and left the room. "It will be returned to you before you leave," Mitch assured Armand.

Completely erased, Cassandra did not doubt. It seemed a superfluous precaution, designed only to prove once again how completely under Mitch's control they were. She stirred slightly on the settee she shared with Seth, chafing at this reminder of just how much her life had changed in the past forty-eight hours. As if sensing her thoughts, Seth settled an arm around her shoulders. Lifting her head, she met his steady gaze and marveled at his ability to soothe her. With a faint smile, she turned her attention back to Mitch.

"Now then, people, listen up," Mitch ordered. "Most of what I'm going to tell you is common sense, but there may be a few things that you haven't considered."

He then proceeded, with the aid of diagrams, slides, and videotape to lecture the Dateline staff for most of the day. As he had said, most of what he told them was common sense—if one lived with the caveat that there were people out there whose aim was to threaten or take one's life.

The most important element was to eliminate the "it can't happen to me" posture that most civilians—as Mitch termed anyone without his expertise—adopted. To demonstrate how flawed that attitude was, he showed several graphic slides of terrorist attacks. Airports, hotels, nightclubs, banks, automobiles, department stores and sidewalk cafés, all flashed onto the screen in grisly, living color.

Since it was unrealistic to assume that any of them would lock themselves inside their apartments and never come out, Mitch told his stunned audience, their best defense was prevention. Thus began the list of "don'ts" that was guaranteed to leave the most well-adjusted psyche sitting just to the right of paranoia.

Don't leave for work at the same time every day.

Don't give any clues that you are about to leave your home.

Don't enter or exit by the same doors at home or work; in addition, don't follow a pattern in your use of alternate doors.

Don't leave your car parked in an insecure location.

Don't take the same route to work each day.

Don't use your home or work telephone to make appointments.

"You forgot to tell us not to talk to strangers," Armand interjected sarcastically when Mitch paused in his recital.

Armand's sarcasm drew a few self-conscious smiles and chuckles from the Dateline people, and a stony look from Mitch.

"I assumed that warning wasn't necessary," Mitch said when an uncomfortable silence fell throughout the room. "I see I was wrong. You may now add that precaution to the others."

Kurt, his long frame lounging in the depths of a wing chair, came to his co-worker's defense. "I think what Armand is trying to say is that none of us are children. Some of your precautions are a bit . . . redundant."

"Really," Mitch drawled lazily. "Tell me, Mr. Leihmann, were you followed to your apartment last night?"

"No." The single word was voiced with supreme confidence.

Mitch turned to the petite young woman assigned to Kurt. "Maureen?"

"Two men in a late-model beige coupe," Maureen replied. "They parked across the street from Leihmann's building and tried to follow us this morning."

"What happened?"

Maureen flashed him a wicked smile that would have charmed the skin off a snake. "They lost me in traffic."

Cassandra was about to ask how something like that could have happened, but Kurt beat her to it.

"Are you talking about the one-way street you turned onto? The one where you were going *against* traffic?" the German asked in a voice that indicated precisely how he felt about that little trick. "We could have been killed."

Maureen looked at him in surprise. "Don't be ridiculous. The danger to us was minimal."

From the expression on Kurt's face, it was plain that he felt Maureen's statement was debatable. He did not press the point, however. Instead, with a withering look for his bodyguard, he retreated to the corner of his chair.

"If there are no further objections?" Mitch looked around the silent group and nodded approvingly. "Wonderful. Now let's discuss how to go about the business of spotting a tail—and what to do once you have decided that you are being followed."

They spent the day in the back parlor, with time off every three hours to make use of the powder room cleverly tucked beneath the staircase. Food was brought to the parlor by the guard who had accompanied Cassandra the previous night, and removed by another man Cassandra had not seen before. By five o'clock, Cassandra had been emotionally and intellectually numbed by both Mitch's recitation and the slide presentation.

"In light of everything you have discussed," Margot said when Mitch finally called it a day, "It is obvious that few, if any, of us are equipped to deal with these people. Would it not be sensible to simply retain our bodyguards until the threat has passed?"

"Given what has been happening the past fifteen years, this type of threat is never totally removed," Mitch answered. "Even if Dateline would consider providing its people with round-the-clock security, can any of you say that you would care to live that way indefinitely?'' A low murmur of dissension ran through the group and he nodded. "You see, that prospect isn't pleasant either. What my staff and I are trying to do is teach each of you how to recognize and minimize the threat organizations such as the Brigade present.''

At a nod from Mitch, Maureen opened the parlor doors. "Dinner is at six-thirty, and you have the evening free," he informed the Dateline people as his staff filed out of the room. "We will resume tomorrow morning at ten.''

"Resume what?" Seth wanted to know.

Mitch raised an eyebrow. "You've paid for the deluxe program, so tomorrow you all get the 'B and B' course—the procedure for locating bugs and bombs. I'm also going to give you a crash course in evasive driving.'' With a nod, he followed his people from the parlor, closing the doors behind him.

Silence reigned in the parlor for a full minute after Mitch departed, and then Seth was deluged with questions. Sighing, he lightly squeezed Cassandra's shoulder and rose to confront his staff. "People," he said loudly, in order to be heard over their voices. "One at a time, if you please.''

Inevitably PJ spoke first, his speech as colorful as ever. "Who the hell is this guy," the photographer demanded. "How long are we going to have to stay here?''

"Mitch is a counterterrorist consultant," he explained evenly. "Since I can't tell you more that that, you'll just have to take my word for it that he knows what he's doing. As for how long we'll be here, we will return to Paris tomorrow evening and work will continue as usual on Monday.''

"What about the office?" Jules asked. "If we are being watched by the Brigade, they are bound to become suspicious when the offices are deserted for two days.''

"They aren't deserted," Seth said patiently. "Mitch has three people at the Dateline office—with New York's blessing, by the way. Obviously they won't file stories, but they will answer the phones and make it seem like business as usual.''

Kurt snorted. "If I was followed, it is probably safe to assume that the others were. The Brigade will know that whoever is in the office, they are not any of the usual staff.''

"Perhaps. On the other hand, it's highly doubtful that any of the terrorists will risk going to the office." Seth shrugged. "And if they suspect we've brought in professional help, so much the better."

"We may have another problem," Margot put in. "Yesterday afternoon the Brigade announced that they were responsible for the bombing, and once the office phones were back in service we had our hands full with reporters calling to demand an interview with either you or Cassandra. Telling these people that neither of you is available and answering the rest of their questions with 'no comment' only heightens their curiosity and hurts Dateline's reputation."

"Let them wonder. The object of this little exercise is to keep you alive, and I frankly don't give a damn about anything else," Seth flared. "Is that understood?"

"Seth, Margot has a point," Cassandra said in the deafening silence that followed his outburst. "I'm going to have to take those phone calls on Monday."

The gaze Seth turned on Cassandra spoke volumes. "And tell them what?"

"That my being at the explosion was a fluke," she replied steadily, her eyes never leaving his. "And that I have never had any contact with the terrorist group taking credit for the bombing." It would be a simple enough fiction to maintain; aside from Seth and Henri, the only person who knew about her prior contact with the Brigade was Kurt, and Cassandra was certain he would back her story. As far as the rest of the Dateline staff knew, the bomb had been her first exposure to the terrorists.

Some of the tension seemed to go out of Seth at her reply and he gave a short nod. "Okay." He turned back to survey the rest of his staff. "Any other questions?"

"I hadn't planned on spending the night," PJ replied. "I didn't even bring a toothbrush."

"I wouldn't worry about that; Mitch is known for his preparation work. Anything else?" When no one answered, Seth crossed the room and opened the doors. "Mitch will have someone show you to your rooms. Remember that you aren't allowed out of the château and keep the drapes closed."

Kurt waited until the others had gone before approaching Cassandra. "You have a slight problem that I didn't want to bring up in front of the others."

She scooted over to give him room to sit down. "Only a slight problem? After everything that has happened, a slight problem will be a relief."

"Everything is relative, I suppose," Kurt answered, glancing up as Seth joined them. "No pun intended."

"I must be a little slower than I thought," Cassandra said with a laugh. "I missed the pun."

Kurt shook his head. "I haven't gotten to it yet. Aside from the various reporters that called yesterday, I took two other interesting calls. Both from the United States."

Cassandra groaned. "Let me guess. My mother and father both burned up the transatlantic lines to find out whether I was alive or dead."

"Not exactly." Kurt sighed. "Your father did call and I assured him that you were fine, just incommunicado for a day or two. He told me to tell you that he was catching the next plane out of Kennedy."

"Oh, hell." Cassandra absently rubbed at the headache that had begun assaulting her temples. "Tell me this is your idea of a sick joke."

"I wish it were." Kurt offered an encouraging smile. "Look, how bad can his visit be?"

"You wouldn't ask that if you had ever met the great Robert Townsend. Hurricanes are more subtle in making their presence known." She shook her head and looked at Seth. "My father's first action when he lands will be to call the Dateline offices and then my apartment. When he doesn't find me, I imagine he'll storm into the embassy and demand to know what has happened to his daughter. Since the embassy has more leaks than a sieve, the Paris papers will have that enticing tidbit in print by Monday, at the latest. What does this do to your plan to keep this incident as quiet as possible?"

Seth shrugged. "Maybe it's better this way. His visit will lend credence to your statement that there was no prior contact between yourself and the Brigade."

Cassandra lit a cigarette and considered that. "I hadn't thought of it that way, but it makes sense. Given my father's profession, he would hardly descend on Paris if he knew that he might be endangering a story." She smiled wryly. "And once he knows exactly what the situation is, he'll leave just as quickly as he can."

"I hate to throw a pall on your rosy scenario," Kurt said quietly, "but I am afraid you have another small problem. Your father called me back an hour later. Ned is accompanying him to Paris."

"Ned? Ned Blake, the scourge of Manhattan?" Cassandra stared at him for several moments before saying calmly, "Go get PJ. I don't have a phrase worthy of this situation."

After seeing Kurt and Cassandra to their rooms, Seth returned to the lower level of the château and, through one of the guards, sent word to Mitch that he needed to see him before dinner. He waited for Mitch in the library, and by the time the ex-CIA agent arrived, Seth had downed two straight Scotches and was refilling his glass.

"Something for you," Seth asked when Mitch strolled into the library.

Mitch shook his head. "Not while I'm working, remember? Anyway, I don't think the supply could withstand the demands if both of us decided to get drunk." He took one of the leather chairs and stretched his long legs out in front of him.

"I don't plan to get drunk," Seth informed him, taking the chair across from Mitch.

A faint glimmer of amusement came and went in Mitch's eyes. "Right. So what's so urgent that you had to talk to me immediately?"

"Cassandra's father and ex-husband are going to show up in Paris." He gestured helplessly. "They may be here already."

Mitch frowned and absentmindedly pulled an unfiltered cigarette from his shirt pocket and lit it. "I take it they could prove to be a problem?"

"Possibly. Cassandra thinks her father is going to raise a big stink at the embassy when he can't locate her."

"Okay, I'll take care of it." Mitch exhaled and studied the other man. "How are you holding up?"

"Don't your cameras and microphones tell you everything?"

"Not what's going on inside a person's head," Mitch replied, unoffended.

Seth thoughtfully rolled the glass between his palms. "Life has a way of sneaking up on you and slapping you right in the face. I've had ten years to come to terms with what happened to my family, and I thought I had—until two days ago. The bombing brought it all back; that's when I realized that I hadn't come to terms with anything. Instead, I'd run away." He leaned back in his chair and met his friend's gaze. "I started dealing with it last night. My reaction to Cassandra's big story was suspicious enough that she had clippings pulled from the morgue detailing my career."

"And among the clippings were the ones from ten years ago."

"Yeah." He managed a grim smile. "Catharsis is a real bitch."

"So I've been told." Mitch concentrated on blowing smoke rings and watching them dissipate. "And Miss Blake?"

Seth raised a questioning eyebrow. "What about her?"

Mitch snorted. "It doesn't take a reporter to see the chemistry between the two of you."

"Spying on us, Mitch?"

"It's what I do for a living." He smiled at the fierce expression on Seth's face. "Relax. I turned off the audio and visual feeds the moment you hauled her onto your lap."

"Thank you so much."

"All part of the service," Mitch said mockingly as he ground out his cigarette and rose. "Just between us, if a woman looked at me the way she looks at you, I'd haul her off to a deserted mountain top and make love to her for at least a month. Now before you go off the deep end," he interjected when the expression on Seth's face turned threatening, "let me say that I like you and I like her. What happens between you and Miss Blake is none of my business. Just keep in mind that the situation you're in has a way of distorting emotions. Take it from someone who knows. I'd hate to see either one of you hurt."

While the Dateline people were served dinner in the formal dining room, and then amused themselves in various rooms in the château, Mitch and his staff ate in shifts in the kitchen and loaded the dirty dishes into the industrial-size dishwasher. The surveillance room was manned on a rotating basis, as were the listening posts in the surrounding forest. The day had proved exhausting for the Dateline people, and by ten o'clock, they had all returned to their bedrooms. At that point, Mitch set the guards on the grounds as well as those inside the château. Once everyone was at their station, the alarms were activated throughout the château, while in the library, Mitch began his meeting with the Dateline bodyguards and the four others who had checked the Dateline offices, telephones and the domiciles of the Dateline employees for any sign of surveillance.

Sipping mineral water and chain-smoking, he listened to the five reports without comment. Anyone unfamiliar with Mitch would have mistaken his silence and faraway look for inattention—in fact, he assimilated everything that was said, mentally sifting through the reports and discarding any opinions that might have emerged in favor of facts. The bodyguards had been with him for several years; their reports contained little or no bias. No notes were taken, nor was the session taped; Mitch's experience had taught him how dangerous it could be to leave any kind of trail.

"So what we have," he summed up when the last person had spoken, "is that Kurt Leihmann was the only one followed. The Dateline telephones have only one tap—the Sûreté's. None of the home telephones have been tampered with, and we couldn't find any bugs." He glanced at the nine people scattered around the room. "Anyone have a comment?"

The man who had supervised Cassandra's culinary endeavor of the night before spoke up from his place beside the closed double doors. "It's rotten."

Mitch shifted his gaze to the guard. "How so?"

He removed the toothpick from the corner of his mouth before answering. "The Brigade went to a lot of trouble to get the

Blake woman involved. Now she's dropped out of sight and they don't even stake out her apartment?" He shook his head. "No way. At the very least they'd want to know where she *isn't*, so that explains why the German was watched. If they've done their homework, they know that Blake and the German are good friends. But why not watch Winter's hotel? He was with her when the bomb detonated, his name was in the papers, and he's her boss. The Brigade has got to figure that those two are involved somehow, but they don't even try to watch his place or bug it?" He shook his head again. "Even terrorists can't be that damn dumb."

"Anyone care to argue?" Mitch asked.

"You said that the Brigade telephoned Blake at a restaurant," Maureen commented musingly. "Which means they were following either her or Winter... or they knew in advance where the two were going. Is it possible the Brigade tapped the office lines, then removed the tap after the explosion?" She looked questioningly at Mitch.

"A nice idea, but Winter didn't phone for reservations, if that's what you're asking."

Maureen sighed. "It was just a thought."

The guard assigned to Margot entered the discussion. "How much do we know about the Dateline staff?"

Mitch lit a cigarette and squinted through the blue haze. "We did a cursory background check—there hasn't been time for an in-depth profile. And Winter gave me copies of the personnel files; they all look to be straightforward enough." He rubbed his free hand across the stubble on his chin. "I see your point. Out of the seven people we're trying to protect, five are possible informants."

"Only five," Maureen questioned. "Why not seven?"

"Winter's past precludes any terrorist leanings," Mitch answered sharply. "As for Blake, she's an ambitious, apolitical reporter who's in over her head—even if she doesn't realize it."

The man guarding the double doors broke the silence that had descended after Mitch's sharp reply. "So after tomorrow on the driving track we just drive them back to Paris and forget about them?"

"That's what we've been hired for, and with the Sûreté in on this, if the officials catch us hanging around the Dateline people they may shoot first and ask questions later."

"I don't like it," the guard maintained, sticking the tooth-pick back into his mouth so that it jutted out at a mutinous angle.

"Neither do I," Mitch admitted, grinding out his cigarette in the overflowing ashtray. "So on Monday, you, Franchot, Maureen and I are going to talk to some of our less savory contacts and see if we can come up with something more sub-stantial than speculation. If there's a rat in the Dateline of-fices, the sooner we find it, the safer everyone will be."

Clad in her nightgown, her pale blond hair falling in waves around her shoulders, Cassandra sat propped up in bed, the first of the files about the upcoming war-crimes trial Seth had given her earlier in the evening open on her lap. The file on Seth had thankfully disappeared along with the breakfast cart. For the past hour, she had been trying to gather her concentration in order to study the background material but, after a minute or two, her thoughts would inevitably wander back to the knowledge that both her father and ex-husband would soon be in Paris, if they weren't already. Her nice, simple, uncompli-cated life was rapidly taking on Byzantine proportions.

With a muttered imprecation, she tossed the folders aside and left the bed. After turning on the stereo, she took a canned soda from the small refrigerator, threw a handful of ice into a glass and poured the soda over the cubes. Settling into one of the chairs, her gaze wandered to the connecting door and she de-bated knocking to see if Seth was still awake. After what had happened this morning, she had expected to spend the evening with him. Instead, he had handed her the folders and spent the remainder of the evening playing pool with PJ and Kurt. By nine, she had given up and gone to her room, calling a cheer-ful good-night over her shoulder to the occupants of the game room. She had heard Seth enter his room half an hour ago and had waited from him to knock on the door. Now she was left with the conclusion that whatever it was that had passed between them this morning, he obviously had no intention of pursuing it.

Leaning over, she grabbed one of the folders from the bed and determinedly flipped it open. Minutes later she heard the click of the handle of the connecting door; her heart stopped, then doubled its beat, and she forced herself to calmly lift her head to the man framed in the doorway.

Seth made no move to enter her bedroom. "I'm sorry, Cassandra."

"For what?" Her voice had a strangled sound to it and she cleared her throat. "You've done nothing to apologize for."

"After what we shared this morning, the way I treated you tonight doesn't count?"

She colored and made a show of straightening the papers in the folder. "It doesn't matter. I understand. We're both under a lot of pressure right now—"

"Don't you dare lie to me!" He hadn't moved from his place in the doorway, nor had he raised his voice above a low murmur, but it cracked like a whip nonetheless.

Her chin came up and she met his gaze defiantly. "What do you want me to say? That I was hurt by the fact that you ignored me this evening after nearly making love to me this morning? All right, I was. Did it make me feel cheap, dirty? Yes, damn you, it did," she hissed. "Satisfied?"

"Not by half."

He moved so quickly that she had no chance to defend herself. One moment he was silhouetted in the doorway, the next he was in front of her, scooping her up in his arms and carrying her into the bathroom.

"What do you think you're doing?" she demanded, pushing against his shoulders. "Put me down."

He kicked the bathroom door closed before roughly depositing her on the marble counter top. She tried to slide off but his big body was right there, forcing her to retreat until her back was literally against the wall. His eyes were full of black fire, pinning her in place as his hands flattened against the wall on both sides of her head. On some level she was aware of the picture they presented; their lips were only inches apart, and when he had crowded her into the wall, her legs had automatically parted for him. She was well and truly trapped, no matter how frantically her mind sought to construct defenses against him. "Don't bother," he said, seeing the panicked look in her eyes. "We slipped past each other's defenses without even being aware of it. Neither of us can pull back now."

"I don't want—"

"Shut up, Cassandra."

His mouth came down on hers with the same ferocity that had edged his words. When she tried to twist away, his hands held her head in a viselike grip. When she kept her teeth locked against the invasion of his tongue, his mouth turned coaxing, teasing, blasting a hole in her determination with a gentleness that was more powerful than physical force. Her lips parted; she welcomed him with a fierce passion of her own while his hands slid to her back, pulling her away from the cool wall and into the muscled warmth of his chest.

"You see," he whispered, staring into her eyes. "It's too late." When she shook her head in a last attempt to negate what she knew was true, his hands slipped upward and locked in her hair, holding her head still. "Mitch said that if a woman looked at him the way you look at me, he'd take her to bed and keep her there for a month." He bent his head and kissed her possessively. "But this is more than physical, Cassandra; if it wasn't, I wouldn't be so damn scared."

"I know," she answered shakily, admitting the truth. "But I keep thinking—"

"You think too much," he admonished, running a finger along the lace of her gown and watching her shiver in response. "So do I, for that matter. Let's just take this one step at a time."

"Does this mean you won't be spending the night with me?" she asked in an inviting whisper as her fingers worked at the buttons of his shirt.

Her hands slipped beneath the material into the mat of hair on his chest and he groaned. "I thought you didn't indulge."

"I don't," she replied, undoing the rest of the buttons so that he was exposed to her gaze. "But in your case I'll make an exception." She leaned forward and tempted him with feather-light kisses across his collarbone.

His breathing grew tortured and he briefly closed his eyes, summoning his willpower. "What about the cameras?"

"I don't care."

When she delicately scraped a fingernail across his nipple, he nearly lost his mind. "Stop that," he ordered, but the words sounded more like an invitation.

She pulled away, tilting her head back to look at him. "Look at us, Seth."

He followed her gaze, seeing her hands nestled familiarly in the wedge of hair on his chest, then lower, to the place his hips had made for him between her thighs, and trembled at the sight.

"Seth?"

He dragged his gaze back to her face, all too aware of the way his lower body was throbbing with desire. He framed her face in his hands. "Is it safe?" When she frowned at him in confusion, he clarified, "Are you on the pill?"

"I . . . no." Color washed through her cheeks. "I haven't—I mean, there hasn't been a need . . ." Her words trailed off and she gazed at him helplessly.

He managed a wry smile. "And I don't make a habit of carrying handy little packets in my wallet. We have to wait."

She nodded shakily, warmed by his consideration. "I'm sorry, Seth."

"Don't be," he said, giving her a provocative look that sent shivers of arousal down her spine. "Anticipation is half the fun."

He lifted her in his arms and carried her back to the bedroom, mindful of the camera tracking their movements. "Sleep well, love."

His parting endearment warmed her heart, as did the fact that he left the door open between their two rooms.

Chapter 6

At six o'clock Sunday morning, Cassandra was once again awakened by the pounding on her door. Having learned her lesson the day before, Cassandra reacted to the demand by asking the identity of the person on the other side; she had barely gotten the query out when Seth was through the connecting doorway of their rooms and roughly pushing her away from the door. He had been through this test years earlier, and even though he was ninety-nine percent certain that the château was still secure, he wasn't about to take any chances. Recognizing the name of the man in the hallway, he cracked the door to confirm his identity before allowing it to open fully. Mitch's people, Cassandra discovered, were in the process of running the same test on the rest of the Dateline employees. The Dateline staff reacted the way Cassandra originally had. Bleary-eyed, they threw open their doors to discover the source of the disturbance and were confronted by the sight of their bodyguards aiming a very large weapon at them.

Since her room was closest to the staircase, Cassandra had been awakened first, and instead of following Seth when he wheeled the breakfast cart into her room, she peered around the door frame to watch the progress of Mitch's team. Kurt opened his door and simply stared like a beached fish at the pistol Maureen had trained on him.

Margot gave a shriek and slammed the door in her body-guard's face. Cassandra gave her five points for her quick re-action. Unfortunately, the man had been overconfident about his charge's reaction and was standing a bit too close to the door when Margot slammed it. The end result was that the bodyguard had a broken nose, and when he knocked on her door again, explaining that she was in no danger and should open her door so that he could wheel the breakfast cart into her room, Margot refused. Seth, wearing only a pair of pants, brushed past Cassandra and began the task of assuring Mar-got that what had happened was really only a drill and it was safe to open her door.

PJ's reaction began typically for the photographer. He was less than pleased at being roused at such an early hour and was, Cassandra had time to notice, naked as a jaybird. He took one look at the revolver pointed at his chest by the woman who had been assigned to him and turned the air blue with some partic-ularly descriptive phrases. What happened next astonished everyone. PJ shoved the breakfast cart into the bodyguard, forcing both the woman and the cart against the opposite wall. Her head hit the plaster with an emphatic crack, and then PJ had literally thrown the cart aside one-handed, grabbed his as-sailant's wrist and twisted her arm and the revolver behind her back. She fell to her knees in order to avoid having her shoul-der dislocated by the pressure PJ exerted.

"What the hell is wrong with you?" the photographer bel-lowed, wrenching the revolver out of her hand and taking a step away from her. "I told you yesterday morning not to even talk to me before I've had my coffee!" With a loud, blatant com-ment regarding the intelligence level of whoever had decided on such a maneuver, he rescued the coffee thermos and a cup from the ruin of the breakfast cart and stalked back into his room. The sound of the door slamming behind him reverberated through the hallway.

His bodyguard struggled to her feet and hammered on PJ's door. "Give me back my revolver, you little twerp!" When he didn't answer, she tried the doorknob and found the door locked. "Damn it, open this door right now!"

"Go to hell." PJ's voice was muted by the door, but the taunt in it carried clearly through the hall. "Come and get it if you're so damn tough!"

She launched into a vivid verbal description of what she was going to do to PJ once she got her hands on the wiry photographer, and the list astounded and amused Cassandra. The woman drew back a foot in order to kick in the door when Mitch's voice halted her. Cassandra jerked around, startled by Mitch's unexpected appearance behind her in the hallway.

"Leave it, Amanda. It's not important."

"But he—"

"I said leave it," Mitch reiterated in a cold tone. "You underestimated the man. He'll give up the weapon when he's good and ready and not before." He turned his attention to Margot's bodyguard. "What happened to you?"

Mitch's switch to French, Cassandra noticed, was effortless, causing her to wonder if she was the only one in the world who had trouble learning a foreign language.

The man started to explain what had happened, but the blood-soaked handkerchief he held to his nose was quicker and more effective than words.

"Never mind," Mitch told the man with a sigh. "Get cleaned up, we've got a long day ahead of us." He shook his head as his people filed down the corridor.

"New recruits?" Cassandra asked, the chuckle in her voice not quite hidden.

Mitch turned to her, his eyes and expression as austere as ever. "No. In fact they're quite good." He looked over her shoulder to Seth. "I would appreciate it if you would allow me to prepare Cassandra in my own way. Don't interfere again. You have forty-five minutes, then I expect to see you and your employees in the parlor." He turned sharply on his heel and strode back to the staircase.

Seth and Cassandra ate together in her room and then Seth returned to his own room to shower and dress. Cassandra did the same, hurrying through the shower in order to have a few minutes left in which to lightly apply the eyeshadow, mascara, blush and powder she had exhumed from the depths of her purse. Satisfied with her reflection, she dressed in jeans and a bright red shirt and stepped back into her bedroom.

Seth was waiting, finishing the last of the coffee with his second cigarette of the day. Cassandra glanced at the opened carton of cigarettes on the shelf of the entertainment unit.

"He really is thorough, isn't he?" She mused. "Right down to the brand of cigarettes I smoke."

Dropping the cigarette pack and her gold lighter into his pocket, Seth rose. "It's his job."

"I know I'm going to regret asking this, but how did he know what size clothing and shoes I wear?"

"He went through your apartment the night of the bombing. One of the women he employs bought the clothes and suitcases the next morning."

Cassandra nodded, having expected something of the sort. "Why didn't he just throw a few of my things into one of my suitcases? It would have saved his people a lot of trouble."

"Mitch didn't want anyone who might be watching your apartment to suspect that you were dropping out of sight for a few days. He did the same thing for me." He glanced at his watch. "Come on, it's getting late."

When everyone was assembled in the parlor, Mitch paired one of his people with one of Dateline's and assigned each pair a room in the château for the "B and B" lesson. It came as something of a shock to Cassandra to discover that she was assigned to Mitch, but she obediently followed him through the lower level of the château to a room she hadn't seen before. The room held a complete, if small, kitchen, a bed, a sofa and a chair, a stereo and a television.

"It's designed on the principle of an efficiency apartment," he told her when they entered. "First I'm going to tell you about the various shapes and sizes bombs and bugs can come in, and then you'll learn how to find them."

"Sort of like a game of Hide the Thimble," she commented as she surveyed the room.

"Only if your thimble can blow you sky high," he replied repressively.

"Right." She made no further attempts to lighten the atmosphere.

Mitch talked for over two hours, describing the most commonly used explosives and electronic bugs. Telephone wire taps he touched on only briefly, explaining that his people had installed a device that screwed into the mouthpieces of the Dateline staff's home and office phones. The device was connected to a little red light affixed to the phone base that would blink if anyone tried to listen in on an extension—it would also discover most taps. They had had to play around a little to get it to ignore the Sûreté's wire tap; but if someone else tried to add a tap, the light would blink. As an added precaution, however, the phone lines would be swept by his people every two days. The bad thing about phone taps was that the more sophisticated ones could be used not only to eavesdrop on a telephone conversation, but to listen to what was going on in the room it occupied. In order to frustrate any would-be eavesdroppers, he suggested either playing the radio or running water in order to have a modicum of privacy for any conversations.

To bug a room without using the telephone had one major drawback. Whoever planted the bug had to have access either to the premises, or at least to an adjacent room, for a long period of time in order to install the microphone. In Cassandra's case, that was a distinct disadvantage since her neighbors were a mixture of retired couples and young mothers at home with their children; both groups tended to come and go at odd hours, which made the risk of detection greater for the Brigade.

"Do you sing?" he asked.

Cassandra blinked at this sudden change of topic. "I'm no Beverly Sills, but I sound pretty good in the shower."

"Good." Mitch handed her a transistor radio. "Turn on the radio and walk around the room while you sing to yourself."

"Are you serious?" she laughed.

"Very. And change frequencies on the radio while you walk."

Certain he had been hit in the head once too often, she took the radio and did as he had instructed. The only song that came to mind was a hymn and she felt more than a little ridiculous singing "Amazing Grace" as she walked around the room. She felt even more ridiculous five minutes later when she heard her own voice come over the radio's speaker as she passed in front of a mirror. She stopped dead in her tracks and looked over her shoulder at Mitch.

"Congratulations, you've just found a real live bug." Crossing the room, he lifted the mirror from the wall and turned it over. On the back was a small microphone, complete with batteries for power and a thin wire antenna. He disconnected the batteries and set everything on the dinette table. "Keep going. You have five more to find."

It was a long, painstaking process, but an hour later she had managed to find the other five. Her elation was short-lived.

"It's a nice little trick," he said when she handed over the fifth bug with a triumphant smile. "And if the Brigade is cash poor, this may be the type of bug they use. If they're flush, however, you're out of luck. The only way you can detect one of the new refined models is with a nine-thousand-dollar countermeasures receiver."

Cassandra plopped down on one of the dinette chairs and glared at him. "Then why put me through this," she asked, waving her hand at the bugs on the table.

"The Brigade has had a lot of expenses the past couple of months. Because of that there is a good chance they might use this type of bug." He opened one of the cabinets in the kitchen and removed several packages of varying sizes. "Now for the bombs."

Unlike the empty pistols that had been used to drive home a lesson on security, the explosives were all too real. Actual bombs had been constructed of TNT, plastique, mercury fulminate, and RDX, an explosive extracted from plastique. She listened, horrified, as Mitch casually explained that a combination of flour and RDX could be mixed with eggs and milk and made into pancakes. Electric and nonelectric blasting caps were displayed next, then detonators. Mitch showed her her tension-release mechanisms while relating the different activities that could trigger the explosives—turning a doorknob, opening a drawer, answering the phone, starting a car.... The list was endless, he said, watching her reactions. But the worst bomb was the one that was detonated by a radio transmitter. Since the bomber was undoubtedly watching the victim in order to time the detonation of the explosives, there was little chance of successfully defusing the bomb. At the first hint that the victim had discovered the bomb, the user would detonate it.

"So what do I do?" Cassandra asked as Mitch replaced the bombs in the cabinet. "Stay in my apartment until I die?"

Mitch shook his head. "The thing about bombs is that they're fairly bulky—the exception being a letter bomb—so if you know what to look for, and take the time to look carefully, you'll be okay." He leaned against the kitchen counter and continued. "Your best defense is prevention. When you get home from work, close all the drapes and use a flashlight to check your lamps. Once you're sure they haven't been tampered with, turn on all the lights in your apartment and check the rest of the place. Keep your car off the street, and even if it stays in a private, patrolled garage, check the engine compartment, trunk, glove compartment and undercarriage."

"It would be easier to sell the car," she commented, unnerved. "I rarely use it, anyway."

"It's not that bad," he replied. "Remember, they're not out to kill you."

"Yet," she added dismally.

"Look, there are a few little tricks to all this. The easiest thing in the world is to purchase alarms for your car and apartment. For added insurance, put a small piece of cellophane on your front door, down low near the floor, so that it adheres to both the door and the doorjamb, and check to make sure it's in place before you enter your apartment. If it isn't, get the hell out of there and call the Sûreté. You can use the tape on your car as well. Just remember to keep the tape alarms as small as possible."

She nodded. "How do you live, knowing what you know?"

He was silent for several moments before answering. "I'm careful; I take precautions. And I never fully trust anyone because man is, by nature, untrustworthy."

"What a horrible way to exist."

He raised an eyebrow. "I'm alive." He left the kitchen to take the other chair at the table, shook out a cigarette and offered it to her.

Cassandra eyed it warily. "Is this another lesson?"

"No," he assured her. "I'm trying to get rid of some of the tension in you."

She accepted the cigarette and light. "May I ask you a question?"

"Sure."

"What did Seth mean the other day when he called me 'live bait'?" The term had bothered her then, but given his hostility, she hadn't had the courage to ask him about it. And then their relationship had changed, and she had been afraid to ask and risk losing the fragile bond forming between them.

"Seth believes—as I do—that the Sûreté is using you to locate the Brigade."

"That's ridiculous!"

"Is it?" Mitch smiled mirthlessly. "Until last weekend the Sûreté hadn't been able to identify a single member of the Brigade, let alone make an arrest. And then along comes Cassandra Blake; not only does the Brigade send you a tape recording, they even put on a show for you. Even if Rocheleau was an idiot—which he isn't—the chance of you leading the Sûreté to the Brigade is just too good to pass up."

"Inspector Rocheleau offered to protect me—"

"And at the same time managed to tell you just how limited his manpower was," Mitch reminded her. "So if you had accepted his offer and something unpleasant happened to you, the good Inspector would be off the hook with his government, the Dateline hierarchy, and the media. It's called 'plausible deniability,' and I can tell you from past experience that it works.

"In the meantime, they dangle you in front of the Brigade and wait for the terrorists to bite."

"Wheels within wheels," Cassandra murmured. "The Brigade watches me, the Sûreté watches me and I have to figure out who's who." She rubbed a hand over her forehead. "So then the people who followed Kurt could very well have been Sûreté, not Brigade."

Mitch nodded. "That's a possibility I'm checking out. Remember, you dropped out of sight not only from the Brigade's surveillance but the Sûreté's as well."

"Do you ever deliver good news?" she asked wryly.

"You want sweetness and light, find a fairy godmother. You want to survive, listen to what I have to say." He stubbed out his cigarette and rose. "Come on. It's time for driving school."

The driving course—a brisk, twenty minute walk along a rough path—was laid out in the heart of, and concealed by, the forest surrounding the château. Expecting to find the course laid out like a racetrack, Cassandra was surprised to find a dirt road that had been judiciously carved out of the forest and wound through the trees. To guard against aerial observation, a minimum of trees had been felled—just enough to allow for the two-lane road—and as a result sunlight fell through the canopy of leaves in a dappled design. Two cars stood nearby—one was designated as the target vehicle, the other as the pursuit.

In the meager time remaining, Mitch and his people taught the Dateline staff some very rudimentary evasive driving techniques and precautions. They were driven through the track once in order to get their bearings; half-concealed side routes were pointed out; sharp bends were noted, as was the placement of three forks in the course.

Each Dateline employee then took his or her turn at the wheel of the target vehicle and was chased down the dirt track by the pursuit car. Although Mitch had instructed the journalists not to exceed the speed at which they would travel the Paris streets, Cassandra still considered the weaving twists and turns among the huge trees perilous. If the target driver was too slow or too cautious, the driver of the pursuit car would close the distance between them and deliver a reprimand by nudging the back bumper of the target car.

By the time everyone had had a turn at the wheel, the morning and part of the afternoon were gone. Watching the training, Mitch wished again that he had a week instead of two days with this group. While they had been appropriately cowed by the "B and B" session, they seemed to view the evasive maneuvers as nothing more than sport. They did what they were told, but remained unconvinced that what they learned might one day save their lives. It was an attitude that worried him.

When the session was finished, he led his charges back to the château for the final session. They wouldn't be any good in a high-speed chase, Mitch informed them, but what he was teaching them would probably get them to a friendly police station in one piece. He did not mention that any tail they might have could just as easily be Sûreté as Brigade. He trained people to anticipate the worst and act accordingly; there was no point in telling them something that could cause them to lower their guard.

After a late lunch, the Dateline staff left the château at intervals so as not to draw attention to their departure, and were taken back to Paris by different routes. PJ was once again assigned to Amanda, and before climbing into the car he nonchalantly handed over the revolver he had taken from her that morning. Amanda took it with ill-disguised poor grace and nearly slammed the passenger door on PJ's foot. Witnessing the exchange, Mitch slowly shook his head and returned to the château. Amanda was good, but she had yet to learn to control her emotions rather than the other way around. Either she was going to change, and quickly, or he would have to cut her loose.

Seth and Cassandra were the last to leave, and the only ones not to be accompanied by one of Mitch's people. When Cassandra mentioned that, Mitch smiled mirthlessly. "If you are being watched, the Mercedes is going to draw enough attention to the two of you. Being in the company of someone who can't be identified or traced would only serve to alter suspicions to certainties. That's the last thing we want—right now you're safer with unconfirmed suspicions."

Seth handed Cassandra into the gray Mercedes before turning to shake Mitch's hand. "Thanks, Mitch."

"Don't thank me; you're not out of the woods yet," Mitch replied. "None of your people truly believes anything they were told this weekend. They're still clinging to their invulnerability—even Cassandra."

"Not your problem," Seth said quietly. "You've done everything I asked. I'll keep them all on very short leashes."

"You do that. In the meantime we'll maintain a low-level presence, keeping the office and residences secure until something breaks one way or the other."

"At least I get to drive a Mercedes," Seth quipped.

"Just remember that it's a loaner," Mitch retorted. "I want it back in the same condition it's in now." He accompanied Seth around the car to the driver's side. "One last thing," he said when Seth put his hand on the door handle. "Cassandra takes the Metro to and from work. Discourage that if you can. She'll be a lot safer in the Mercedes."

Mitch watched the car disappear around the bend in the drive before walking slowly back to the château. Franchot was setting the window alarms in the library when Mitch entered the room and poured a hefty amount of Scotch into a crystal tumbler.

"All the windows are secure," Franchot announced.

"Good." Mitch strolled to the window and contemplated the horseshoe expanse of lawn fronting the château. "Call in the listening posts and tell them to replace the trip wires on the claymores and deadfalls as they withdraw." When Franchot started for the door, Mitch added, "Do you still see that pretty little clerk from the Sûreté?"

Franchot smiled. "Occasionally. She is no longer a clerk; now she is the secretary to one of the directors."

"Even better." Mitch smiled coldly. "I want you to find out if the Sûreté has laid out any long-term plans for staking out Mademoiselle Blake and if so, who has the assignment."

"No problem. Can I leave tonight?"

"Yes. We're closing up the château tonight, so if you find out anything, you can reach me at the Paris number." Carrying his drink, Mitch walked to the butler's pantry off the kitchen.

Looking straight into the camera positioned above the hardened steel door, he pressed the buzzer concealed in the wood frame. A five-second interval elapsed before he heard the faint buzz that indicated the release of the electronic dead bolt. He opened the door and descended the stairway to the communications center. A glance at the bank of interior monitors showed the black-and-white images of empty rooms with dust covers draped protectively over furnishings. A sad, abandoned air now permeated the château, as it always did at the conclusion of a successful operation. Mitch mentally shook off the feeling and shifted his attention to the exterior monitors, watching his people set the booby traps as they withdrew from their posts.

Satisfied, he crossed the room to a desk tucked into one corner and pulled the telephone toward him. After taking a hefty pull on his drink, he punched out a number.

"Extension 314," he requested when the connection was made. He heard the call being transferred and smiled slightly as he recalled the code to use on an unscrambled line.

"Greg Talbott."

"Monsieur Talbott," Mitch replied in French. "This is Monsieur Saint Germain. A package addressed to you was mistakenly delivered to my address. I am returning it to you this afternoon by special messenger. It should arrive about five."

In his borrowed office at Orly Airport, Greg leaned back in his chair, his gaze fixed on the two men seated on the other side of the glass wall separating the office from the reception area. "Merci. The mails have been particularly unreliable this week. In fact, I myself am returning a package damaged in transit."

Mitch quietly replaced the receiver, breaking the connection between the château and airport. Opening the bottom desk drawer, he removed all documents relating to Dateline and its employees and dumped them into a chemically treated bag. Rising, he carried the bag to the far side of the room where what appeared to be an oversize garbage can stood. The major difference between this fireproof can and its aluminum cousins that were toted out once a week for collection, was the ducts, one of which ran from the cylinder to an outside vent while the other was connected to a small propane bottle.

Lifting the hinged lid, he dropped the bag into the container. When the lid had hissed back into place, Mitch locked down the hasps and walked the half dozen steps to the propane bottle. He opened the valve, allowed the gas to run for several seconds before shutting it down, then pressed the red ignition button on the side of the can. He was rewarded by a muted whoosh as the contents of the incinerator ignited. The propane was exhausted within seconds, but by then the chemicals in the burn bag had taken over the task of destruction. Within five minutes, what remained of the paper trail that could connect Mitch and any of his employees to Dateline was eradicated. All that remained was a handful of gray ash.

Greg Talbott hung up, pushed himself out of his desk chair and took the four steps that enabled him to open the door to the reception area. "Gentlemen, if you would step inside, I have some answers for you."

"About time," Ned Blake threw at the man who had introduced himself as an undersecretary at the American Embassy. Taking one of the chairs facing the desk, Ned tugged at his cuffs and smoothed a hand over the front of his vest. "I don't understand why we have been detained here. If my wife has come to any harm—"

"Ex-wife, I believe, and I assure you, she is fine," Greg interrupted, irritated by the man and the way he fussed with his three-piece suit. Ushering Robert Townsend to the second chair, before taking his own seat behind the desk, he continued, "I've just spoken with the immigration department, Mr. Townsend. You are free to enter France." He smiled genially at the older man before returning his attention to Ned Blake.

"Unfortunately, Mr. Blake, you pose a problem."

"And just why is that?" Ned Blake asked with a slight sneer. "My passport and visa are both in order, despite what we were told."

In his best officious manner, Greg shuffled a pile of empty forms into a neat stack before replying. "The present government considers your politics rather...unsavory. Since you have been in D.C., you have written several articles about the French government which they consider to be less than flattering."

Greg cleared his throat and offered Ned Blake his most apologetic expression. "Given the trouble the government has had with the Freedom Brigade during the past few weeks, they are understandably concerned that you are taking the opportunity to capitalize, at their expense, on a story about the danger to foreign nationals."

"I only report the news; I don't make it," Ned replied arrogantly, smoothing his expensively styled brown hair into place.

"Be that as it may," Greg said regretfully, "the French do not consider you to be just another reporter, and have decided to revoke your visa."

Ned was caught between preening at what he assumed was a compliment and distress at being denied entry into the country. "As flattering as that may be, I can assure you that any thoughts of a story take a distant back seat to my concern for Cassandra. If you would simply explain to the French authorities—"

"Mr. Blake, I have explained your situation. The fact remains that since you and Ms. Blake no longer have a formal relationship, the French consider your claim of concern for her welfare invalid."

"I intend to register a complaint," Ned warned.

"That is an option, of course," Greg replied easily. "But you will have to do so once you are back in the United States."

Ned eyed the younger, composed man suspiciously. "I suppose it was pure luck that had you at Orly when our flight landed."

"Not at all; the French were good enough to voice their concerns about your arrival early this morning. In the interest of maintaining good diplomatic relations between the United States and France, I agreed to meet your plane."

Ned turned to his former father-in-law. "Do you believe this story, Robert?"

Robert Townsend ran a hand through his wild mane of silver hair and sighed. "I have no reason to disbelieve him."

"You don't—" Ned stammered incredulously. "Robert, do you mean to tell me you don't find it odd that barely forty-eight hours after issuing our visas, the French suddenly decide to revoke mine because my occupation poses some sort of threat?"

"I've seen it happen before," Robert said quietly, studying the man across the desk.

"So have I," Ned concurred, "and it has usually happened when a government—ours included—is trying to hide something. What are you hiding, Mr. Talbott?"

"I am hiding nothing," Greg responded with a show of forbearance. "I am simply a member of the diplomatic corps stationed here, trying to handle what is a very delicate situation.

Your ex-wife has already been involved, however accidentally, with the Freedom Brigade; the French, quite rightly, want to minimize the chance of a foreign national becoming a terrorist target a second time. As I have said, the French government had its reservations about your occupation and your reasons for coming here. Now, in light of the amount of publicity you generated before leaving the United States, they feel they have no choice but to revoke your visa."

"Ned," Robert Townsend said when his daughter's former husband opened his mouth to continue the argument, "stop proving what an ass you are and thank the man for his help."

In answer, Blake favored both men with a glare. Springing out of his chair, he stalked to the door. "Very well. As I have no choice in the matter, I will be on the next available flight to Washington. But believe me, Mr. Talbott, neither you nor the French have heard the end of this." The door slammed behind him.

Shaking his head, Robert Townsend rose. "To think I actually approved of his marrying my daughter." He shook Greg's hand. "I won't ask why you kept us here for nearly twenty-four hours, Mr. Talbott, but I assume it had to do with Cassandra's safety." When Greg merely smiled, Robert chuckled.

"I do hope your daughter will refuse to answer any questions Mr. Blake may put to her until a resolution has been reached in this Brigade affair," Greg commented as Robert scooped up the single carryon with which he always traveled.

"I wouldn't worry about that," Robert grinned. "Ned doesn't have Cassandra's phone number or address. And even if he did, my daughter hasn't spoken to the man since their divorce. I doubt his sudden reappearance in her life would cause her to alter her stance."

For Cassandra and Seth, the drive back to Paris was accomplished in a far different atmosphere from the one that had prevailed during their journey to the château. As the Mercedes purred along the rural roads he took her hand, holding it warmly as they talked. The present threat of the Freedom Brigade was, by tacit agreement, ignored, but no other topic was forbidden. Cassandra encouraged him to talk about his last assignment in Paris, and it seemed the most natural thing in the world that he found himself telling her about his wife and child. They were—and always would be—a part of him; now, however, the pain of their loss was diminishing, their images blurring in his memory. He felt a moment's guilt at the dimming of pain and then Cassandra squeezed his hand and he realized that this ending was also a beginning. His heart was alive again, willing to explore whatever the future held.

He talked about his family, how his father, a lawyer, had instilled idealistic goals in his three children, but particularly in his only son. His mother, on the other hand, was something of a dreamy romantic. She wept at sad endings and beautiful poetry and insisted that her children know as much about the arts as they did about world affairs. She had even forced piano lessons upon Seth until the day his piano teacher called to say that he had brought the family pet—a harmless gerbil—to his lessons. The normally well-behaved pet had peeked out of Seth's schoolbag, realized that here were new horizons to explore, and leaped to the floor to do exactly that. It had taken Seth an hour to corner the elated gerbil, which was, oddly enough, exactly the amount of time allocated for his lesson. Given his attitude, the teacher had continued, she was resigning the questionable honor of teaching scales to a boy who would rather play with a pet rat than study the piano.

"Actually, what I really wanted to do was play football," Seth confessed, "but Mother wouldn't hear of it. I was the only thirteen-year-old boy I knew who had to memorize etudes instead of formations. The solution to my problem seemed obvious—if I couldn't quit, I had to get the teacher to do so. And I did."

Cassandra laughed and leaned her head against the seat. "So, did you get to play football?"

"Yep. Unfortunately I broke my leg in the second game and was sidelined for the rest of the year. Not the most auspicious beginning for a would-be professional player, I have to admit. There I was, my leg in a cast and lacking any extracurricular activity which, in my father's eyes, was a cardinal sin. So to keep him happy, I joined the junior-high-school newspaper and, since no one else wanted the job, I got to report the sports. It was fun, but I was sure that the following year I'd be making the sports page, not writing it. Instead I did both.

"The year after that JFK was assassinated, Vietnam started making headlines, and I joined the debate team. I began devouring news in any shape or form, trying to sort out truth from propaganda. That's when the thought of a career in journalism first reared its ugly head. My senior year I was captain of the debate team, quarterback of the football team and editor of the school paper.

"Everything was rolling along nicely, and I had just decided to follow in my father's footsteps when the faculty advisor yanked my editorial on the inequity of the selective service system, and something in my gut said this was it. The rest of the staff and I broke into the school one night and printed up bootleg copies of the paper containing not only my censored editorial, but a front-page story of the attempt to suppress it." He shook his head, remembering. "The next day the paper's staff was hauled into the superintendent's office and suspended for a week. The administration was going to file a criminal complaint as well, since we were plainly guilty of breaking and entering, but my father crashed a meeting of the school board and delivered a lecture on freedom of the press. The board members were so impressed that they settled for placing an official letter of reprimand in each of our files. That's when I knew I didn't want to be a lawyer."

"Was your father disappointed?"

Seth shook his head. "He told me that if I got into this much trouble for following my conscience once I had my degree, then we'd both know I'd made the right choice." He sent her an amused look. "Besides, one of my sisters ended up carrying on the family practice."

"Only one? What does the other do?"

"Would you believe she's an interior designer?"

Cassandra smiled, wondering if Seth could feel the erratic beat of the pulse in her wrist. Suddenly nothing seemed impossible and, briefly, she questioned her own sanity. In the space of two weeks, her world had turned upside down and yet she couldn't rid herself of the rosy optimism that colored her emotions. She felt twenty-two again, standing on the edge of forever and ready to embrace life.

She told Seth of the ups and downs of being Robert Townsend's daughter—of the upheaval in her life when she learned of her parents' divorce; of the summer that she was twelve and her father decided it was time she see some of the world. Robert had burst back into her life in June and, over her mother's objections, told her to pack a bag. They had a plane to catch. It was the summer of 1968, and within three hours she and her father were in a pressurized cabin, traversing the United States en route to Los Angeles where her father would cover the California Primary.

Robert used the primary to begin a crash course in politics for his oldest child. In their hotel room she studied the daily papers each morning and then accompanied her photographer/father as he trailed after the candidates. She was even given her own press pass, an honor so enthralling that while her father manipulated two cameras and roll after roll of film, she took notes on the candidates' speeches. She still had her first "dispatches" and could laugh at their simplicity now. Her father, however, had seen something in her work that caused him to fan the ember of promise, and treat her stories with utmost respect. Within days, the press corps had made her their unofficial mascot. She shared their meals, imitated their deadlines and, finally, standing beside her father in the crush of reporters jockeying for position in the doorway of the pressroom, she witnessed the nihilistic action of Sirhan Sirhan. The sight of her father snapping off shot after shot through the tears standing in his eyes was forever engraved in her memory.

"I saw it on television," Seth recalled. "College students had a rough time dealing with the reality of the assassination. How did you manage it?"

"Dad, typically, tried to explain the unexplainable, in between fending off my mother's orders that he bring me home." She smiled faintly. "Finally Dad told Mom that he hoped she wasn't raising a coward and would she agree to allow me to make the decision? She did, and as far as I was concerned there was no choice to be made."

"You stayed with Robert."

"I stayed with Robert," she concurred. "Our next stop was the Poor People's March in Washington. After that Dad took me home just long enough to get my birth certificate. He had a friend who rushed me and my passport through bureaucratic channels, and the next thing I knew, we were stepping off a plane in Saigon.

"We stayed for two weeks, spent another two weeks in a whirlwind tour of Southeast Asia, during which I learned some very sad truths, and were back in time to cover the Republican Convention and then get pictures of the riots at the Democratic Convention. It was pretty heady stuff. By the time Dad dropped me back into my comfortable, protected existence, it wasn't so comfortable anymore. I was suddenly aware of The World."

Seth chuckled. "You give new meaning to the term 'cub reporter'."

"I suppose that's true. All I knew then was that I was well and truly hooked on the idea of following in my father's footsteps. For the next few years I nearly drove Mom out of her mind; she could see the way the wind was blowing and did her level best to convince me that working as a salesclerk in a department store was preferable to being a gofer at the local newspaper office. All to no avail; I could be pretty stubborn."

"You still can be," he threw in laughingly.

"Thank you very much," she returned. "Anyway, I ended up spending summers and vacations with Dad from then on. My sister wanted nothing to do with journalism, so Mom finally stopped beating her head against my brick wall and let Dad have his way. When I was twenty-one he gave me—" She broke off with a small gasp. "Oh no. Seth, my camera!"

"Battered looking Nikon?" he queried. At the pained expression in her eyes, he carried her hand to his lips and kissed her fingers. "I found it at the park. The shutter mechanism didn't take kindly to the explosion, but PJ says he can fix it."

"Thank goodness," she sighed.

"Aren't you the same woman who claimed she didn't know an f-stop from nuclear fission?"

Cassandra looked sheepish. "I bent the truth a little." When he raised a disbelieving eyebrow at her statement she admitted, "Okay, I bent the truth a lot."

"Why didn't you become a photographer?"

"Photographers—the good ones like my father and PJ—are able to capture everything in a single frame, reaffirming the adage about one picture being worth a thousand words. Mine, on the other hand, were only worth ten." She shrugged indifferently. "Fortunately, I had already discovered that my writing was equal to any photograph, so the transition was fairly painless."

"So painless that you still carry the camera around?"

She flashed him a smile. "You know our business. There's never a photographer around when you need one, so I figure better my picture than none. I just follow Dad's advice about giving the shot 500 at f/11 and pray that PJ can save me in the darkroom."

They were on the Boulevard Peripherique now, on the outskirts of Paris. Seth changed lanes and headed into the city proper. "Speaking of fathers, I imagine yours is waiting less than patiently."

Cassandra groaned and slipped her hand out of his to light a cigarette. "With everything that went on today, I'd almost forgotten that Dad and Ned were coming here."

"As you said yesterday, your father's a veteran. He'll make sure you're all right and then slip quietly out of Paris."

She nodded, her eyes on the passing city. "Dad doesn't worry me."

"I guessed that much," he returned dryly. "I even considered taking you to my hotel instead of your apartment, but that is definitely not the way to divert anyone's attention, particularly an ex-husband's."

"What I don't understand is why Ned is suddenly so concerned about my well-being." Looking over at Seth she added, "Any thoughts on that subject?"

"Since I don't know him, my speculations reflect rather unfairly upon him."

"Don't worry; if you knew Ned your speculations would be even worse, so tell me what you think."

"How's his career doing?"

Cassandra tilted her head, considering the question. "The last I heard, he was doing just fine. He'd been assigned to his paper's Washington Bureau and seemed to be on the fast track to success in the nation's capital. Why?"

Drawing a breath, he said baldly, "I was just thinking that if his career had somehow derailed, the perfect way to recover would be the inside story on the Freedom Brigade and his ex-wife."

"I don't think even Ned..." she hesitated and then sighed. "Then again, it sounds like something he would do. I'm certain that he hasn't suddenly discovered that he's madly in love with me."

Seth felt his equilibrium slip at the thought of Ned Blake wanting to be part of Cassandra's life again. "Stranger things have been known to happen. He may have decided that the divorce was a mistake."

Her lips curved into a smile that Seth could only describe as contemptuous. "If you knew why I divorced him..." Her words tailed off and she shook her head.

Aware of the slow, painful throb in his heart, he said quietly, "I asked you once if you were over him, and you gave me a typically flippant answer." When she didn't reply, simply bit her lip and stared intently at the road ahead of them, he gently brushed his hand over her cheek. "I'd like to ask the question again and receive an honest reply. If I'm running in second place, I want to know."

In a voice hushed with remembered pain, she said, "My marriage to Ned was never great, but, in spite of my parents' example, I truly believed that marriage was something enduring. Ned and I had problems, but so did several of our friends. I thought we could work everything out—right up to the day I came home early from visiting my mother and found Ned in bed with another woman."

"Cassandra," Seth breathed softly, hearing the pain in her voice.

"I ran out of the house and got into my car intending to go...I don't know where I thought I was going. I was crying and it was raining, and the next thing I knew I was heading broadside into a semitrailer. I don't remember hitting it." She paused to crush out her cigarette. "When I came to, Ned was sitting on one side of my bed, my mom and dad on the other. He'd fed them some feeble story about the brakes on my car failing and at the time I was too weak and too hurt to argue."

"That's when you left him?"

She shook her head. "No, I wasn't smart enough for that. When my parents left, Ned cried, saying that the accident was all his fault and that he didn't deserve me." She gave a hoarse little sound that was a parody of her normal laughter. "He was right, but I didn't see it; so when he begged for a second chance, I agreed. When I was discharged from the hospital, I went home with Ned and tried to pretend that nothing had happened. I could have saved myself the effort.

"There were other women—four that I know of and God knows how many others. Ned simply didn't care enough about me to be discreet. I found out about the four from expenses for New York hotels that he put on our credit card. When I checked the dates, they coincided with the days that Ned had told me he had to be out of town on a story. I didn't say a word about the first three, but when it happened the fourth time, something in me snapped. I packed my suitcases and waited for him to come home. I foolishly thought that nothing could hurt me as much as the knowledge that my husband was unfaithful. I was wrong."

Seth's hands tightened around the steering wheel until his knuckles whitened. "Did he hurt you?"

The restrained violence in his voice brought her gaze around and she understood the track his thoughts had taken. "Not physically. We argued, but this time he didn't even try to talk me into staying. That's when I learned that he was being promoted, and that the woman he was seeing was the publisher's daughter. I also discovered that Ned had married me to cash in on my father's name. I filed for divorce the next day, on grounds of mutual incompatibility."

"Does your father know?"

"If so, he found out on his own. I never told anyone the truth." She lightly touched the back of his right hand. "Until now."

He caught her hand in a crushing grip. "Does it still hurt?"

"No. I told you the truth when I said I was over Ned five minutes after I walked out the door. He had managed to kill any tender feelings I might have harbored for him. For which I will be eternally grateful," she added fervently.

"I will never hurt you that way," Seth vowed.

"I know." Cassandra smiled. "The one thing I've learned about you is that you are an honorable man."

The tension in him eased. "Do you like honorable men?"

"Very much."

He kept a firm grip on her hand for the remainder of the drive.

"There he is," Cassandra muttered as Seth wheeled the Mercedes into a parking spot across the street from her building. "Jeez, do you think he could make himself any more conspicuous?"

After shifting into Park and turning the ignition key, Seth followed her gaze to the man waiting at the top of the building's steps. Robert was immediately recognizable by the mane of silver hair.

Seth slid out of the seat and used the seconds it took to walk around the front of the Mercedes to assess the street and its occupants. He saw no immediate threat to either himself or Cassandra, including the man who might be Cassandra's ex-husband. While Robert Townsend might move heaven and earth fo find out what had happened to his daughter and where she had been, he was less of a problem than Ned Blake would be.

Aware that he had drawn Robert's attention, Seth opened the passenger door and assisted Cassandra out of the car. The effect on Townsend was instantaneous; he straightened and stared hard at the approaching pair.

Robert waited patiently, his expression reflecting nothing of his feelings at finding his daughter unharmed and holding the hand of a male companion, when he had spent the past three days worrying over her safety. When Cassandra reached the bottom of the steps and looked up at him, Robert shoved his hands into the pockets of his worn jeans and scowled back. "You could call your mother; she's scared half to death."

"That's rich, coming from the man who said he never called home because he couldn't understand the international dialing codes," Cassandra shot back as she started up the steps. "For that matter, I know the office told you I was fine. Didn't you bother to relay that little fact to Mother?"

"I told her."

"And?"

"And she made the airline reservation for me. She would have come, too, but your sister is due to produce my third grandchild in a week or so, and the news that you had been the victim of a terrorist bomb wasn't doing her state of mind any good, either." His eyes narrowed assessingly when Cassandra came to a stop in front of him. "Joanie says if you don't make it home for this baptism she's disowning you as a sister."

"I'll be there," she promised.

"Good. Now come here and give your old man a hug." When she did so, he wrapped his arms around his daughter and held on tight. "You sure gave everyone a good scare, honey."

"Believe me, it wasn't my idea." Cassandra rested her cheek against the battered tweed jacket that her father always wore when he traveled.

Robert gave a throaty growl of amusement and held her at arm's length. "Sure you're all right?"

"Positive." Her smile was the feminine version of Robert's devastating one. "A few bruises and a slight concussion is all."

"Not enough to keep a good reporter down." He hugged her once more before releasing her. "Well, honey, offer me a drink, a place to sleep for tonight and I'll be out of your hair as soon as I can book a flight out of here." He turned and shook hands with the man waiting patiently behind his daughter. "Good to see you again, Seth."

"Same here, Robert," Seth replied.

"Could we save the amenities until we're in my apartment," Cassandra asked as she fitted her key into the door and led the way into the vestibule.

"I would have waited inside," Robert explained as he grabbed his flight bag and followed her into the building, "but your concierge wouldn't hear of it. She wouldn't believe I was your father, even after I showed her your baby picture."

Cassandra made a "tsking" sound. "You must be losing your touch."

Hearing the commotion, the concierge opened her door and poked her head into the corridor. Seeing Cassandra, she stepped into the hallway and launched into a series of rapid questions to which Cassandra had no choice but to reply. The concierge was a dear woman, in her early sixties, with an insatiable curiosity about each of her tenants and their lives. Yes, Cassandra answered patiently, the story in the papers had been true; she had been hurt in a bombing, but not seriously. Yes, she should have called to let the woman know that she would be gone for the weekend, an offense for which she profusely apologized. No, she did not have any plans to leave Paris. And finally, yes, the silver-haired man beside her was indeed her father.

The concierge apologized to Robert before ducking back into her own apartment to retrieve the mail she had held for Cassandra. The woman smiled, bid the three *bonsoir* and firmly closed the door in their faces. Cassandra hid a smile at the woman's eccentricities as she started up the stairway to her third-floor apartment and unlocked the door.

"I don't think you'll fit on the couch, Dad, but you're welcome to a piece of the floor." Cassandra dropped her purse and keys on the kitchen counter. "By the way, where is the Fifth Horseman of the Apocalypse? Kurt said he was coming with you."

"If by that crack you mean where is your former husband," Robert said with a frown, "the answer is that he ran into a slight problem at the airport."

"Oh? What happened? Couldn't his ego make it through the customs check?"

"Casey," Robert sighed, using his pet name for his daughter. "If you would stop sniping about the man, I could tell you that his visa was revoked."

That brought Cassandra up short. "Why?"

Robert shrugged. "Supposedly because of some rather unflattering pieces he's written about the French government, plus the fact that he generated a lot of unfavorable publicity about your being the victim of a terrorist attack." He looked from his daughter's surprised expression to Seth's calm one. "Those were the reasons a very diplomatic young man from the embassy gave us, and I don't have any cause to disbelieve him. Do you?"

"This is all news to us," Seth replied as the memory of his meeting with Mitch flashed through his mind. Was this what Mitch had meant when he had said he would take care of the problem? Seth calmly met Robert's gaze. "The authorities are understandably touchy about the present situation."

"Umm," was all Robert said.

Cassandra had heard that tone of voice before. Her father used it when he was convinced there was more to a story than he had heard, and his insatiable curiosity worried her. If he decided to stay in Paris to protect her, there was a very real possibility that he might be hurt. Stepping around the counter and into the kitchen, she masked her sudden attack of nerves by asking brightly, "Can I offer anyone a drink?"

Deciding to let the question of Ned's revoked visa rest for the moment, Robert called over his shoulder, "Bourbon, on the rocks," while he explored the apartment.

Cassandra pulled a glass and a bottle of bourbon from a cabinet.

"I'll take care of the bourbon if you'll make coffee," Seth offered, moving into the tiny kitchen to stand beside her and lay a reassuring hand on her shoulder.

"It's a deal," she agreed with a grateful smile. A search of a bottom cabinet uncovered her coffee maker, still in its box.

"Do you know how to use that thing?" Seth asked as he watched her open the box and set the various elements of the machine on the counter.

"Yes," she replied sharply, bristling at the implied criticism. "But when it's just me, I make do with instant."

Seth studied her for a moment, aware of the tension that radiated from her. How was it possible that he could be so attuned to her emotions after such a short acquaintance? The answer flickered through his mind and was gone before he could acknowledge the veracity of it. "So do I, even though I don't like the taste." He dropped ice into a glass and poured the bourbon over the cubes. "Maybe we should start having breakfast together, that way you won't have to repack the coffee maker."

His offhand comment nearly caused her to drop the glass decanter. She turned slowly. Seth was smiling, and his eyes were warm with a look that promised a great deal more than fresh coffee. She stood motionless against the counter, the coffee decanter clutched in trembling hands as he took the single step that separated them and brushed his lips against hers.

"Make the coffee," he ordered affectionately.

"Yes, Seth."

He smiled, picked up Robert's drink, and walked into the living room. Cassandra caught her father staring at her and busied herself with the coffee. By the time the machine was merrily gurgling away, she had recovered enough of her composure to grab her cigarettes and lighter from her purse and join her guests.

Robert had taken the sofa, and Seth occupied the chair. When he made to rise in order to give her the seat, she waved him back down and settled herself cross-legged on the floor in front of him. Seth's hand drifted through her hair and then began to gently massage the tension out of the muscles in the back of her neck. She smiled at her father, unaware of the intimate picture she and Seth presented.

Robert cleared his throat. "There's been a lot of speculation in the papers about this latest bombing. I want to hear your version of it," he told his daughter.

"It was just a case of being in the wrong place at the wrong time," Cassandra said a little too breezily.

"There was a rumor that the terrorists had contacted you," Robert informed her. "That you were meeting with them when the bomb went off."

"Dad, that's crazy," she responded. "Who told you that?"

The wicker gave a rather alarming creak as Robert searched for and found a more comfortable position on the sofa. "Ned heard it."

Seth's hand stilled and came to rest on her shoulder. Cassandra looked inquisitively at her father. "Exactly what did he hear?"

"That you had been in touch with the Freedom Brigade before the last bombing."

Cassandra's heart sank. She had hoped that her father would be satisfied with her version of what had happened, but Ned, typically, had managed to arouse all of Robert's paternal and journalistic instincts.

She fumbled for a cigarette, buying time to compose herself, and met Seth's eyes above the flame of the lighter he held for her. He gave an almost imperceptible nod of his head and she resigned herself to the inevitable.

"Look, Dad," she began gently, "a lot has happened in the past few days."

"So I gathered," Robert said wryly.

Cassandra frowned at him and continued. "The bomb wasn't exactly an accident, but it wasn't an attempt on my life, either. What I am about to tell you must remain in the strictest confidence." Robert nodded and she smiled. "What Ned heard was true; I have been in contact with the Brigade. Or, more accurately, they have been in touch with me. A week ago I received an anonymous phone call from a man who claimed to be a member of the terrorist organization responsible for the violence in Paris. That was followed by a tape recording that had been made by the leader of the terrorists and gave their name as the Freedom Brigade. They have, it seems, chosen me to write their story."

Within fifteen minutes, she had sketched out her connection to the terrorists for her father. Seth poured coffee for the two of them and a second bourbon for Robert while she talked. It was a carefully edited version of the truth—she did not tell her father about Mitch and his people, nor did she discuss the extraordinary château outside Paris, not even when it became obvious that he thought she and Seth had slipped away for the weekend.

Robert downed the last of his drink and carefully set the glass aside on the brass-and-glass end table nearest him. "So now what are you going to do?"

"Do?" Cassandra eyed him quizzically. "I intend to go to work tomorrow, finish the research for the upcoming warcrimes trial, and cover any other assignment Seth gives me."

"Casey," Robert said in an admonishing tone. "Don't try to con the guy who taught you all his con artist's tricks. What are you going to do about the terrorist story?"

"If it's assigned to me, I'll cover it," she answered calmly.

"And if Dateline decides to send you back to the States?" he asked.

"That would be my decision," Seth said before Cassandra could reply. "At the present time, I don't see that happening."

"Seth, you're a good man and a good reporter and, believe me, I deeply regret the fact that you have to go through this business with terrorists a second time. However—" Robert paused and folded his arms across his chest in a familiar gesture that Cassandra recognized as his prelude to the delivery of an edict "—However, Casey is my primary concern."

"And mine," Seth agreed.

"I would hate to go over your head, Seth, but I will if necessary."

Frowning, Cassandra said slowly, "What exactly do you mean, Dad?"

"I mean," Robert replied with a faintly apologetic air, "that if Seth won't send you back to the States, I'm sure Tom Burroughs will."

Seth sensed, rather than saw, the effect her father's words had upon Cassandra. The determination that had carried her through the past few days seemed to collapse in the face of Robert's warning.

"Oh, Dad, you wouldn't."

"Yes, he would," Seth stated. "And he has enough clout that Tom would undoubtedly agree."

"That's not fair," Cassandra bitterly told her father.

"And who told you life was fair?" Robert asked. "Not me, Casey."

"No, you didn't," she retorted. "You were the one who always said journalism was a higher calling, remember? Seize the opportunity; get the story; find an edge over the others and move before they do—that's what you told me. And now that there's a little danger—"

"A little danger?" Robert queried in a low voice that was all the more impressive for the wealth of emotion it contained. "A little danger is the same as a little bit pregnant—there ain't no such animal. And if you think for one minute that I'm going to leave my daughter in the middle of some mess with a bunch of homicidal maniacs, you, my dear, don't know me as well as you think you do."

"I know you very well," Cassandra argued. Springing to her feet, she paced around the living room before saying accusingly, "If I were a man you would have stayed in Connecticut, holding Mom's hand and telling her not to worry instead of deciding to play the worried father."

Robert's aquamarine eyes darkened. "That's probably true, but it doesn't alter your situation."

"Dad, if you get me recalled I'll be forced to resign from Dateline, you know that. And you know what the industry gossip mill will do to my reputation. After that you can forget my reporting anything that vaguely resembles hard news; I'll be lucky to get a job on the society page. I've worked hard to get where I am. One phone call from you will wipe it all out."

Robert sighed and leaned back in his chair to survey his daughter. "You don't fight fair."

Cassandra's lips curved in a shaky smile. "Did you expect anything less? I fight the way you taught me to."

"All those summers you spent with me, I never thought twice about the situations I was putting you in. Because you were with me, I thought that you were protected. Your mother felt differently, of course, but until three days ago I couldn't understand why she would get so worked up. Now I do."

Cassandra swallowed the lump in her throat. "I'm sorry you're worried, Dad, but it comes with the territory. If you didn't want me to follow in your footsteps, you shouldn't have showed me your world."

Robert nodded reluctantly. "I would at least like your promise that you won't place yourself in a position where you can be taken hostage by these poeple—or worse."

"I promise," she immediately conceded. "Having a bomb explode in front of you does wonders for your self-preservation instinct."

With a slight chuckle, Robert threw up his hands in defeat. "I don't know how I'm going to explain this to your mother.

She made me promise that you would be on the next flight back to the States.''

"You'll manage, Dad," Cassandra said dryly. "You always have.''

"True. Just the same, I think I'll stay in Paris for a while. Maybe your mother will take the news better if she knows that I'm here.''

"Dad," Cassandra began warningly.

"I won't interfere," he vowed. "But after all, there is a story breaking, and I am one of the best photographers around. It would be a pity if I missed it. Besides," he mused aloud, "it makes it harder for your mother to find me, particularly if she doesn't know what hotel I'm staying in." He picked up his glass and gave it to his daughter. "Get me another drink, Casey, while I call around and find myself a room."

Seth followed Cassandra into the kitchen while her father made use of the telephone. If Robert noticed the unblinking red light on the phone's base, he said nothing.

"What are we going to do now?" she asked him as she dropped ice into the glass. "I was sure he would leave."

"We'll make the best of it," Seth replied, handing her the bourbon. "As long as he doesn't interfere or generate any publicity, I think it will work out."

"And that's another thing. What about this business with Ned? When did the French start revoking journalists' visas on such flimsy pretexts?"

"Beats me," he answered honestly. "Let's just be grateful for the new policy; your ex-husband is one less problem to deal with."

Cassandra shrugged and shoved Ned and his problems to the back of her mind. She had enough to deal with without worrying about his visa troubles.

Chapter 7

Your father is really something," Seth commented to Cassandra as they took the stairs back to her apartment. Just moments before they had watched Robert—who had refused Seth's offer of a ride—depart in a taxi bound for the hotel he frequented when he stayed in Paris. "Until now, I've only seen him in a professional setting. It's interesting to watch how he deals with his family."

Cassandra smiled gently. "I wonder if he was serious about talking to Tom Burroughs."

"I'm sure he was," Seth affirmed. "And I'm surprised he decided against it."

"Why?"

Seth opened the apartment door and headed to the kitchen, where he searched the cupboards hopefully for a bottle of Scotch. When his search proved fruitless, he settled for the bourbon Robert had been drinking.

"He's caught between his heart and his head," he explained as he made himself a drink. He raised the bottle in mute question to Cassandra and when she shook her head, he continued. "Intellectually, he knows that you're all grown up and able to take care of yourself. Emotionally, however, he feels that you're still the little girl he's supposed to protect from the big bad world—the same world, incidentally, to which he introduced you. He would never forgive himself if anything happened to you because of a story."

A chill ran up Cassandra's spine at his words, and she paused in the midst of collecting the dirty dishes in the living room. They had been talking about Robert, but the observation fit Seth as well. "Have you forgiven yourself for Angela?" she asked softly, afraid to open old wounds, but more afraid of the haunted look on his face.

His eyes met hers. "I'm not sure," he said finally. "Angela was still a baby, depending on her mother and me to keep her safe."

She moved into the kitchen, deposited the dishes in the sink, and leaned back against the counter. Ghosts flitted in the depths of his black eyes—memories of what he had had and lost. He had admitted to being frightened of the attraction between them, but how deep did that fear run?

The powerful chemistry between Seth and herself was undeniable, but she wanted more than a relationship built on sexual attraction. She wanted—needed—the same kind of emotional commitment from him that she was capable of offering in return. Until he relinquished the past, he would be incapable of anything beyond physical intimacy, and instinct told her that she dared not fall into that trap. The knowledge that she was ready to hand this man her heart on a silver platter while his own was held inviolate terrified her.

"Absolution is out of my province, Seth." She held her breath, waiting for the explosion.

His face registered first surprise, then anger. "I'm not looking for forgiveness," he stated coldly.

"Aren't you?" Her aquamarine eyes gleamed in the dimly lit room.

"No."

"You've been wearing your guilt over Rachel and Angela like a hair shirt for ten years. Isn't it time to give up the role of martyr?"

A muscle worked in his jaw. "You don't know what you're saying."

"Yes, I do, and that's why you're angry. You're very big on opening other people's eyes to unpleasant truths; I think it's time you face a few truths of your own."

His eyes burned with black fire. "Is this some new barrier you've found to keep me at arm's length? If so, it's a good one, lady. Be careful that it doesn't work too well."

For just a moment her courage wavered. She could apologize now, blame the hurtful words on the pressure they had been under for the past few days. He would understand and forgive. But intuition told her that their future together depended upon Seth forgiving himself for the death of his wife and child. Until he did, there would be no room for her in his heart.

Trembling inwardly, she said, "Go ahead and run, Seth; you've been waiting for an excuse to do just that ever since you came back to Paris." Straightening, she walked around him to the apartment door. "I didn't frighten you at the beginning because at first you thought I was too ambitious, then too irresponsible, and you didn't *have* to run because my flaws gave you the upper hand. You could save me from myself and everyone would look at you and say, 'How noble, how self-sacrificing, and after all the poor man has been through.'"

Her eyes narrowed. "Well, now that you've corrected all my character flaws to your satisfaction, what are you going to do? Stay or run?"

He stalked across the room to her. "You're the one who wants to run," he growled. "And I'm getting damn tired of chasing you."

"No you're not. You *like* the fact that I run; it saves you from confronting the truth, which is that you buried yourself in the grave with Rachel and Angela," she taunted. "My ex-husband was a real bastard, but I give him credit, he never lied to himself the way you have." She threw open the apartment door. "You reach for me with one hand while you push me away with the other, and it's tearing me apart."

The sound of his own breathing distorted Seth's hearing; the floor seemed to tilt precariously as he reached for her shoulders.

Cassandra flinched as his fingers bit into her flesh. "Now what, Seth? Are you going to kiss me? Hit me?" His fingers tightened and she blinked against the tears that flooded her eyes. "Just what are you going to do now that I'm not running?"

He swore feelingly and threw her aside. Cassandra cried out as the edge of the counter slammed into her ribs, but Seth didn't hear. For several moments, all he could see were the faces of Rachel and Angela and the car turning into a fireball around them.

Gasping, Cassandra pulled herself upright, pressing a hand over her abused ribs. She had gone too far, she thought despairingly; unwilling to settle for less than a whole man, she had now lost whatever part of himself Seth had been willing to give. This time he was going to walk out and she wanted to weep for what might have been. Instead she bit down hard on her bottom lip and watched Seth's hands clench as he battled the past.

The memories receded, leaving him weak but strangely at peace with himself. This was what he had feared from the first—that those compelling, aquamarine eyes would see through his confident facade to the terrified man beneath. Cassandra was right; caught in the physical attraction between them, he had unconsciously tried to keep his heart uninvolved. His acceptance of this ugly truth precluded his walking away. He carefully closed the door and relocked it. Turning, he leaned against the wood, his hands shoved into his trouser pockets. Enough space remained between them that Cassandra wouldn't feel threatened. He hoped.

"Do you believe everything you've just said?" When she nodded, he sighed. "You would think that after ten years I would have worked through all my guilt, but I haven't. I still feel responsible for their deaths." His dark, imploring gaze settled upon her. "It's complicated between us, isn't it?"

"Yes, I suppose it is." Her vision swam with tears but she forced herself to say calmly, "I think our involvement with the Brigade is making matters more difficult for you; so until this business is finished one way or the other, I think it might be best if we don't see each other."

"That's going to be difficult, isn't it? Considering that we work in the same office?"

"You know what I mean," she cried. "You constantly compare me to Rachel, and I know I suffer by comparison."

He exhaled heavily. "There may be some truth in that," he confessed quietly, "but not in the way you think. What frightens me is not the fact that I want you in my life, but the very real possibility of losing you. Emotionally, I don't think I could survive that."

For just a moment her heart seemed to stop beating, and then it resumed with a heavy lurch that shook her from head to toe. She could do nothing more than stare at him as he stretched out a hand to her. "Don't turn me away, Cassandra. Please."

It was the way he said "please" that crumbled all resistance—his voice poured a wealth of meaning into the word. Slowly, through a mist of tears, she saw her own arm reach toward him until just the tips of their fingers touched and her gaze lifted to his. They were both scarred, though the scars were buried deep, hidden away from the world. Perhaps what drew them to each other was the knowledge that each could understand and forgive the other's all too human failings.

"No ghosts," he promised, his fingers flexing ever so slightly, drawing her forward. "Not mine, not yours." She was watching him almost fearfully and his heart ached for both of them, for the pain they must survive in order to trust each other.

She stopped with just inches remaining between them. His hand engulfed her own, warm and alluring, but otherwise he did not touch her. She studied his face, his eyes, seeking the truth, and found desire and need, amazement and wariness—mirror images of her own emotions. His free hand gently touched her hair, her cheek, and she took the last step that brought her against his chest.

"Seth—"

"Shh." He pressed her head into his shoulder and closed his eyes; his cheek came to rest upon the top of her head.

Cassandra nestled closer, content to listen to the deep, even rhythm of his heartbeat.

"I'm not capable of promising you forever," he whispered. "Not yet."

She nodded slightly. "I know."

"But I do care for you, Cassandra," he continued, his arms tightening around her. "And I'll do my best not to hurt you."

"I know," she repeated, her arms stealing around him. They were both avoiding the word love, she realized, perhaps because they both knew how much pain was involved with the word. It didn't matter; in time, perhaps they would heal enough to forget their fear.

His lips moved against her temple and Cassandra abandoned her analysis in favor of the sweet pleasure of Seth's mouth. She tilted her head, allowing him access to the curve of her neck, then shivered as he nipped gently at her flesh and laved the spot with his tongue. He bent slightly, slid an arm under her knees and lifted her high against his chest.

Her eyes opened languorously, and she traced the shape of his mouth with a fingertip as he carried her into the bedroom. The room was dark, save for the light that spilled through the doorway from the living room. The indirect lighting showed him the bed, and a moment later the springs groaned under their combined weight. Propped against the brass spindles at the head of the bed with Cassandra on his lap, Seth bent one leg so that his foot rested flat upon the spread. Bracing Cassandra against his thigh, his mouth searched blindly for hers while his hands tangled in the mass of blond hair falling like a veil around her shoulders.

Cassandra sighed as their lips met; her fingernails kneaded his shoulders, a primitive response to the invasion of his tongue. The heady scent of sandalwood cologne surrounded her. He tasted pleasantly of coffee and bourbon, and the mating of his tongue with hers was the most seductive encounter of her life. She heard the low whimper she made, felt the tautening of the muscles in his thigh and belly as her hands unconsciously clutched his shirt in an effort to draw their bodies closer together. A wild heat suffused her, melting her curves into the harder planes of his frame. She was kindling to his flame, and when his fingers released their hold in her hair to repeatedly brush the outside curves of her breasts, the fire threatened to burn out of control. She gasped and pulled back slightly, offering herself to his questing touch.

"S-Seth..."

"I know," he answered shakily, watching her through eyes grown heavy-lidded with passion. "I ache, too." He pressed an index finger against the generous curve of her bottom lip, then caught his breath when the tip of her tongue brushed sensuously along the pad. His free hand glided across her rib cage, slid upward between her breasts and slowly, deliberately, began undoing the buttons of her shirt.

When the last button had been released, he parted the sides of the shirt, absorbing the sight of the satin and lace that cupped her breasts. The heavy thrum of his heartbeat shuddered through his frame as his fingertip defined the scalloped edge of the lace before insinuating itself inside the protective barrier to touch the flesh beneath.

Cassandra's head fell back against his upraised knee as the heat of his hand scorched her. Her breasts felt full and heavy, the nipple puckering in anticipation of his touch. Her lips moved against the finger he had kept pressed against her, then spontaneously parted and closed, drawing him into her mouth.

His breath hissed between his teeth; every muscle turned to iron as she provoked the primitive side of him. Groaning, he cupped his hand beneath her breast and skimmed his thumb over the impudent nipple. She cried out softly and shivered. Her nails bit through his shirt and into flesh, threatening the last of his self-control.

"Sweetheart, listen to me." The words lacked urgency; rather, they flowed like molasses, sweet and thick with desire. "Cassandra, please," he beseeched her when she melted weakly against his chest and sought his mouth with hers.

Reluctantly she tipped her head back and forced her eyes open. Her voice, normally as clear and precise as a clarion, emerged on a low, breathless note. "Don't run now, Seth; I couldn't bear it."

He swallowed convulsively, aware that his tenuous hold on reality was slipping away. "I'm not going anywhere, sweetheart, but you have to listen to me." Her lips formed a moue that was almost his undoing. "We have to think about protecting you," he grated. Comprehension flared in her eyes and he nodded. "If you don't have anything, I have to stop now... or I won't be able to stop at all."

She smiled and pressed her lips against his in a kiss that spoke of tenderness and understanding. "Wait," was all she said.

He watched as she slid from the bed and entered the adjoining bathroom. There was a sharp click and light audaciously flooded the bedroom before she closed the door. His breath was rasping in his ears and Seth took advantage of the brief separation to regain some semblance of control. Trying to steady his erratic heartbeat, he listened to the hushed sounds of Cassandra's movements. There was the sound of a cabinet opening, an interval of silence, then the cabinet closed and he heard water running.

In the old-fashioned bathroom, Cassandra took care of the necessary precaution before catching sight of her reflection in the mirror over the sink. Her mouth had a swollen appearance, and her eyes had darkened to an intense color. She touched a shaking hand to her lips, wondering, for the first time, if what she was about to do was insane. She had known Seth for barely a week. Was it the act of a rational woman to invite a virtual stranger into her bed? She turned off the taps and reached for a towel, her gaze never wavering from the mirror, as if her reflection could give her the answer she sought. And perhaps it did, because she knew with a certainty that came from the depths of her soul, that this was probably the sanest thing she had ever done in her life. Being with Seth was inexplicably *right*.

The door opened, the harsh light blinding Seth before it was turned off. His eyes had barely adjusted to the shadows again when he realized Cassandra was beside the bed.

Reaching for her, his lips curved in silent welcome, he discovered that she had discarded her jeans. The shirt still hung from her shoulders, diminishing the effect of the pale bands that delineated her bra and panties. He caught her hands. "Cassandra...."

She settled beside him, her fingers going to his shirt. "One of us is wearing too many clothes," she teased. Cupping the back of her head in one large hand, he managed an amorphous reply and pulled her down for his kiss.

With a small whimper of pleasure, she braced herself against his chest as his mouth and tongue renewed their assault on her senses. Her deft fingers made short work of the buttons on his shirt and she impatiently tugged the material free of his waistband. Gently disengaging herself, she pulled back and surveyed the broad expanse of his chest now exposed to her gaze. Murmuring her appreciation, she combed her fingers through the thick, dark hair that covered his chest in an unabashed display of hedonism.

"You're beautiful," she whispered, leaning forward to sprinkle kisses along his torso.

Seth couldn't answer; his heartbeat was threatening to tear him apart. Her hair fell against his chest, the perfect counterpoint to the searing brand of her mouth. He was trapped, borne along on a wave of desire that banished all other considerations. When Cassandra found the flat nipple harbored within a whorl of hair, she sighed and turned her attention to it. His reaction was electrifying. He stiffened and arched toward her, his hands curling around the brass spindles at the head of the bed as he gave a harsh, masculine cry of passion.

Smiling slightly, she trailed kisses up the sturdy column of his neck to his jawline. He turned toward her, capturing her lips as an iron arm went around her waist and drew her closer. His free hand caught hers and carried it to the blatant proof of his arousal. He cried out again, softer this time, as she caressed him.

"Help me, sweetheart," he breathed. He slid the shirt down her arms and carelessly tossed it away. Bending forward, he nuzzled the satin and lace covering her breasts as his hands searched for the snap.

"In front," she murmured as her fingers worked on his belt. He was quicker than she. The sensations his hands created as they cupped her made her clumsy, and when his mouth surrounded her she could do nothing more than revel in the response he created so easily.

In the end, Seth dealt with his own clothing as well as hers. She watched him through half-closed eyes, watched as he stripped away their civilized veneers with gentle, adoring hands and then stretched out on his side next to her. Their gazes met as their bodies brushed together, his alive with wonder, hers almost shy now that no barriers, physical or emotional, existed between them.

He smiled, caught her chin when she would have buried her face in the hollow of his shoulder. "Don't," he murmured. "I want to see your eyes when it happens."

She caught her breath as his hand slipped from her face to her throat and beyond. His fingers found the blond triangle of hair at the juncture of her thighs and hesitated. She saw the question in his eyes, felt the sting of tears in her own at his consideration. With a tremulous smile she granted him entry.

"I adore you," he said as he found the center of her desire and stroked it gently. She shuddered beneath his ministrations and he bent his head to her breast to stoke the fire higher.

Her hands ranged helplessly over his shoulders, his back, his chest. The stubble of his beard against her flesh abraded, aroused. "Please," she whispered. "I don't think—" Her words died as his fingers teased her.

Seth raised his head. "What do you think, love?"

"That I want you," she answered in a throaty voice that she didn't recognize. "Oh, Seth, please—I need you."

"I know, sweetheart; I can feel it." His mouth caught hers as he turned her onto her back and rose above her. "Look at me, Cassandra."

As if she could do anything else, she thought incredulously. The planes of his face had grown harsh with desire, but his dark eyes remained tender. She pressed her palm against his cheek as he made a place for himself between her thighs. His hands moved to her hips—holding her, positioning her—and, as she felt the heaviness of him, she knew a moment's unease. He waited, giving her time to adjust to him. His mouth teased hers and he felt the change in her.

"No ghosts," he reminded her, breathing the words into her mouth. "Not yours, not mine. Tonight we start over."

"Yes." The word had barely emerged before he took possession of her body with a slow, rocking motion that drove the past away. She watched him as he watched her, saw his eyes widen when he felt her body conform to the needs of his own. "Seth . . ."

"You feel so right, love, so very right. And I want you so badly." He was at the very edge of his control. Instinct demanded release; his heart said otherwise. He wanted Cassandra to feel the same aching hunger that was consuming him.

Seth began to move and Cassandra gave a small gasp of amazement. A desire unlike any she had ever known caught her in its relentless grip and swept her along. Her body stretched to accommodate Seth's demands as he murmured words of passion and possession that burned themselves into her soul.

She wrapped her arms around his neck, out of control, feeling as if she would burst into a million pieces at any moment.

"Yes, that's right," he groaned, gathering her close. "Hold on to me, love; I'll take you where you want to go. I'll wait, just, please . . ." Words deserted him and he nipped the sensitive area where her throat met her shoulder.

Her breasts sank into the mat of hair on his chest and she shuddered at the exquisite sensations the meeting produced. She turned blindly toward his mouth, delighting in its familiar texture as passion spiraled them higher. She was reaching for something just out of reach, something she would recognize only when it was within her grasp. Suddenly Seth's rhythm altered and the next moment the world spun crazily away. Every nerve ruptured with unbearable pleasure and she uttered a wordless cry of fulfillment. Seth was saying her name over and over again in a litany that ended abruptly when he gave a hoarse cry and followed her over the edge.

The last of his strength had been expended and he collapsed against her. Cassandra welcomed his weight. She held him close and traced the straight line of his spine with her fingertips. The aftershocks vibrated through them, leaving them almost painfully sensitized. Seth's uneven breathing rasped in her ear, bringing a wistful smile to her mouth.

Instinct had not failed her. What had begun as pure physical attraction had metamorphosed into a bond that was as unbreakable as it was new. At least for her. Seth might feel otherwise.

Reluctantly, Seth lifted himself away from the delicate frame he had been crushing into the mattress and rolled to his side, carrying her with him. Smiling, he kissed her gently and brushed a strand of damp hair away from her cheek. The quiet enchantment that radiated from her made him want to growl in triumph. He resisted the urge to play the satisfied male and said, "You're beautiful."

Cassandra laughed, a deep, throaty sound that bespoke contentment and satisfaction. "You are supposed to tell me that *before* we get into bed."

"Oh?" He raised an eyebrow at her. "Should we get dressed and start all over again?"

She grinned. "I'm game if you are."

He curled an arm around her waist when she made to rise. "Down, sweetheart, I'm not as young as I used to be."

"You couldn't prove it by me," she retorted archly.

"That has to be the best news I've heard in quite some time." He propped himself up on one elbow and combed his fingers through her hair so that it formed a blond halo against the jade green bedspread. "I like your hair," he said quietly.

"So I see."

He tapped her lightly on the nose. "Behave yourself. There's something incredibly erotic about a woman with long hair." She reached out a hand to toy with the dark hair that covered his chest, and discovered what she had missed during their heated lovemaking. His torso was a mass of ridged and gouged flesh.

Seth watched the changing expressions on her face before saying, "A little memento of the PRCF. The bomb turned my automobile into shrapnel, and I was standing close enough to catch some of it."

Cassandra blinked away tears and continued her investigation, as if her touch could erase both the trauma and his scars. "Does it hurt?"

"Once in a while," he admitted. "The doctors couldn't remove all the metal, so from time to time a piece will shift."

"Then what do you do?"

"Go to a doctor, get an X ray to see if anything vital is in danger of being damaged." Seth touched her cheek, bringing her gaze up to his. "Sometimes the doctor will remove it; sometimes he leaves it alone."

"That's why you don't go through the metal detector at work," she said softly as comprehension dawned.

He nodded. "I'd set it off. I can't use the detectors at airports either, so I carry a medical ID with my picture on it, explaining the problem. Sometimes I'm subjected to a body search if the guards think the ID is fake. It's just a minor inconvenience." When she did not comment, he looked at her searchingly. "Revolting, isn't it?"

Frowning, Cassandra raised a hand to his face and said simply, "No."

The smile returned to Seth's face. "That was short and to the point."

"I have this boss, you see, who's constantly trimming my copy—ouch!" Her impudence had earned her a slap to the backside but she grinned unrepentantly. "I'm going to take a shower. Care to join me?"

She was off the bed before Seth could answer. Feeling satiated and utterly content, he rolled off the mattress and followed her into the bathroom. The water was running when he yanked back the shower curtain to step into the claw-foot tub. Smiling, she drew him under the spray with one hand while she utilized the bar of soap with the other.

She liked touching Seth, Cassandra thought as she worked the soap over the mat of hair on his chest and then had him turn so that she could do his back. His body was as she had imagined it—deeply tanned, save for the area that would be covered by bikini bathing trunks, with well-developed musculature. His stomach was like a washboard.

When her hands faltered to a stop, Seth turned back so they were face-to-face. "My turn." His voice was a low growl as he took the soap from her hand and drew it over the top of her breasts. Her eyes darkened in renewed passion as his hand traveled lower.

"I thought your advanced years had caught up to you," she murmured, looping an arm around his neck when her legs began to tremble.

"My recuperative powers are better than I thought," he returned. He caught his breath as her hand boldly cupped him.

The tub was small, reinforcing their intimacy. Scant inches separated them, and the slightest movement allowed his hair-roughened flesh to slide against its satiny, feminine counterpart. Fingertips brushed lightly, tracing patterns in the white lather, eliciting gasps and murmurs of encouragement. The soap fell to the bottom of the tub, unnoticed. Eyes glowing with seductive purpose, Seth caught Cassandra around the waist and lifted her against him. She cried out softly when he entered her, then gasped as he began to move. The noise of the shower drowned out their cries of pleasure.

When it was over, it was Seth who turned off the shower and toweled them both dry before carrying Cassandra back to the bedroom. He settled her in the bed, retraced his steps to flip off the bathroom light, and then slid between the sheets.

She smiled into the darkness as his arm pulled her back against his chest. Tomorrow she might doubt the wisdom of what they had just done, but for now the reality of falling asleep in his arms held all her misgivings at bay.

Cassandra woke the next morning to find herself nestled so close to Seth that the pelt of hair on his chest tickled her nose. One of his legs was thrown over hers, pinning her to the bed. She smiled at the wall of his chest, considering the various aches of her body that spoke of shared passion and possession. Lifting her head in order to see the alarm clock over his shoulder, she realized that she had awakened an hour earlier than normal. Not that she minded, she thought happily. Waking up in Seth's arms was every bit as enjoyable as falling asleep in his arms. It could definitely become habit-forming.

Moving slowly and carefully so as not to awaken him, she extricated herself from his embrace and tiptoed into the bathroom. After a quick shower, she brushed her teeth and shrugged into the floor-length robe hanging on the back of the door. She searched the drawers of the small vanity until she found the toothbrush she hadn't yet opened. She placed it next to the sink for Seth and then tiptoed back through the bedroom and into the kitchen.

Last night's used dishes greeted her, but, fortunately, Seth had turned off the coffee maker at some point. She quickly disposed of the dirty cups and glasses and when the coffee maker was clean, filled it and slid the switch into the drip position. The scent of fresh coffee wafted through her apartment as she sliced bread for toast and then frowned at the contents of her refrigerator. She rarely ate breakfast, but she had the feeling Seth would want more than a cup of coffee. Her hand paused in midair as she lifted the carton of eggs. Where had this sudden surge of domesticity come from? Brewed coffee instead of instant? Scrambled eggs *and* toast?

She placed the eggs on the counter and stared at them, searching for an answer. She remembered spending a weekend with Joanie shortly after her sister had met, and fallen for, Craig. Her husband-to-be would be joining them for dinner and Joanie had bustled around her apartment, preparing the dishes she knew Craig liked and straightening this and that until Cassandra had been ready to scream. Joanie had laughed and apologized, explaining that the nesting instinct must have caught up with her. Now, standing in her Paris apartment, Cassandra swallowed nervously and reached for her cigarettes. Was it possible that she had been inundated with the same instinct?

Of course not, she told herself bracingly. It wasn't as if she were in love with Seth...although there was no denying that she already cared more deeply for him than she ever had for Ned. But that didn't mean anything. And neither did the fact that her heart gave a joyful leap whenever she saw him.

Seth woke to the smell of coffee and the discovery that the other half of the bed was empty. That was a pity, he thought, because he had hoped to start the day by kissing Cassandra awake. But there would be other mornings, he consoled himself as he glanced at the clock on the nightstand. The thought made him smile. He was still smiling when Cassandra tentatively poked her head around the door.

"I'm sorry. I didn't mean to wake you," she said quietly.

"You didn't." He levered himself up on one elbow as she moved across the room. When she perched on the edge of the bed, he slid a hand around the back of her neck and brought her lips down to his. "Last night was incredible," he murmured at last. He fell back against the pillow with Cassandra sprawled across his chest.

She propped her chin on her hands and studied him with troubled eyes. "No regrets?"

"None," he answered firmly. "You?"

She gave careful consideration to the question, although she knew the answer. She had agonized over it and her own conflicting emotions while she worked in the kitchen and had discovered that it was too late to waste energy on transparent denials. She had fallen head over heels in love with Seth Winter. A slow smile lit her face. "Only that this is a working day."

"We could call in sick."

"Tempting," she drawled, "but Kurt and I have a trial to cover today. Remember?"

He thoughtfully combed his fingers through her hair. "I remember. I just don't like the idea of your being out of my sight for hours at a time."

She stiffened slightly. "If you're thinking of pulling me—"

"I'm not," he assured her. "As bureau chief, I've assigned the story to my two best reporters. But as your lover, I would worry less if you were in the office until..." His words trailed off when he saw the triumphant expression on her face. "What?"

"Lover," she echoed, turning the word over and over in her mind. "I like the way that sounds when you say it. I don't think I've ever been anyone's lover before."

His heart contracted and then expanded with wonder until it seemed to fill his chest. "Well you are now."

"Yes," she agreed softly, aquamarine eyes shining. "I'm going to enjoy being your lover." She kissed him tenderly and then pushed herself upright. "If we keep this up, breakfast will be late."

His grin was wickedly inviting. "I won't mind."

"But I will," she retorted, rising. "Get dressed while I start scrambling the eggs."

Seth showered and dressed quickly. Ten minutes later they were sitting at the oval table devouring the meal of scrambled eggs and toast. He volunteered to clear the table while she dressed, and when Cassandra emerged from the bedroom she found that the dishes had been washed, with the exception of the two cups of coffee sitting side by side on the table.

"I have forty-five minutes before I have to leave for the Metro." She took her chair and slipped her feet into the sling-back pumps she carried.

"I thought you could ride to work with me today," he commented idly, admiring the graceful expanse of leg her softly gathered white skirt exposed. The shocking-pink blouse she wore complimented her coloring, and her hair was swept into a topknot and pinned securely in place. She looked coolly professional, scarcely resembling the passionate woman he had held in his arms the night before.

Cassandra lit a cigarette, and smiled. "Don't you think that would be a tad obvious?"

Shrugging, he took a cigarette from the pack on the table. "So we arrive in the office at the same time. What's obvious about that?"

"Nothing, I guess," she conceded, turning her attention to her coffee cup.

"Cassandra," he said patiently, understanding what was troubling her. "I'm not about to carry you into the office over my shoulder or swagger around your desk. To do so would do just as much damage to my reputation as it would to yours. But I also refuse to slink out of here as if what we've done is something to be ashamed of."

In spite of her fears, Cassandra chuckled. "You win. I'll ride to work with you."

He reached for her hand. "I don't want to *win* anything. Don't mistake me for your ex-husband; I don't consider this a contest."

"I know you don't," she replied, relaxing under the warmth of his gaze. "I don't either, but everything has happened so fast that it's going to take me some time to adjust."

"It will be worth the time," he promised her. "Now, finish your coffee. We have to stop at my hotel on the way to the office so I can change clothes."

In the end, none of their co-workers seemed to find it strange that they were both late in arriving at the Dateline office. De-

spite the upheaval of the past few days, the office routine
seemed not to have changed. Margot was on the phone, chattering brightly to a famous fashion designer who had called to
invite her to the unveiling of his winter line. Jules was putting
the finishing touches on his interview with France's most popular soccer player; he barely noticed when the two of them
walked through the door. Kurt was in the teleprinter room,
sipping coffee and watching something print out. PJ had made
himself at home at Cassandra's desk and was muttering a string
of imprecations into his mustache as he worked on her damaged camera. He glanced up and shook his head as Cassandra
approached him.

"Try to avoid falling on the camera next time," he growled
at her. "You damn near ruined the shutter."

"Sorry," she replied airily. "I'll be more careful in the future." She perched on the corner of her desk to watch him
work. "Are you coming to court with us?"

PJ nodded. "Just long enough to get some photos of the defendant. Unless you want me to stick around to take pictures
of the state's witnesses."

"I don't think so. From what I've been able to gather from
the files, most of these people value their privacy. Digging up
the past is going to be painful enough for them without our
turning them into a media circus."

"What a noble sentiment," he mocked. "Noble, but mis-
guided. Come on, Cassandra, these people are *news*. It can't
hurt to have photos to run with your sidebars."

She blinked, as stunned by her changed attitude as the photographer was. "Let me talk to the people first. If they're
agreeable to pictures I'll let you know."

"Suit yourself." PJ made a final adjustment with a tiny
screwdriver and laid her camera on her desk. "There you go.
Should work fine now."

"Thanks, PJ."

The photographer snorted. "Look, if you decide you need
photos and can't find me, use the Nikon. I can work wonders
in the darkroom." Rising, he strolled over to the coffeepot.

Cassandra put her camera in her shoulder bag and walked back to the teleprinter room. "Anything interesting?" she asked Kurt, peering over his shoulder.

"Possibly." The printer rattled to a stop and he tore the copy out of the machine. "Take a look."

It was a flash message from the Madrid bureau, transmitted simultaneously to all Dateline offices, reporting a gun battle between Spanish border guards and two men, one of whom was known to be a member of the IRA. The men had been trying to enter Spain from France, using counterfeit passports, when a customs official had recognized the IRA member from a circular distributed by the Spanish authorities. The two men had apparently panicked and tried to retrieve their phony documents when the customs officer had delayed their entry into Spain. A fight had ensued and the IRA suspect had pulled a gun. The border guards had drawn their weapons and, in the exchange of fire, the two men had been killed and one border guard had been seriously injured.

A search of the terrorists' effects had revealed a substantial amount of cash, in both French and Spanish currency, several photographs, and tapes and pamphlets acclaiming the recent wave of terror in France. Although, officially, the Spanish authorities refused to comment on the photographs, there was speculation that they were of possible victims targeted by the highly active group who claimed responsibility for the rash of bombings in Paris—the Freedom Brigade.

"What do you think?" Kurt asked when she had read the transmission.

"I think it deserves investigation," she answered thoughtfully. "Let's show it to Seth."

Seth was editing a story when they entered his office. His suit jacket hung on the coat tree and his shirtsleeves were neatly folded up above his elbow. Cassandra shivered at the dark hair sprinkling his arms and the back of his hands as she passed him the story. The memory of the strength of his hands and how it felt to be held tightly in his arms practically turned her legs to jelly.

Seth read the story without comment, his only outward display of emotion the repeated tic of the muscle in his jaw. When he was done he handed the paper back to Cassandra. "It's definitely an important story, but the two of you have a trial to cover, remember?"

"I was thinking that it might be a good idea for me to fly to Madrid," Cassandra began. "If I can get permission to listen to the tapes, I might be able to identify the voice as matching the one on the tape that was delivered to me."

"I'm sure you could," Seth said reasonably, smiling. "But the fact remains that the trial takes priority over this."

"But—"

"I'm also sure that the Sûreté has already sent a man to Madrid with a copy of your tape," he continued, literally trampling her argument under his own reasoning. "No doubt he will do an adequate job of matching the voices—if they can be matched."

"Yes, but it's a continuation of the Brigade story—my story," she interjected. "If there's a connection between the Brigade and those two dead men I want to write about it."

He leaned back in his chair, the smile vanishing. "No."

Cassandra stared at him. "Why?"

Seth raised his index finger. "One, Dateline's Madrid bureau is perfectly capable of handling this on their own. Call them if you like, and let them know that you want to be notified of any possible connection to the Brigade. I'm sure they will be happy to accommodate you." A second finger joined the first. "Two, I need at least one background piece on the trial by deadline." A third finger was raised. "Three, the Brigade is not the only story happening in France. I warned you once that our job is to report the news, not make it, and I'm warning you again. I won't warn you a third time." His look encompassed both of the people standing before his desk. "I trust I make myself clear?"

"Perfectly," Cassandra ground out, angry at being treated like a mischievous schoolgirl. She pivoted on her heel and stalked back to her desk without another word.

Kurt couldn't conceal his amusement. "My congratulations. Henri usually had a devil of a time getting her to drop whatever bone she had between her teeth."

Seth grunted. "Henri has the patience of a saint; I don't." He plucked a pen from its holder and turned his attention back to the story he had been editing before the interruption.

Cassandra couldn't help glaring at Kurt over her cigarette as, grinning, he sauntered back to his desk to retrieve his coffee. "Don't look so damn smug," she hissed at him. "Just wait until you want to follow up a story and he tells *you* no."

"Still, he is right."

"What does being right have to do with any of this?" she grumbled.

"I'll buy lunch today," Kurt cajoled. "You can pick the restaurant, too."

The hard set of her jaw eased fractionally. "I'm immune to bribery."

"No you're not," he cheerfully contradicted her.

The smile that had been lurking at the corners of her mouth burst through. "All right, I'm not." The sharp bell of her phone interrupted their conversation.

"We have to leave in fifteen minutes," Kurt reminded her as she reached for the receiver.

Nodding, she crushed out her cigarette and answered her phone.

The caller was Renaud Malat, wanting an interview for an article on terrorism he was writing for *Le Matin*. Instead of an interview, Cassandra offered him a brief statement, in which she said that she had had no contact with the Freedom Brigade prior to, or after, the bombing. Her presence in the park when the bomb was detonated was purely coincidental. When Renaud pressed for more details, Cassandra politely told him she had nothing more to say and hung up. The hounding by the press had begun.

Before her phone could ring again, Cassandra quickly scribbled out her statement and made copies for Margot and Jules. "If anyone wants a comment," she told Margot, "this is all I have to say on the matter."

"They will not be happy," Margot observed.

Cassandra shrugged. "I'm sorry to dump this in your lap."

"We will survive." Margot grinned conspiratorially.

"I'm sure you will." Cassandra's phone rang again and, sighing, she picked up the receiver. "Cassandra Blake."

"I told you it was complicated between us." Seth's voice came warm and rich through the line.

She glanced at his office. He was bent over his desk, apparently studying the copy he had been working on earlier, holding the receiver in his free hand. His office door was closed and he did nothing to even vaguely indicate that he had called her. Trapping the phone between her shoulder and cheek, she stuffed the background files on the trial into her bag. "You were right."

"I would have made the same decision even if I hadn't spent last night in your bed."

The color in her cheeks suddenly rivaled that of her blouse. She glanced at the red light that Mitch's people had installed on all the phones they had checked, in the office as well as in the employees' homes. The light remained off, a reassuring sign that no one was eavesdropping on their conversation.

"Cassandra," he said when she remained speechless. "Did you assume you would be able to manipulate me because we were sleeping together?"

"N-no," she choked out, appalled by his speculation.

"I didn't think so." Despite his confident words, there was no mistaking the note of relief in his voice. "Can we argue about this over dinner?"

"If you like." Kurt was frowning at her and pointing at his watch.

"Does that mean you're angry?"

"No," she replied carefully, all too aware of Kurt standing only a few feet away. "I have to go."

"Be careful, sweetheart," he cautioned affectionately. "I'll miss you."

Before she could frame a suitable reply, he broke the connection. For Kurt's benefit she spoke into the dead receiver. "Right, Dad, I'll talk to you later." She replaced the receiver and reached for her shoulder bag. "Ready?"

"I was waiting for you," Kurt reminded her archly. "Did you bring your car? Why would I even ask such a thing?" he asked of the room at large. "If she drives the trial will be over before we get there.'' He shrugged into a navy blazer. ''We'll take my car; it's parked in the lot across the street. Is PJ coming with us?''

Cassandra shrugged and hurried to the darkroom. ''PJ,'' she called through the closed door. ''Kurt and I are leaving now. Do you want a ride?''

''Me ride with that manic German?'' the photographer shouted back. ''Have you lost your mind?'' The remainder of his reply was incredibly rude and perfectly clear. He would rather crawl there on his hands and knees than trust his life to Kurt's driving skills.

''If he misses something because he is late, I will never forgive him,'' Kurt told Cassandra, but not loud enough to be heard by the man behind the darkroom door.

They swept through the office together, Cassandra hurrying to keep up with Kurt's longer stride as she checked the power of the batteries in the small tape recorder she had grabbed at the last minute. She preferred taking notes, but the recorder would make sure she didn't miss anything.

Caught up in the excitement of covering a new story, they talked nonstop on the way to court. The weekend and all of Mitch's lectures and warnings seemed far away now, nothing more than an aberration.

The Palace of Justice stood in the midst of a sea of humanity. People had waited for hours—some overnight—outside the main entrance in order to be assured of a place in the courtroom's gallery. All of the building's entrances were guarded; plainclothes police circulated through the crowd, listening and looking for the one fanatic that could turn the chaotic scene into tragedy.

The press was accorded its own entrance at the side of the building, and the security precautions there were more stringent than those at the main entrance. The four well-armed policemen posted at the door regarded the reporters with blatant suspicion. A fifth man, apparently in charge of this area, ran through the rules that the press would follow.

The journalists must display their press passes at all times, they were told; also, when they reached the courtroom, they must remain in the area that had been roped off for them. No television cameras would be allowed in the courtroom; the television media would have to rely on artists' depictions of witnesses. The final official warning was that the press was to keep its distance from the witnesses until after they had testified. With that, the doors behind him were thrown open and, one by one, the journalists and their possessions were inspected before being waved on.

Metal detectors were used; purses were upended, cameras opened and inspected, camera cases were searched, resulting in several yards of ruined film. The more experienced press photographers waited until they had passed the checkpoint to load their cameras.

Kurt went through the checkpoint first and waited for Cassandra to catch up. Once she was inside, they hurried to the courtroom, taking note of the added guards prowling the corridors.

Outside the second-floor courtroom, oak benches lined both sides of the hall, empty still, since the doors had not yet been opened to the general public. Selecting the bench facing the courtroom's double doors, Cassandra sat down and pulled the folders from her purse as she told Kurt, "I'm going to wait out here this morning."

"You will not be allowed near the witnesses until they have testified," he reminded her.

"I know, but I want to study the background material before I interview anyone and it will be easier to read the files out here."

Kurt frowned, less than pleased with the idea that Cassandra would be out of his sight. If he disregarded the threat the Brigade posed to himself, he did not underestimate the danger to Cassandra. "It might be better if we stay together."

Giving him a look of pure disdain, she replied, "Kurt, look at the way this place is guarded. Do you really think the Brigade would be foolish enough to try anything here?"

He had to admit that she was probably right. The sound of voices and hurrying feet carried clearly up the stairwell. The doors had just opened to the public, and within moments they would join the string of reporters filing into the courtroom.

"Get in there before you end up in the back row," she prodded. "I'll be right here."

With a last anxious glance in her direction, he nodded and ducked into the courtroom. Cassandra grinned and then turned her attention to the folders on her lap. She should be able to get enough background from the files to conduct a worthwhile interview.

Franchot met Mitch at an outdoor café. To any passerby, they were nothing more than two friends whiling away a beautiful summer morning enjoying the sunlight and the small cups of black coffee.

"Something very odd is happening at the Sûreté," Franchot said as he leaned back in his chair and admired the swaying hips of the woman who had just walked past him.

"Odd how?"

"According to my friend, her director and Inspector Rocheleau have been spending quite a bit of time talking with the CIA."

"Does she have any idea what they discuss?"

"Unfortunately, no. The meetings have been very hush-hush. No notes and no tape recordings."

Mitch thoughtfully sipped his coffee. "Has your friend heard the Blake woman mentioned?"

"Not directly. But there is something else—one of the Inspector's favorite agents, who happens to be in my friend's department, has been gone for nearly a month."

"That doesn't necessarily mean that he's connected to Blake. He could have taken an early vacation."

"My friend thought of that, but then she remembered the necessary paperwork for a vacation had not been put through. Not wanting the man to get into trouble, she decided to fill out the required forms and put them in his file. The only problem was that his file had disappeared."

"Interesting. Is your friend willing to reveal the agent's name if the money is right?"

Franchot raised his hands, palms up. "I can ask."

"Please do." Mitch put money on the table to pay for their coffee and rose. "I'll be in touch."

Franchot didn't watch him leave.

Chapter 8

The first day of the trial was a harbinger of July—the temperature soared and Paris steamed. Inside the Palace of Justice, the corridors on the second floor grew crowded and the high ceilings threw back echoes of assorted conversations in an acoustical nightmare that threatened to permanently impair Cassandra's hearing. Given the overabundance of bodies and the paucity of ventilation, the atmosphere in the corridor rapidly became oppressive. Gallic tempers flared.

To her left, a high-school teacher argued with one of the guards. His class had been promised seating in the gallery, but their bus had been caught in traffic and they were thirty minutes late. The guard shrugged and explained that their seats had been held until just minutes before the proceedings were to begin, and then released to those waiting in the corridor. The guard was sorry, but there was nothing he could do. No seating remained for the general public. The teacher, casting aspersions upon the guard's parentage under his breath, herded his class back down the staircase.

Cassandra shared her bench with a white-haired grandmotherly type who smelled of lavender and an alien who sported a green mohawk, wore leather pants and simply smelled, period.

Examining the research files occupied most of the morning. The accused was a man in his early seventies, a member of the Gestapo during World War II. He was charged with five "crimes against humanity", the abridged version which left Cassandra chilled. The state had wanted to charge him with other crimes as well, but the statute of limitations had run out years earlier. One of the folders contained copies of the evidence the state had previously released, and she paged through photographs, victims' statements and translations of Gestapo records.

Tucking the folders back into her shoulder bag, Cassandra turned to the alien, pointed out her press ID and asked him if he would mind answering a few questions. He blushed bright red—a rather amusing hue, given the color of his hair—and stammered out an affirmative reply.

She found him eager to please, but sadly lacking in any historical basis on which to form an opinion. He knew about the Nazis and the famous French Resistance, but was vague on what role the Gestapo had played. Besides, he answered, when asked his opinion of the trial, the prisoner was an old man. What harm could he do now?

The grandmother turned at that and proceeded to deliver a quick, emotional lecture regarding her encounters with the Gestapo. The young man beat a hasty retreat, leaving Cassandra with the prospect of a remarkable interview. The woman found Cassandra's French understandable, albeit terribly amusing, and was soon immersed in resurrecting the past. A few people overheard the interview, listened attentively and slowly, one by one, other survivors came forward, offering their memories as well. When the court recessed for lunch, PJ and Kurt found Cassandra at the center of a very vocal, but polite, knot of twenty or so individuals. Her tape recorder was running, but voices might be lost in the background noise, so she was frantically scribbling on her pad in an effort to support the verbal record with written notes.

Kurt waved, gesturing at the crowd to indicate that he and Cassandra had to leave if they were to get a table at a nearby restaurant. Cassandra shook her head, mouthed that he should go without her, and returned to her interview subjects.

They had come prepared, these people who had lived through the devastation of war. Cheese appeared as if by magic, and freshly baked bread. Several people had brought coffee, and the alien—who had been fascinated by the stories in spite of himself—volunteered to buy disposable cups. By the time he returned, the courtroom had been locked and the crowd in the corridor had thinned. He passed out the Styrofoam cups to the members of the group that had found seats either on the floor or on vacated benches. Food and drink were shared and conversation continued nonstop during the two hour recess.

When PJ returned early, he found Cassandra still holding court in the corridor. His mustache twitched as he smiled and circled around the band, snapping off pictures in rapid succession.

Cassandra looked up at the sound of a shutter clicking and glared at him. She started to apologize for the overzealous photographer, but her explanations were waved aside. Mirrors were produced, lipstick reapplied, hair patted into place—everyone flattered by the idea of having their picture in the press. Cassandra couldn't help smiling as PJ worked his way through the group without a harsh word passing his lips.

"What's going on in the courtroom?" she asked when the photographer seated himself on the floor at her feet and unloaded the film he had just shot.

"The state showed blowups of deportations and Gestapo roundups this morning," PJ replied. "Then called the survivors of the defendant's alleged crimes to authenticate the scenes. It's going to get rough." He snapped his camera together and looked up at Cassandra. "I suggest that after Kurt has filed his story tonight, you take him out and get him drunk. He's going to need the release."

"That bad?"

PJ nodded. "And judging by the state's opening statements, it's going to get worse." He patted her hand before getting to his feet. "I'm going back to the office. Need a ride?"

"No, I'll come back with Kurt."

"See you later, then." PJ trotted toward the staircase.

Smiling brightly, Cassandra set about ending the mass interview. By the time Kurt returned from lunch, she was ready to accompany him into the courtroom. They sat together in the press section, taking notes on the testimony. When the court adjourned for the day, they fought their way to Kurt's car and rushed back to the office to file their stories.

Seth met them at the door when they returned, as did Robert Townsend. Cassandra glanced from one man to the other; Robert was wearing his traveling clothes and a serious expression and his sole carryon sat by the door. Seth looked grim. Cassandra introduced her father to Kurt, trying to ignore the sinking feeling in her stomach. Kurt shook Robert's hand and then excused himself, making a beeline for his desk. For several moments, no one spoke.

"I know you'd like a little privacy, Robert. Use my office," Seth offered, breaking the silence. Avoiding Cassandra's questioning gaze, he followed Kurt.

Cassandra led the way into Seth's office. "Well, Dad, what brings you here?" she asked when Robert closed the door.

"I came to say goodbye. Your mother called this afternoon to tell me Joanie just gave birth to a baby boy." The smile he wore faltered under his daughter's steady regard. Giving a sigh of resignation, he said, "I also wanted to see if there was any chance that you would fly home with me tonight."

It took a few seconds for Cassandra to realize what her father was asking. Once she did, she dropped her bag on Seth's desk and began to calmly pull the pins out of her hair. "I'm afraid not, Dad."

"I didn't think so, but your mother insisted that I ask." He studied his older daughter intently. "I wish you would reconsider. I don't like the idea of leaving you here, at the mercy of a group of maniacs. I've talked with Seth about this; he's more than willing to authorize a vacation for you until this whole thing blows over."

Cassandra combed her fingers through her hair, struggling to hold on to her temper so that she would not say something rash. "That's very big of him, but I don't need a vacation. What I *do* need is to file my story before deadline."

"Your mother would feel better—hell, so would I—if you would come back to the States for a few weeks."

"Would you run?" she asked baldy.

"It's not running, Casey—"

"Of course it is," she argued, trampling his protest. "I'm not exactly thrilled that the Brigade knows my face and my name, but I refuse to let them run my life. I won't leave Paris."

Robert studied the toes of his tennis shoes. "I can't drag you onto the plane, although I think I should, and Seth has pointed out that if I stay in Paris I may complicate your situation."

She bit her lip. "There's some truth in that."

He lifted his eyes to hers and Cassandra saw the concern in their depths. "Level with your old man, honey. Are you in danger?"

"I don't think so," she answered, shading the truth just enough to comfort her father. "Seth retained a security consultant to protect the staff; the security man thinks—God knows why—that the Brigade will make its big move in the next seven-to-ten days. All of us will be fine if we just do what this man tells us to."

Robert did not look entirely convinced, but some of the fear had left his eyes. "Is this security consultant on duty twenty-four hours a day?"

"Believe me, Dad, nothing will happen to me . . . or anyone else for that matter. The staff is protected both here and at home." It was a blatant lie, but it was for his own good.

"If things get dicey—"

"I'll fly back home," she promised. Smiling, she hooked her arm in his and walked with him out of Seth's office to the door. "What time is your flight?"

"Eight o'clock."

"Want me to drive you to the airport?"

Robert shook his head. "You're on deadline. Don't worry about your old man, I'll grab a cab.

"I'll walk you down."

Seth walked up to them as Robert bent to retrieve his suitcase. "Leaving, Robert?"

Robert nodded and offered the younger man his hand. "Casey's going to walk me downstairs and put me into a cab. Thanks for everything, Seth."

"My pleasure." Seth raised an eyebrow at Cassandra. "Are you sure you don't want to go with your father?"

"I'm sure," she told him in a tone that dared him to start an argument.

"In that case, you're on deadline," Seth replied easily. "Goodbye, Robert."

Cabs were plentiful at this hour and they flagged one immediately. Throwing his carryon in the back seat, Robert turned and pulled his daughter into his arms. "Take care of yourself, Casey."

"I will," she assured him, smiling. "And be sure to tell Mom and Joanie I'm fine and happy about being an aunt again."

"Will do," he promised, then added, "I like Seth."

"So do I," Cassandra answered blandly. "He's a good editor."

"Uh-huh." Robert gave her a knowing look that raised the color in her cheeks. "Grab him, Casey; he's a far cry from what you dragged home last time."

"Dad—"

Robert was already closing the back door. "I'm proud of you, honey." He gave her a final wave as the cab lurched into rush-hour traffic. Cassandra watched until the cab was out of sight before she walked back inside and took the elevator to the fifth-floor office.

Seth was lounging in the hallway outside the office door, one shoulder braced against the wall, as she turned the corner from the elevator. "That was quick."

"My father isn't given to long goodbyes." She crossed her arms over her chest and looked at him with barely concealed menace. "I understand the two of you had quite a talk today."

"I just told him the truth."

"And added to his worries." She shook her head in disgust.

"He was more worried *before* we talked," Seth replied. "And he was entitled to the truth."

"I told him the Dateline staff was under twenty-four-hour protection," she said quietly. "If I hadn't, he might have changed his mind and stayed in Paris indefinitely."

Glancing over his shoulder to make certain the office door was closed, Seth then leaned forward and brushed a quick, hard kiss over Cassandra's mouth. "Part of me wishes you had gone with him," he admitted. "But part of me is very glad you stayed."

Cassandra smiled tremulously and reached toward him. He caught her hand and carried it to his lips. "I missed you today," she confessed in a whisper as his mouth rubbed against her knuckles.

His eyes burned into hers as he drew her toward him. "We'll make up for it tonight."

Her heart pounded at the sensual promise in his gaze. A slow heat rose from deep inside her, making her legs tremble. Her thoughts ran wild, picturing them together in bed.

His face hardened with desire. "I want you, love. You *will* invite me home tonight, won't you?"

"Yes." How could she not? She swayed toward him, bracing herself against his chest.

His lips hovered a mere breath away from hers, and in that moment came the sound of the elevator opening on their floor. "Damn!" Seth straightened and let go of her hand.

Reality returned with a jolt. Cassandra took a step backward and tried to still the tremor running through her. A security guard on his rounds walked by them, acknowledging their presence with a polite nod. They watched him until he turned the corner of the hallway.

"I have a story to write," Cassandra said unsteadily.

Seth nodded, controlling with an effort the flood of desire that had swept through him. He opened the office door and held it for her. "Show me what you got today."

Cassandra, Kurt and Seth were still working when Armand came on duty at six. The stringer exchanged pleasantries with them before retiring to the teleprinter room to transmit the day's stories to the New York office. When the machines were busy, he worked on the weather reports for the following day.

By ten o'clock, Kurt and Cassandra had finished their stories, printed them out, and turned them over to Seth. Now Seth, using Cassandra's desk, read their copy. Kurt sat tensely in his chair while Cassandra perched on his desk, smoking nervously; both watched Seth's every nuance, trying to interpret his reactions. The story was a sensitive one; their accounts had to be accurate and balanced.

At last Seth rose and stepped across the aisle to Kurt's desk. "Okay, folks. Give those to Armand for transmission to New York tonight and you can go home."

Kurt closed his eyes and raised his fists in a triumphant salute. Cassandra scrubbed her hands over her face and gave a heartfelt sigh of relief.

"Good work, both of you," Seth complimented them as he scrawled his signature across their stories. "Cassandra, that was a nice angle, juxtaposing the punk rocker with the survivor of Auschwitz in a general-information piece. Tomorrow I want an article on the three judges hearing this case." He looked at Kurt as the German got to his feet and stretched. "If today is any indication, this trial is going to be gruesome. Old hates are going to surface and you're going to be caught right in the middle. I'm giving you the option of sticking with the trial story or doing the background assignments."

"I prefer the trial, but thank you," Kurt answered with a grateful smile. "Besides, Cassandra has stolen enough of my stories." He picked up both their stories and took them back to Armand.

"How is he handling the trial?" Seth asked when Kurt was out of earshot.

"He seems fine to me, but PJ said he was having some problems this morning when the prosecution produced the blowups of the deportations and roundups. In fact, PJ suggested that I take Kurt out tonight and get him drunk."

Seth immediately rejected the photographer's recommendation. "He's going to have to show up in court tomorrow morning in a functioning state. Let's take him to dinner and listen to whatever he has to say."

Cassandra looked up at him with undisguised warmth. "You really are a nice man. A lot of bureau chiefs wouldn't worry about their reporter's reaction to a story."

Shrugging off the praise, Seth replied in a low voice, "Just bear in mind that I have plans for the two of us. We feed him, listen to him, and dump him." Then he grinned at her, assuring her that he had been teasing, and she laughed as she set about straightening up the mess on her desk.

The three of them ate a late dinner at the small café across the street from the Dateline office, one of the gathering places for the press. The food was unremarkable, but it satisfied their hunger, and the bottle of wine Kurt ordered put them in a mellow mood. Seth drank one glass of wine, then turned to coffee. By midnight, Cassandra was delicately yawning behind her hand while Kurt was deep in conversation with a reporter from one of the Paris papers.

Catching her third yawn within five minutes, Seth tapped Kurt on the shoulder. "Cassandra's tired; I'm going to take her home. Do you need a ride?"

Kurt shook his head and exchanged a man-to-man smile with his chief. "I have my car. Besides, Michelle and I are going to discover the merits of the house wine."

Seth's gaze skimmed assessingly over the raven-haired woman. "I take it you two have met before?"

Michelle beamed up at him, although her eyes were slightly out of focus. "We met at dear Henri's party."

"Dear Henri, eh?" Seth echoed wryly. "Take my advice, Kurt; call a cab when you're ready to leave."

Cassandra's gait was slightly unsteady as they left the café, so he wrapped an arm around her shoulders for the walk to his car. "I think you enjoyed the wine a little too much, love."

Smiling, she nestled closer to his side. "I'm slightly tipsy, but that's all. It feels like forever since I've been this relaxed."

"I can see it coming. You'll fall asleep in the car and I'm going to end up carrying you into your apartment."

She laid her head against his shoulder. "Do you know, until last night, my only experience with a man carrying a woman off to bed came from what I read in romance novels?" The shocked look on his face made her laugh. "It's true. You're the only man who's ever carried me off to bed."

"Cassandra, keep your voice down." Her comment had drawn raised eyebrows from the two men they had just passed.

"I liked it," she continued, ignoring his warning. She pressed a warm kiss onto his neck, then teasingly flicked the area with her tongue. "I like you, too."

Seth groaned and tightened his hold on her. His body seemed to have forgotten he was forty years old; it was reacting like that of a passionate teenager. "Could you please try to bear in mind that we're on a public street? You're going to get us arrested."

"In Paris," she demanded incredulously. "Never! Paris loves lovers!" This was said in such ringing tones that several pedestrians came to an abrupt halt and stared at her.

"Oh, God," Seth lamented. Thankfully, that proved to be her last pronouncement during their walk. She did, however, make several whispered suggestions that steadily eroded his self-control and her hands seemed to have taken on a will of their own as well. By the time they reached the parking garage, he was aghast at the thought of what she might do or say in front of the attendant. Happily, Cassandra was content to rest her head on his shoulder. The Mercedes was brought down and he stuffed her into the passenger seat and snapped the seat belt before she could do or say anything outrageous.

Smiling, Cassandra watched as Seth capably negotiated the Paris streets, his stark profile illuminated by the dashboard. "Did I embarrass you back there?"

He flicked a glance in her direction, and the hard line of his mouth softened. "No, but you came damn close."

"I'm not drunk, Seth."

"You're close to it, love."

"Because I said I want to make love with you? It's the truth."

His fingers tightened on the steering wheel. "Sweetheart, you pick the damnedest times to say that."

"I know." Her hand crept across the seat toward his leg. "Do you run?" she asked speculatively, her fingertips flexing against the rock-hard muscles of his thigh.

"No," he said through clenched teeth.

"Lift weights?"

"Yes—Cassandra!" Her hand had come to rest on his inner thigh.

Feeling delightfully wicked, Cassandra merely smiled. She harbored no illusions about her appearance. She was attractive enough, she supposed, but a far cry from drop-dead gorgeous. Seth, however, made her feel beautiful...and incredibly sexy. "Are you staying the night again?"

"If you're agreeable." He had to force the words through his constricted throat.

"Oh, I'm completely agreeable," she assured him. "I like waking up in your arms." She started to work on her seat belt.

"Sweetheart, I can either make love to you or drive. I can't do both." There was a hunted quality to his voice.

She blinked at him, but gave up her efforts with the seat belt. "Will you carry me off to bed again?"

"If I can make it that far," Seth muttered. "Now behave yourself."

"Yes, Seth." But her hand remained on his thigh for the duration of the ride.

Cassandra wasn't overly concerned with the precautions Mitch had drilled into them, but Seth was. He drove around the block, searching for and finding a parking space directly beneath a streetlight. He took her keys, and examined both the outside door and her apartment door before using the key on either. While Cassandra turned on a lamp in the living room and kicked off her shoes, Seth prowled her small apartment, making sure no one was waiting for her.

"Everything's fine," he told her when he returned to the living room. He closed the drapes that he'd opened that morning. A glance at the telephone showed him that the red light had not been activated, and he allowed himself to relax.

Cassandra threw the dead bolt and turned, a sultry smile on her lips. Slowly, she unzipped her skirt and let it fall in a white pool at her feet. Seth's eyes narrowed, his gaze following her hand as it moved upward to free the buttons of her blouse. The pink sides parted, and the blouse and half-slip went the way of the skirt, revealing the flesh-toned teddy she wore.

Seth found it hard to breathe as he watched her approach. The teddy was a frothy confection of lace; the shape and color of her breasts were clearly visible through it. Barefoot, she was several inches shorter than he, and Seth was unexpectedly filled with a sense of protectiveness toward her. She had led him out of hell into heaven, breathed life into a heart that had hung in suspended animation for years. He made his living stringing words together, and yet he could not find a word that embodied what he felt for her.

"Seth?" Cassandra saw the flash of pain come and go in his black eyes.

She was directly in front of him, her delicate, long-fingered hands resting against his chest. "I want you so much, sweetheart," he said thickly.

"I'm right here." She brought her mouth up to his and kissed him hungrily. Her tongue sought his, challenged, cajoled, until she felt him tremble. Her hands learned his body as she stripped away his clothes. Delighted that he was content to let her have the upper hand, she sank to the floor and tugged him down beside her.

Seth gasped as her mouth made forays across his torso. His hands sifted through her hair and clenched, coaxing her to areas she might have missed. The fall of her hair caressed him, tangled erotically with the hair on his chest. Her mouth grazed his hip, sparkled against his thigh. And then she found the quintessence of his desire and he burst into flames.

Clasping her in his arms, he dragged her up his body. He sought her mouth, found it, and plunged into its warm depth even as his hands caught her hips and positioned her over his manhood. He opened his eyes and was instantly trapped by her aquamarine gaze. "Cassandra..." He lost the ability to speak as she sank onto him.

Cassandra smiled at his rapt expression. Their union touched her soul in the same way. His hands tightened on her hips, pleading for release. She rested her hands against his chest and arched her back. The movement tore a low, masculine cry from Seth and she gloried in her power. She moved again, slowly at first, then with increasing urgency as the fire spread through her veins. Through the haze of her own rising passion, she watched Seth's reactions. His head was thrown back, the muscles in his neck standing out as he drove into her. She felt the first spasms of his climax, saw the almost unbearable pleasure contort his features as he called her name and then she was with him, glorying in the consummation.

She crumpled against his chest, too weak to do anything but listen as the wild pounding of his heart subsided to its normal steady beat.

"Lady, the things you do to me," he said hoarsely. Every muscle in his body was trembling. He was weak as a kitten—and ready to take on the world.

She found the strength to rub her cheek against his chest. "I didn't know it could be like this."

"Neither did I," he whispered.

Tears stung her eyes; she ached to tell him of her love, but it was too soon to say the words. Love had once hurt him so badly that she was certain he would run from it now. She had to give him time to adjust to her presence in his life, without the pressure of all that love entailed, and in time—dear God, please—he would be able to love her as well.

"Cassandra, you're crying." The salty tears had slid unnoticed from her eyes to fall in scalding droplets on his chest. "Did I hurt you?"

"Oh, no, Seth! It's just that this was so beautiful...."

"I know, love." He stroked her back comfortingly. "I know."

Chapter 9

Nothing in Cassandra's life had prepared her for the impact that loving Seth would have upon her world as the week passed. When she woke in his arms for the second morning in a row, she knew that she was right where she belonged, and she would fight tooth and nail to keep her place. Her alter ego watched in sardonic amusement as she made room for Seth in her apartment and her life.

Common sense dictated that Seth should move in with her, she told her other self. They were *involved* for heaven's sake; since he had spent three consecutive nights in her bed, neither one of them was naive enough to think that he would sleep in his own apartment, so why not eliminate the struggle of finding a suitable apartment in Paris?

Common sense? Annoyed, her other self embarked upon a campaign of guerrilla warfare as she rode with Seth to the office Wednesday morning. She was starting to use Seth to define her life—the same trap she had fallen into with Ned.

No, there was no comparison, Cassandra argued. Seth supported her career; he didn't expect her to be less than she was. It wasn't as if she were back in suburbia, fighting the war on crabgrass.

Oh, really. Her alter ego gave Cassandra a sharp nudge when she purchased several potted geraniums to brighten their apartment. Remember the Boston ferns? Next you'll be talking about getting a puppy. And what's this about "our" apartment?

"Puppy" sprang out at Cassandra from her computer monitor, jerking her back to reality. She blinked, staring in amazement at the discovery that the argument she had been carrying on with herself had been entered into the computer. Enough was enough, she decided as she pressed a key and erased the conversation from memory. She loved Seth and that was that. So she had a few misgivings. Given the speed with which their relationship had developed, that was only to be expected. It was a week today that the bomb had exploded in the deserted park.

But what about—

"Oh, shut up," Cassandra snapped irritably. "Who asked you anyway?"

Kurt looked up from his terminal. "Did you say something?"

"No—I mean, I was just thinking out loud."

He shrugged and went back to his story. Cassandra rose and walked to the coffeepot to fill her mug, trying to bring some kind of order to her unruly thoughts. She was supposed to be working on the interview that the director of the Summer Festival of Concerts had granted her this morning, but at the moment, she couldn't care less how many world-class orchestras were scheduled to appear. She stared in annoyance at the coffee running into her mug and reached for the cream—Kurt had made the last pot.

Procrastinating, she made a tour of the office, seeing what the other reporters were doing. It was a quiet news day. Even Kurt was in the office for a change; the defendant had fallen ill and the presiding judge had ordered a postponement until the defendant recovered.

Cassandra knocked on the darkroom door and asked PJ if he wanted a fresh cup of coffee. He told her to mind her own business; he was processing a roll of film. Sighing, she strolled over to the open windows and gazed at the street below as her thoughts wandered once more.

In spite of her misgivings and Seth's warning, their relationship was proving less complicated than she had feared. No one knew that they were living together—except Armand, and he knew only because Seth had to be accessible around the clock. It didn't take a genius to realize that the phone number he now left with the stringer was identical to Cassandra's home phone. Armand, however, was the soul of discretion. He hadn't so much as raised an eyebrow. Kurt no doubt had his own suspicions, but they remained unspoken.

Much to Cassandra's surprise, she and Seth were able to separate their private and professional lives without difficulty. At the office, Seth treated her the same way he treated the other reporters. There was no favoritism displayed; Seth was painstakingly fair about that. Every article had to meet his criteria. There were no exceptions.

She shifted her gaze from the street to Seth's office, and was struck anew by her love for him. A tiny smile touched her mouth as she watched him work. It was late afternoon; in another three hours they would be home, putting dinner together in the tiny kitchen. Seth loved to cook and, since he didn't expect her to wait on him, she was rediscovering her own enjoyment of it.

As if her gaze produced a physical sensation in him, Seth looked up and met her eyes. His features softened and he smiled slightly. His phone rang, distracting him, and she sighed again, wondering how long she could keep her love a secret. The expression that settled over his face as he talked on the phone was the one he had worn when they first met; it was a cold, emotionless mask and it sent a prickle of alarm up her spine. She straightened, her hands wrapped around her mug, and saw him turn his back to her as he spoke.

The conversation was brief. He replaced the receiver and stared at it for several moments before turning back to her. He lifted his hand, gesturing for her to come into his office. She did so reluctantly, aware of the fear that gripped her heart. When she entered his office, he closed the door.

"I have to leave for an hour or so," he said flatly. "I want you to cover for me here. Make sure the stories that need to be transmitted do so by deadline."

It bothered her that he didn't meet her eyes as he talked but devoted his attention to rolling down his sleeves and straightening his tie. "All right, Seth; I'll handle it."

"If anything unexpected crops up, use your own judgment. I don't have a number to give you."

Cassandra swallowed. "I understand."

The taut note in her voice got his attention. He met her gaze and tried to smile. "I'm meeting our friend with the château."

A violent tremor assailed her hand, sloshing hot coffee over her fingers. She didn't notice. "Why?"

"He has something to tell me and he doesn't want to do it over the phone." A muscle worked in his jaw. "God, Cassandra, don't look at me like that. I can't stand it."

"I'm sorry," she choked out. "I don't like having him drop back into our lives like this. You know as well as I do that he doesn't deliver good news."

"Don't jump to conclusions—"

"I don't have to," she exclaimed quietly. "I know who he is and what he does, remember?" She bit her lip to keep it from trembling. "Take me with you."

"No." The refusal was reinforced by his steely tone. "He said me, just me."

"Where—"

Seth curtly shook his head. "Don't ask."

Cassandra closed her eyes. Mitch's world was invading hers again. Security was paramount; you never knew who was listening, or how.

"I'll be back as soon as possible."

Drawing a calm breath, she opened her eyes and nodded. "Be careful."

One corner of his mouth kicked upward. "I'm not in any danger. You wait here for me," he ordered.

"I will." She wanted to throw herself into his arms, draw what comfort she could from his embrace. But that wasn't possible. "I'm scared, Seth."

"Don't be; everything's going to be fine." He shrugged into his suit jacket, opened his office door and paused to smile at her. "I wish I could kiss you."

Swallowing the lump in her throat, she said with forced lightness, "Hold that thought."

He nodded and left before one of them succumbed to temptation.

Pasting a carefree expression on her face, Cassandra slowly returned to her desk. "Well, guys, I'm in charge. Anybody have their copy ready for me?" She was answered with groans, for which she was grateful. She wasn't sure she could summon the concentration necessary for editing.

Time passed with agonizing slowness. Kurt handed her his piece about the final stage of the Tour de France cycle race and she read it with one eye on the clock. Having no idea what she had just read, Cassandra signed it off and told Kurt to send it. Margot and Jules were chatting back and forth at their desks, and it was an act of will for her to keep from snapping at them.

An hour and a half had elapsed before Seth came through the door. Cassandra went light-headed with relief.

"Anything exciting happen while I was gone?" he called to the room at large as he dropped his suit jacket on the coatrack.

"Cassandra wanted to move into your office, but I managed to keep her out here," Kurt answered.

Everyone laughed, and Cassandra joined in. Only she noticed that her laughter was tinged with hysteria. Seth grinned and went into his office and Cassandra pretended to work on her article for the rest of the afternoon. The shift changed at six and there was the usual easy banter between the departing day people and the arriving Armand.

"Anyone for a drink?" Jules asked as they walked to the elevator. "It's on me. My wife sold one of her paintings yesterday."

They all offered congratulations, including PJ, and no one thought it curious that Seth and Cassandra begged off. The group split up when they reached the sidewalk and when the others were out of sight, Seth slipped an arm around her waist.

"What happened?" she demanded, once again aware of the incipient hysteria in her voice. "What did Mitch have to say?"

"Do you want a drink?"

"No. I want several drinks," she informed him. "Several *large* drinks. In fact, if you have any tranquilizers on you, I'll take the bottle. My nerves are shot."

He tightened his arm around her and pressed a kiss against her temple. "Come on, I know just the place."

They reclaimed the Mercedes from the garage and he wheeled the car competently through the rush hour traffic to the Rue Vivienne.

"What did Mitch want?" she asked insistently as they sped through Paris.

"I'll tell you later," he promised. "Just relax."

She mumbled dire threats under her breath regarding supercilious males, and tore the cellophane off her second pack of cigarettes of the day.

Parking was at a premium, but as usual, Seth found an impossibly small spot that magically enlarged when he backed the Mercedes into it. He helped her out of the car and led her into a brasserie called Vaudeville.

The brasserie was known for its "twenties" atmosphere, made up of mirrors and marble. The crowd was just starting to gather and they took one of the last tables on the sidewalk terrace facing the Bourse, Paris's stock exchange. Seth ordered a carafe of house Riesling that, thankfully, was delivered immediately. He filled their glasses and touched his glass to hers. "Cheers."

"Remember the Alamo." Cassandra emptied half her glass with one swallow while her toast caused him to choke on the mouthful he had taken.

"So it's going to be one of those nights," he speculated when his cough subsided. A smile tugged at the corner of his mouth.

"Will you kindly tell me what Mitch wanted?" she hissed, fumbling through her bag for her cigarettes.

"You should carry a smaller purse," he advised as she searched for the lighter.

"A small purse is of no use," she retorted. Her fingers closed around the lighter and she held it up triumphantly. The flint obligingly produced a flame, but her hands were shaking so badly that she couldn't touch the flame to the end of the cigarette.

"Give me that before you set your blouse on fire." He held the lighter for her, then lit a cigarette for himself. "Calm down, love; I promise you the world isn't going to end tonight."

"What did he *want*?" Cassandra reiterated, clearly exasperated.

"Just to let me know that the Sûreté has taken the taps off your phone—both home and office."

"That's it? That's all he had to say?" Her aquamarine eyes widened in rage. "I'll kill him!"

Seth smiled and took a sip of his wine. "Remember the flash that came through on Monday?"

"How could I forget," she asked with a saccharine smile. "I wanted to fly to Madrid, but my bureau chief disagreed."

"We are not going to gnaw at that old bone. Now listen. Mitch has heard that one of the men killed at the border was the leader of the Freedom Brigade."

Cassandra's hand paused in the act of raising the glass to her mouth. "How reliable is his source?"

"So-so." He exhaled a cloud of smoke. "Mitch is going to do some more checking and get back to me, but given what he knows now, he thinks we may be home free."

She closed her eyes briefly and uttered a heartfelt, "Hallelujah."

"My sentiments, exactly." He leaned forward and took her hand in his. The cold wine had chilled her fingers and he pressed her cool flesh to his mouth. "Now will you relax?"

She smiled and squeezed his hand in answer. Without the complication of the terrorists, and the painful memories they brought back, surely Seth would find it easier to come to terms with what he felt for her. She was finding it increasingly difficult to keep from blurting out her love for him.

That night their lovemaking was leisurely, unhurried. They had all the time in the world to explore the bonds that were drawing them ever closer.

"Goddamn it, that's not good enough!" Mitch whirled on Greg. "Can't you Company men ever come up with a definite answer on anything? Was the dead man a member of the Freedom Brigade, or wasn't he?"

It was three in the morning, and the apartment they occupied was in one of the less fashionable districts of Paris.

Greg ran his hands through his hair and repeated the answer that had provoked the uncharacteristic outburst. "We don't *know*. And neither does the Sûreté. Or if they do, they're not saying."

Mitch shook his head and lit another unfiltered cigarette. "Why did they pull the phone tap?"

"According to my opposite number, the deadline on their permit expired and since the Blake woman hadn't been contacted again, the judge refused to extend it."

"Hell, Greg, you don't really believe that, do you? The Sûreté wouldn't let a little thing like legal niceties pressure them."

"I can only tell you what I've been told."

Swearing, Mitch paced the room. "There's something wrong, something I'm missing. Something you're missing."

Greg raised his hands. "The Brigade has gone to ground. Whatever trail the Sûreté may have had is stone-cold dead."

"What about the agent that I told you about, the one who disappeared a month ago without filing his vacation paperwork?"

"Nothing. No one I talk to even knows his name."

"Right," Mitch sneered. "They're stonewalling you, kid."

"What would you like me to do, teach?" Greg retorted sarcastically. "Break into their offices and search their files?" He drew a hand over his face. "I get the feeling they're holding out on me, but I can't force the issue, particularly now when the Blake woman appears to be out of danger."

Mitch stared out the grimy window. "I wonder..." He turned back to Greg. "Did you find out anything about that Dateline photographer?"

"The guy who disarmed one of your key people?" Greg couldn't resist the opportunity to tweak his mentor's nose. "Yeah, I did. He's not your run-of-the-mill camera jockey. In fact, he came late to the profession. From the age of twenty-one to thirty-one he was a resident of the Duke of York's barracks in Chelsea." He grinned at the stunned look on Mitch's face. "That's right, teach. The photographer was a highly trained member of the British Special Air Service—the unit Her Majesty depends upon to deal with any terrorist threat."

Friday dawned with oppressive humidity and the promise of rain in the air. In defiance of the weather, Cassandra chose the bright tangerine linen suit she had purchased several weeks earlier and had yet to wear. Beneath the jacket she wore a white silk shell and instead of her usual bun, she pulled her hair back into an alligator clip so that it fell in a wild cascade down her back. Pearl studs graced her earlobes and her feet were encased in low-heeled white pumps. Glancing at her reflection in the full-length mirror that hung on the back of the bedroom door, she smiled; the tangerine accented her coloring and gave her a coolly elegant look. By quitting time she should appear just as fresh as she did now, or so she hoped. Apparently Seth was also reacting to the diminished tension, for he had abandoned his usual black suit; today he wore a pair of pleated khaki trousers and a short-sleeved shirt done in muted, contrasting stripes.

Cassandra gave him a long, admiring stare when he emerged from the bedroom. "No tie?"

"Not today. I don't have a lunch scheduled, or any meetings outside the office, so I decided to go casual. What do you think?"

"I like it." She wrapped her arms around his waist and dropped a kiss in the hollow at the base of his throat. "But then, I like you even when you're not wearing anything."

"So I've noticed." Placing a fingertip beneath her chin, he raised her face to his for a long, drugging kiss. When he released her mouth, they were both trembling.

"Let's play hooky," he suggested in a sexy purr. "We'll hop in the car and drive into the country, find a little inn and spend the day in bed."

She nuzzled the springy thatch of hair that peeped through his open collar. "The office will worry."

"We'll call in sick."

"Umm." Her head lolled to the right as he pressed a string of kisses down the side of her neck. "That might look suspicious."

"I don't care. They're eventually going to find out that we're living together."

"Will that bother you?" she asked almost idly.

He framed her face in his hands and gazed into her eyes. "No. In fact, it will be a relief once they know. This is going to sound medieval, but I'll say it, anyway. I like the idea of everyone knowing you're mine, off limits to any predatory male with dishonorable intentions." He raised an eyebrow. "Will it bother you?"

She studied his shirt, afraid that her love would shine like a beacon and drive him back into his shell. "No."

Seth frowned and gently forced her to meet his eyes. "Are you sure?"

"Of course," she managed to say with the proper degree of confidence. "After all, Paris is full of sexy women; I'd better stake my claim before some pretty mademoiselle turns your head."

"As if she could." He drew her back into his arms and passionately assaulted her mouth. When Cassandra was leaning weakly against him, her cheek resting against his shoulder, he said, "So do we play hooky today?"

She pulled away with a rueful sigh. "I can't. I have to finish that piece on the Summer Festival."

"How much do you have left to write?"

"Only the entire article," she admitted. "My concentration wasn't the best yesterday."

"If you can finish by noon, we can still take the afternoon off. I'll just tell Kurt to send his coverage of the trial to New York before deadline. He's good enough that my signature is just a rubber stamp."

"I'll do my best," she promised.

By the time Seth pulled into the parking garage across from the Dateline office, several large drops of rain had splattered against the windshield. Hand in hand, they dashed across the street and just avoided the cloudburst that let loose as they entered the building. They rode the elevator up to the fifth floor, exchanging looks in the crowded car.

Kurt and Margot were in the office, and one of them had started the percolator; the smell of fresh-brewed coffee filled the room. Seth went directly to his office while Cassandra headed for her desk.

"Good morning, Margot, Kurt." She beamed at her colleagues. Margot was resting her head in her hands and wriggled a fingertip in acknowledgment. Kurt's head was resting on his desk, cradled in his arms; he gave no indication that he had heard Cassandra. "Did you have a nice evening?"

Margot winced. "Too nice," she said in a whisper. "We ended up celebrating with Jules and his wife. Everyone was ready to go home when PJ quit swearing and started ordering rounds of vodka. *Mon Dieu,* no wonder the Soviets are always invading some poor country. They are looking for a civilized liquor. My head is threatening to explode."

"Take some aspirin," Cassandra advised. "Where's Jules?"

"He called in sick," Margot replied.

"Great minds think alike," Cassandra murmured, picking up her mug and heading for the coffee. "Want some coffee, Margot?"

"Kurt made it again," the Frenchwoman lamented, summoning the energy to send a withering glance in his general direction. "I took one sip and gave up. *He's* had two cups. I hope he dies."

Cassandra hid a grin as she filled her cup. The coffee looked even worse than Kurt's usual brew. She wrinkled her nose and added twice as much cream as usual. "Is PJ in?" she called to Margot, then instantly regretted her action when the brunette pressed her hands over her ears. "Sorry." She tiptoed to Margot's desk. "Is PJ in?" she reiterated in a stage whisper.

"I have not checked," Margot said with great dignity. "I hope he dies, too."

Chuckling softly, Cassandra veered toward Kurt. *"Guten Tag, Herr Leihmann."* He groaned and she bent to peer at his face. If his pallor was any indication, he had one hell of a hangover. "Kurt, can I get you anything?"

He struggled to raise his head but the effort was too much. "Cas—"

His voice was raspy, as if he weren't getting enough air. Frowning, she brushed back a lock of blond hair that had fallen over his forehead. Her hand came away wet with sweat. A frisson of alarm ran through her; whatever was wrong with her friend wasn't a simple hangover.

Setting her cup aside, she took one of his hands in hers; it was cold and clammy. She felt for his pulse and found it thready. "Seth!" Not even her yell brought a reaction from Kurt. "Seth, I need you!"

"Cassandra, *s'il vous plaît*," Margot gasped.

The panic in Cassandra's voice brought Seth out of his office at a dead run. "What's the matter?"

"It's Kurt. Something's wrong with him." She knelt beside the chair and gently slapped his cheek. "Kurt? Kurt, can you hear me?"

Margot had forgotten her hangover and was hovering behind Seth. "Call for an ambulance. Move!" Seth snapped at her when she froze at the sight of Kurt's ashen face.

"Kurt!" Cassandra pulled him upright, bracing him against the back of his chair. "Damn it, Kurt, *wake up!*"

His eyelids flickered and opened briefly. His mouth worked soundlessly and his fingers locked convulsively in the folds of Cassandra's tangerine skirt. The fear in his eyes tore at her heart.

"What the hell is going on out here?" PJ stormed out of his beloved darkroom, filling the air with curses.

"Shut up," Seth yelled at the photographer. "Your mouth is the last thing we need right now!"

Ignoring the bureau chief, PJ took in the scene at a glance, and sprinted toward the desk. "Help me get him upright," he ordered Seth, grabbing the German under his arms. "He's starting to vomit. If he aspirates he'll be in real trouble."

Cassandra stepped back, letting the men muscle Kurt around. When his stomach was empty, they lifted Kurt from the chair and deposited him on the floor. "Cassie, I've got a couple of blankets in the darkroom. Go get them."

She ran to the darkroom, located the blankets and returned in under thirty seconds. Margot had called for an ambulance but now was doubled over her wastebasket, gagging. PJ glanced briefly at Cassandra as he reached for the blankets. "See what's wrong with Margot, Cassie."

"But Kurt—"

"Seth and I can take care of Kurt," he told her bluntly. "See what you can do for Margot."

Margot collapsed into Cassandra's arms. Her face had taken on the same ashen hue as Kurt's and she was wringing wet with perspiration, but conscious. Memories of Margot's recent bout with food poisoning sprang to mind as Cassandra carefully lowered the trembling woman to the floor.

Reaching to the desk behind her, Cassandra grabbed a handful of tissues and gently dabbed the perspiration from Margot's face. "You'll be fine," she assured her petite co-worker.

Margot's breathing was becoming labored. "How...is... Kurt?"

Cassandra glanced across the room. Seth was slapping Kurt with greater temerity than she had displayed and shouting at him to stay awake while PJ tore through Kurt's desk. "Fine," she answered shakily. "Seth's with him."

Margot started to gag again and Cassandra rolled her onto her side. After what seemed like hours, but was in reality no longer than fifteen minutes, the ambulance crew arrived. Seeing two patients instead of the one they had expected, they detailed Seth and PJ to bring a second collapsible gurney from the ambulance.

Holding Margot's hand, Cassandra watched as the paramedics made certain Kurt's airway was clear before they slapped an oxygen mask over his face. She tried to follow their conversation as they talked to each other and into the radiophone they had brought with them—it was linked to a hospital, she assumed—but they were too far away.

Seth and PJ burst through the frosted double doors with the second gurney and headed straight for Cassandra. While one of the paramedics was starting an IV in Kurt's arm, his partner hurried toward Margot.

"What's wrong with them?" Cassandra asked the man when he had finished listening to Margot's heart. He looked at her blankly and she fumbled for the French translation of her question.

"Let the man do his job, sweetheart." Seth's hands closed around her arms and lifted her away from Margot.

"I don't understand this," she said, fighting back tears. "Margot was just talking to me. How could she be fine one minute and sick the next?"

Seth wrapped his arms around her. "I don't know." Like her, his mind sought answers and remembered the confusing outbreak in the seventies of what was later termed Legionnaire's Disease.

PJ was still rifling Kurt's desk and Cassandra turned on him. "What do you think you're doing? Leave Kurt's things alone."

The photographer paused and looked up from his task. "Kurt and Margot are being treated by professionals. I am trying to react in a manner that might help our friends, instead of falling apart. If you care about these people, I advise you to do the same," he told her icily. When she glared at him but remained silent, he continued, "Doesn't it strike you as odd that only Margot and Kurt are ill?"

"Of course, but I don't see what that has to do with you going through Kurt's things."

"Wait a minute, sweetheart," Seth advised. "Go on, PJ."

"I was with both of these people last night," PJ informed them as he continued his search of the desk's drawers. "We tied one on, no doubt about it, but we all drank the same thing. So why am I not in the same state as Kurt?" He opened the final drawer. "Answer: they obviously ingested something I did not."

Cassandra forced her mind to ignore the sight of Kurt lying unmoving on the floor. She could help him most by remaining calm. "What about Jules? Margot said he called in sick."

"Jules and his wife did not drink or eat anything different than I did—at least, not while we were together." He slammed the last drawer shut with enough force to shake the entire desk; the action was the only outward sign of his anger. "My guess is Jules is simply suffering from a hangover. These two aren't."

Nodding in agreement, Cassandra brushed at her wet cheeks. PJ's dissertation was interrupted briefly when one of the paramedics questioned him.

"He wants to know if you saw either Kurt or Margot eat anything," he translated for Cassandra.

"No. Kurt was just sitting there, with his head on his desk, and Margot was complaining about her headache."

PJ rapidly translated her answer for the paramedic. The man shrugged and spoke into the radiophone.

"It has to be something they ate," PJ insisted, worrying the ends of his mustache.

"You think it's food poisoning?" Cassandra asked.

"That's as good a theory as any," he conceded. "Their symptoms appeared almost simultaneously, which means whatever they ate, they ate it at about the same time."

"But Margot isn't as bad as Kurt," Cassandra pointed out, her mind starting to function now. "Why?"

The photographer shrugged. "I don't know; maybe she didn't eat as much of whatever was tainted as he did. Or maybe my theory's wrong. Bloody hell!" He delivered a kick to the side of Kurt's desk that tipped Cassandra's mug on its side. "If I didn't know better, I'd *swear* Kurt was poisoned. He has the classic symptoms: vomiting, weak pulse, clammy skin...."

Cassandra stared as her mug rolled off the edge of the desk and shattered against the floor. She shifted her gaze back to the top of the desk. Spilled coffee from her mug pooled around papers and files and was absorbed by the fibers. Kurt's mug lay on its side, adding its contents to the mess. A feeling of indescribable horror spread through her.

"PJ," she whispered, hoping against hope that what she was thinking was impossible. "Did you have any coffee this morning?"

"Sure, three cups."

"From the office pot?"

"No, from my thermos." He scowled at her. "Why?"

On legs that felt as if they were made of wood, she pulled away from Seth and started toward the coffeepot. "Margot said that Kurt made the coffee this morning and that it tasted worse than usual. She only managed one sip. Kurt, however, drank three cups." She stopped in front of the percolator. "What if someone... for some reason, poisoned the coffee?" Turning around, she found the two men regarding her with expressions of dawning comprehension. "It fits your theory, doesn't it, PJ? It fits!"

Seth was the first one to move. He explained Cassandra's theory to one of the paramedics in rapid, precise French while PJ ran to his darkroom. When he returned, he had an empty glass bottle in his hand.

"My developer comes in these," he explained as he filled the bottle with coffee. "I wash them out and keep them. God knows why. It's the pack rat in me, I suppose." When she stared vacantly at him, he grabbed her arm with his free hand and shook her roughly. "Come on, Cassie, stay with me! The hospital can test the coffee to determine what poison was used, but if it's not the coffee, we're going to need you to repeat everything Margot said and did. Oh, hell!"

PJ whirled and strode to where Seth was helping lift Margot onto one of the gurneys. "We're going to need Cassie at the hospital and she's going catatonic on us. See what you can do with her. I'll help our friends here."

Reeling with the shock of what had happened to her friends, Cassandra hadn't heard a word PJ had said. She felt numb; her mind retreated, refusing to accept any further realities. Seth saw the emptiness in her eyes and recognized it; the same emptiness had stared back at him from his reflection in the months following his family's death. The memory flitted through his consciousness, then dissolved. His concern was all for Cassandra now. When he reached her, he pulled her unresisting form into his arms.

"Sweetheart, don't fold up on me; I need you to pick up your purse and get the Mercedes out of the garage." He pulled back far enough to look into her eyes. "Cassandra? Come on, baby. You have to help me. PJ and I can't do this alone."

The emptiness in her eyes reluctantly receded, and was replaced by incredible sorrow. "Oh, Seth."

"Cassandra, I know this is rough, but you have to hang on." Framing her face in his hands, he used his thumbs to brush away the fresh tears rolling from her eyes. "I want you to get the Mercedes and bring it around to the front of the building. Can you do that, sweetheart?"

She nodded shakily.

"Okay." Digging into his pocket, he pulled out the car keys and parking chit and folded her hand around them. "PJ and I are going to help carry Margot and Kurt to the ambulance. You get the Mercedes and meet us in front."

She nodded again, stepped around him and walked to her desk. She deliberately averted her eyes from the sight of her friends lying on the gurneys; if she looked at them, she was sure she would collapse.

She had no memory of leaving the office and running across the street to the garage. One moment she was standing in the office, aware of the obscene mockery of the scent of freshly brewed coffee, and the next she was sliding from underneath the steering wheel of the Mercedes into the passenger seat to make room for Seth. The trip to the hospital remained a merciful blank as well.

Nothing could erase the hours spent in the hospital corridor outside the emergency treatment stalls. Cassandra remained leaning against the wall and chain-smoking while Seth and PJ alternated their time between the treatment stalls and checking on her.

From her place in the hall, she watched through the open doors of the emergency entrance as the rain gave way to full sun. Time was passing, she knew, but it had no meaning, nor did the progress reports PJ and Seth carried to her. She simply waited, constructing a wall of ice around the rage that had begun to build within her.

It was midafternoon before both Seth and PJ emerged from the treatment rooms—the strain of the past few hours stark upon their features—smiling.

"They did it, sweetheart," Seth told her as he scooped her up in his arms and twirled her around. "Margot has been moved to a private room; she'll be released in a couple of days. Kurt is in intensive care, but the doctor says he should recover without any complications."

Cassandra hugged Seth back, "I'm so glad."

"So am I." PJ favored her with one of his rare heart-stopping grins. "Kurt owes me a hundred francs from our last poker game." He raised an eyebrow at the couple's lingering embrace. "If no one has any objections, I'm going home."

"Go ahead," Seth said agreeably. "We'll see you Monday morning. And, PJ," he called when the photographer started to saunter off, "thanks."

"Any time." He raised a hand and continued through the door.

"Kurt's been asking for you," Seth informed her quietly, curling an arm around her waist and leading her down the corridor to the elevators. "I told him I'd bring you up as soon as he was settled."

"How is he?"

"Weak, and he looks like hell, but all things considered, he's in better shape than I thought he would be."

Their stay in the intensive care unit was brief, but long enough to convince Cassandra that Kurt really would live. When he reached for her, his strong hand so frail and trembling in the aftermath of the poisoning, she started to cry.

Kurt smiled weakly. "Some women look seductive when they cry.... Not her."

Cassandra gave a hiccup of laughter through her tears. "Just for that, I'm going to find a snail and put it in your geranium pot again." She held his hand for the few seconds it took for him to fall asleep.

They dropped by Margot's room on their way out. The pretty brunette was pale, but as mad as the proverbial wet hen.

"Who would do such a thing?" she demanded, gesturing so violently with her arm that Cassandra was afraid she would dislodge her IV.

"Some psychopath," Cassandra said. "It takes a sick mind to think of something like this."

"I hope the police find the *cochon*," Margot intoned venomously.

"Margot, do you need anything?" Cassandra asked in an effort to calm her.

Margot informed them that she had already called her parents and they were bringing her things to the hospital. "You both look exhausted," she said. "Go on, get out of here. Seth, you must take Cassandra out for dinner. And order a good bottle of wine," she called as they walked out of the room.

Chapter 10

Do you want to go out for dinner tonight?" Seth asked when they were in the Mercedes.

"No." She stared out her window, feeling the ice around her heart begin to crack.

He turned the ignition key and backed out of the lot. "We'll stop at the market on the way home then," he said when she remained silent. "What sounds good to you?"

She massaged her temples with her fingertips. "I want to call Mitch."

"What?"

"You heard me, Seth; I want to talk to Mr. Wonderful, your so-called security expert. I'd like to thank him for nearly getting two of my friends killed."

"What happened today is not Mitch's fault," he said carefully.

"Oh, of course not. He was just so busy teaching us about bombs and bugs that he forgot to mention poison." Cassandra snorted. "You don't buy that bunch of bull I told Margot about a psychopath, do you?"

"Not exactly."

"Damn right," she muttered angrily. "We both know who's responsible for this, don't we?"

Seth sighed. "It doesn't make any sense for the Brigade to poison the Dateline staff."

"No? Can you think of a better way to get headlines without running any physical risk?" Her hands clenched in her lap. "All the time we thought it was me they were after. It wasn't me; it was us, the entire bureau! If they had pulled it off, they would have been guaranteed headlines from now until Christmas! They would be heroes, for God's sake." The outburst had drained some of her anger and she sank back in the seat. "They almost did it, Seth. If Kurt hadn't drunk so much coffee and if we hadn't been a few minutes late—"

"That's enough of that," he said sharply. "What's important is that the hospital was able to identify the poison and both Margot and Kurt are going to be fine."

"What's important is that those maniacs are running around free," she burst out. "The Sûreté, Mitch—the Brigade fooled them all! We have to do something...."

"I agree, but not now. We're both exhausted. What we are going to do is go home, get something to eat and figure out what to do next."

"We have to tell the Sûreté."

"The Sûreté pulled the taps on our phones, remember? If we go running to Inspector Rocheleau with a wild story about the Brigade trying to poison the Dateline staff—"

"It's not a wild story. It's the truth. Two of our people are in the hospital, for God's sake. How much proof does Rocheleau need?"

"Apparently more than he has, since he's the one who authorized, then pulled, the phone taps." He forced himself to calm down. Shouting at each other wasn't going to settle anything. "Light a cigarette for me, sweetheart."

Cassandra did so. When she handed it to him, he gave her a weary smile. "I'm sorry; I didn't mean to snap at you."

"Don't apologize, it's been a hell of a day for both of us." She reached out to touch his hand. "I just keep thinking this whole thing is my fault. If I hadn't been so insistent on getting this story, the Brigade would have left us alone."

"Don't start thinking that you are responsible for those murderers. They sent you the tape. They called you, not the other way around."

"But if I hadn't been so eager—"

"You're a reporter. No reporter worth the title would willingly walk away from the story of the year."

"You would."

What had he done? Seth asked himself, hearing the guilt in her voice. All the warnings he had given her, his own admissions of guilt, all had returned to haunt him. He had wanted her to drop the story for her own safety, but instead she now blamed herself for Kurt and Margot. Cursing silently, he turned onto a side street and pulled into the first available parking space. Crushing his cigarette in the ashtray, he turned and caught her by the shoulders. "Don't be so sure I would have walked away from this story."

Her eyes filled with tears. "Of course you would have. You did before."

"No. Ten years ago the story was *taken* away from me. It took me months to recover from my injuries and somehow, during the time I spent brooding over my loss, I convinced myself that I was responsible for everything the PRCF did, and I lived with that guilt for ten years."

"But it wasn't your fault!"

"That's right. The responsibility wasn't mine, it belonged to the PRCF." His fingers tightened. "It took me ten years to figure that out. I wasn't responsible then, and you aren't responsible now. Do you hear me? Nothing that has happened is your fault!"

The tears spilled down her cheeks and her slender body shook with sobs as she buried her head in his shoulder. Fear, horror, rage, guilt, all spilled out of her with the shedding of her tears. She felt as if she would cry forever.

Ruthlessly, Seth jerked her upright. "I want to hear you say that you are not responsible for what the Brigade has done." When she only cried harder he gave her a brutal shake. "Say it! I am not responsible for what the Brigade has done."

"I—I—" She choked on her tears, pressed her lips together to try to regain some of her lost control. "Am not r-responsible...."

Her eyes pleaded with him; he felt her pain as if it were his own. He shook his head. "All of it," he ordered, shaking her again, but more gently than before.

"N-not responsible f-f-for the Br-Brigade."

He caught her in his arms, crushing her against his chest. "That's right," he whispered savagely. "You aren't responsible."

He held her close until her tears were exhausted, soothing her with meaningless words and the warmth of his presence. When she had calmed, he lifted her away from his shoulder and smiled tenderly at her ravaged appearance.

"Kurt was right," she said, wiping ineffectually at her cheeks. "I don't look seductive when I cry."

"I don't agree. I find honest emotion seductive as hell."

She gave a weepy laugh. "I don't know about seductive, but it sure is messy." She searched her shoulder bag for the tissues she always carried.

When she unearthed them, Seth took them out of her hand and blotted up the last of her tears. "Seductive," he said firmly. "And I don't want to hear any arguments." He kissed the tip of her nose. "Let's go home."

Cassandra nodded and relaxed into the upholstery. She didn't care where they went, as long as they went there together.

Seth took her straight home and, much to the delight of the concierge and over Cassandra's protests, he lifted her out of the car and carried her up to her apartment. He knew all too well how guilt could drain a person.

Inside the apartment, he carried her into the bedroom, undressed her with loving hands and took down her hair. He found a nightgown in the armoire and slipped it over her head. "You rest, sweetheart. I'm going to make a couple of phone calls and then I am going to prepare the best chicken soup you've ever tasted." He neatly folded the sheet over her.

She caught his hand when he started to leave. "Seth."

He bent over her and smiled. "What is it, love?"

"Thank you."

"Anytime." His black eyes glowed as he brushed a kiss across her lips. "Go to sleep now."

Seth poured himself a hefty portion of Scotch from the bottle he had bought two days earlier and took his drink into the living room. Sinking onto the wicker sofa, he sipped his drink and calmed down before pulling a list of phone numbers out of his wallet and settling in to make the first in a series of calls.

The first person he called was Armand. He told the stringer what had happened and asked if he could come in early to the office today.

"Of course," Armand replied. "If there is anything else I can do—"

Seth suddenly remembered something he and PJ had overlooked. "And, Armand, for God's sake, don't use the coffee in that open can. Put it in my office; the police intend to pick it up this afternoon or tonight."

His next call was to Jules. The stringer was appalled at Seth's story.

"You are certain Margot and Kurt are fine?"

"Yes, Jules, I'm certain. I'm sorry, but I need you to work this weekend since—"

"Do not apologize," Jules protested. "I will open the offices at eight tomorrow morning."

Seth had finished his drink and he definitely felt the need for another. He cracked the bedroom door on his way to the kitchen and found Cassandra fast asleep. Smiling, he poured himself another Scotch, added a handful of ice and returned to the sofa.

It was five o'clock, Paris time, which meant it was noon in New York. With any luck he would catch Tom Burroughs before he left his office for lunch.

The choking noise Tom made when Seth told him what had happened carried clearly over the transatlantic line, as did the ensuing silence. For a moment, Seth was afraid the other man had suffered a heart attack.

"I'm speechless," Tom said at last. "Do the police have any leads?"

Seth glanced at the unblinking red bulb on the phone. "They feel the suspects are obvious—the same people who contacted Ms. Blake."

"I imagine this is going to hit all the wire services tonight," Tom mused. "This is the kind of publicity Dateline can do without."

"I'm sure neither Mr. Leihmann nor Ms. Lemay are exactly thrilled with this latest development."

Tom cleared his throat nervously. "I'm sorry, Seth. Naturally my primary concern is for our staff."

Seth took a long swallow of Scotch before replying. "I need you to authorize another transfer of funds."

Tom's hesitation stretched to a full minute. "Do you really feel that's necessary?"

"If I didn't think it was necessary I wouldn't ask," Seth growled. "Give me a break, Tom; corporate can afford it."

"Your friend comes highly recommended, but he is also high priced."

"You get what you pay for."

Tom coughed. "Yes, of course. Let me get back to you on that. You're at the office?"

"No."

"Ah, I understand. You're still at the hotel, then."

"No, Tom. I've taken an apartment, but I would rather you didn't call back tonight. I plan to have another drink and then go to bed. Call me at the office tomorrow morning. If I'm not there, leave a message with the stringer." He slammed the receiver back on the cradle before Tom could protest. "Jerk."

His last task was to call the number he had used only eight days ago. His call was answered by a man's voice repeating the phone number he had just dialed.

Even though he understood the need for security, Seth still felt a bit silly giving the coded reply. "I would like to place an order for a birthday cake."

"Wait one."

A series of clicks sounded as the call was routed and re-routed to its final destination.

"Yes."

The clipped affirmative was meant to discourage identification, but Seth recognized Mitch's voice. "I am in the clear and without backing. I need a meeting."

There was the briefest of hesitations. "Two a.m., Sunday. Number ten."

The connection was broken.

Exhaling, Seth leaned back in the sofa and downed the last of his drink as he flipped open his wallet and extracted the second slip of paper Mitch had given him at their first meeting. Number ten was Le Train Bleu, a brasserie on the Boulevard Diderot. Seth had been there once several years before; the decor was Belle Epoque; the waiters were very formal, as were the starched white linens on the tables, and the food was mediocre. Its principle attraction was that it was listed in every Paris guidebook and was usually inundated with tourists. In that, it was a perfect place for a meeting.

Seth smiled to himself. If someone had found a way to tap Cassandra's phone and bypass Mitch's red light at the same time, they would have a hell of a time figuring out where the meeting was to be held unless they had a piece of paper identical to the one in his possession—which Mitch had assured him no one did. Each slip was unique, computer generated, and used only once.

No, if the Brigade were listening in, he was about to lead them on a merry chase. Particularly if they were expecting him to leave the apartment at two in the morning on Sunday. Mitch's code system for time and day was to drop back twenty-four hours—which would make the meeting on Saturday—and add twelve for the time—two in the afternoon.

Seth replaced the pieces of paper in his wallet and carried his glass into the kitchen. He quietly let himself out of the apartment and went to the market.

He returned an hour later and prepared the soup. While it simmered, he took a shower, changed into his jeans, and sat and watched the news on television. There was no mention of the poisonings. When the soup was ready, he filled a bowl and carried it into the bedroom.

Setting the bowl on the nightstand, he gently shook Cassandra awake. "Hungry?"

She gave him a sleepy smile and let him pull her upright and plump the pillows behind her back. "I can feed myself," she said around a yawn.

"Let me pamper you, you deserve it." He spooned soup into her mouth.

"What about you? Your day has been every bit as bad as mine—probably worse."

"We can discuss it later. Eat up."

When she was finished, he tucked her back under the covers. She was asleep before he closed the bedroom door.

After eating a bowl of soup, Seth cleaned up the kitchen and filled the coffee maker. It was amazing how comfortable he felt in Cassandra's apartment—their apartment now. They were going to have to discuss sharing the rent and utilities.

He raised an eyebrow when he opened the coffee can and started to measure the coffee into the basket. Was there a possibility that whoever had tampered with the coffee at the office had been here?

Seth shook his head; there was such a thing as being too paranoid. He did, however, trash the open coffee can and its contents, open a new can and use the fresh grounds to fill the basket. He set the timer on the coffee maker and then settled on the sofa and read until ten. Yawning, he checked the door and windows, brushed his teeth, and crawled into bed beside Cassandra. Still sleeping peacefully, she instinctively turned toward him and nestled close. Smiling at the pleasure he derived from just cuddling with her, he touched his lips to her forehead and fell asleep.

They both awoke early on Saturday morning. Cassandra ran a possessive hand through his thick chest hair and kissed his jaw. Grinning, Seth caught the hem of her nightgown, stripped it off in one smooth motion and pinned her beneath him.

"I didn't hear you come to bed."

"That's the way I planned it." He leered at her. "I would, however, like to take advantage of this opportunity to discuss my turn at being pampered."

She slid her foot over the calf of his leg. "Did you have something definite in mind?"

"As a matter of fact—" ducking his head, he ran the tip of his tongue across the tops of her breasts, before continuing "—I had something like this in mind...."

"Oh!" She locked her hands in his hair and guided his mouth. "You have such good ideas."

The only sounds that emerged from the bedroom for quite some time were half-spoken words of passion and need.

"I have to go into the office," Seth told her over a breakfast of fresh orange juice, croissants and coffee. His short, black hair glistened with droplets of water from their shared shower, and he was casually dressed.

"I'll go with you. I need to work on the concert article anyway."

"That's not all." He reached for her hand. "I have another meeting, and I can't take you along."

"Why not?"

"Please, sweetheart, just trust me."

"It really isn't fair," she sighed. "You get that look in your eye and say please and I do whatever you ask."

He smiled. "Thank you."

"May I ask if you're going to see our friend from the château?" It seemed silly to refer to Mitch that way, but unless they were in a public place or in the car, Seth insisted upon discretion.

"Got it in one." He kissed the back of her hand, then turned her hand over and flicked his tongue against her palm.

The breath caught in her throat as she felt the first stirrings of renewed passion.

He watched her reaction through half-closed eyes. "I like what we do to each other. I just have to look at you and I want you so bad that I start aching like a green kid."

"I know. You do the same thing to me."

"How fortunate that we're so compatible."

Cassandra nodded. "When do you have to leave?" she asked wistfully.

He trailed a playful finger along the vee neckline of her robe. "Too soon for what you're thinking," he teased. "But I think we'll stay in tonight."

Aquamarine eyes sparkled wickedly. "In that case, I'm going shopping. Something in black, I think."

"Just don't buy anything that requires a lot of effort. You won't be in it that long."

After Seth left, Cassandra decided she would stop at the hospital before going shopping. Not knowing precisely how long Seth would be gone, she ran the vacuum cleaner over the carpet and dusted.

Dressed in a strapless red sundress and matching red sandals, she piled her hair on the top of her head and applied her cosmetics sparingly before studying her reflection. She looked a little pale, so she added a bit more blusher. Satisfied, she grabbed her shoulder bag and left the apartment.

She had just locked the door when she heard her phone ring. "Rats." She considered ignoring it, but she had never been able to ignore a ringing phone.

By the time she dug her keys out of the bottom of her shoulder bag and unlocked the door she had counted six rings. "Don't hang up," she ordered as she burst into the apartment. She lifted the receiver on the seventh ring. "Hello?"

"Cassandra, it's Armand."

Her annoyance faded. "Is something wrong?"

"No, nothing. I am at a café just a few blocks from your place and I was wondering if you would join me for lunch."

"Armand, ordinarily I would, but I was just on my way to the hospital."

"Is Seth going as well?"

"No, he's at the office." She glanced at her watch. "I'm sorry, Armand, but I'm running late. Maybe another time?"

"I will look forward to it."

Shaking her head at the unexpected invitation she left the apartment before the phone could delay her further. The walk to the Metro was as enjoyable as ever, and Cassandra smiled as she strode briskly along. Yesterday had to be the nadir of her experience with the Brigade, she thought. Surely now the Sûreté would do *something* to catch the terrorists. Seth's refusal to contact Inspector Rocheleau didn't worry her; she was certain Mitch would insist that they notify the Sûreté. Or the Sûreté might already know; the police may have reported the incident to them.

She was nearing the steps to the Metro when a figure came out of nowhere and blocked her path. For a moment she panicked, and then she recognized the man. "Armand!" She laughed. "You gave me a scare. I didn't realize you were so close to the station."

"Come with me, I have a car."

Her smile faltered. "What are you talking about? I told you I don't have time for lunch—" He threw an arm around her shoulders, drawing her up tightly against his side. "What do you think you're doing?" she began angrily, only to feel something very hard jabbed into her ribs.

"I have a gun, and I won't hesitate to use it. Don't try to struggle; don't try to get away; just pretend that we are lovers out for a stroll."

Stunned, she fell into step beside him. "I don't know what this is all about—"

Armand smiled coldly. "You are an ambitious woman. I am certain you'll be pleased to know that you are about to participate in the story of the decade."

"What are you talking about?" To keep him from seeing how badly her hands were shaking, she wrapped them around the straps of her shoulder bag.

"Congratulations, *Mademoiselle*. You are the first prisoner of the Freedom Brigade."

The building's maintenance crew had cleaned the Dateline offices before Armand had arrived on Friday. When Seth came through the double doors, he was assailed by the scent of disinfectant. Jules had opened several windows, but the smell was pervasive.

"Seth, I just took a message for you," the stringer said when he saw his chief.

What now? he thought warily. He wasn't up to dealing with any more shocks. "What is it?" he asked, taking the message slip from Jules.

"The police called. They said to tell you that the coffee grounds tested negative for poison."

"That's impossible. The sample of coffee we took to the hospital was loaded with the stuff."

Jules shrugged and returned to his desk.

Seth went into his office and dialed the number the police had left. The man who answered identified himself as a detective and repeated what Jules had just said.

"Look, detective, I don't mean to tell you your business, but the percolated coffee was poisoned. The hospital tests proved it. One of my people made a fresh pot of coffee yesterday morning, and two of my staff ended up in the hospital, poisoned. The only way they could have been poisoned is if the coffee grounds were poisoned."

"I understand," the detective answered. "But our tests were also conclusive. This tin of coffee is just that—coffee. I suggest you check your supplies to determine if this was the only opened tin."

"Fine. I'll do just that. If I find another opened can I'll call you." Seth pulled a cigarette out of his pocket and lit it as he walked to Jules's desk. "Where do we keep the coffee supply?"

"There is no supply. When a tin is empty, one of us buys another. Everyone takes their turn buying the coffee."

"So there isn't another can around here?"

"No. I am positive there is not because I threw the old one out a week ago. Kurt brought in the last one."

Puzzled, Seth called the detective and relayed the information. In that case, the detective said, whoever poisoned the coffee obviously removed the evidence—unless Monsieur Winter thought that Monsieur Leihmann had poisoned himself.

Seth analyzed the disappearance of the poisoned coffee on his way to meet Mitch. Kurt had definitely not poisoned himself, which meant the detective's first possibility was the right one. Someone had entered the Dateline office, removed the incriminating can and replaced it with another.

That did nothing to limit the field of suspects. All the guards in the building had master keys, as did the maintenance staff. Anyone could have waltzed in and out of that office.

Le Train Bleu was just as Seth remembered it. He was shown to a corner table and five minutes later Mitch arrived.

"Have you ordered yet?"

"No."

Their waiter appeared with the menus and they both ordered the grilled salmon and coffee. Neither of them wanted wine.

Mitch lit a cigarette and leaned back in his chair. "Your people made the morning papers. What can I do for you?"

"First, I have to tell you that I don't have your fee. New York seems to have their doubts about investing any more money in the protection of their Paris staff."

Mitch waved aside the consideration. "In my business, word of mouth is the best advertising—in fact it's nearly the only advertising. If you happen to know anyone who needs a security analyst you can mention my name. Besides, we go back a long time."

"I appreciate it." Without wasting anymore time, Seth brought Mitch up to date.

Their salmon arrived and Mitch waited until the waiter was gone before speaking. "You have trouble, my friend, no doubt about it."

"Why do you think I called you?"

"Miss Blake hasn't received any more tapes or phone calls?"

"Nothing."

"How about at home? Are the two of you close enough that she'd confide in you?"

"You might say that. We're living together."

Mitch smiled briefly. "Congratulations. Okay, let's eat and then get out of here."

When they were finished, Seth paid the bill and joined Mitch on the street.

"The excuse the Sûreté gave for pulling the taps on your phones is that their warrants expired. I don't buy it."

"Look, Mitch, should I close down the Dateline office? These people are after my entire staff!"

"Much as I hate to say it, I think it's time we paid a visit to Rocheleau. But there's one stop I want to make first." The route Mitch had chosen led directly to the gray Mercedes. "I'm glad to see you're taking care of my car."

When they reached the car, Armand dropped all pretense of courtesy. Forcing her to slide under the steering wheel to the passenger seat so that the gun would remain trained on her, he slid in beside her and quickly slapped a pair of handcuffs on her wrists.

"Enjoy the ride, Cassandra," he said as he gunned the car's motor into life. "You're about to meet the leader of the Freedom Brigade."

He pulled into traffic with a great deal of speed and daring, but little competence. At this rate, Cassandra told herself, she wouldn't have to worry about meeting anyone. Armand would get them both killed before they reached their destination.

Armand failed to notice the nondescript brown compact that trailed three car lengths behind them.

Inspector Rocheleau's office was crowded. One of his deputies was standing in front of the door, but between the Inspector and his deputy stood three very large, very angry Americans, one of them the CIA liaison from the American Embassy.

Seth's voice vibrated with fury. "What do you mean you have a man on the inside?"

Rocheleau sighed and motioned them to take a seat. "The Freedom Brigade first came to our attention a little over a year ago. At the time, it was decided to try to plant an officer within their ranks." He folded his hands over his potbelly. "We had a very eager, very capable young man working in another department who badly wanted to work in the counterintelligence end of things.

"As you know, the best cover is always the one that adheres as closely to the truth as possible. We followed that principle. Our man presented himself to the terrorists as a disillusioned member of the Sûreté. In order to prove himself, he had to feed them some information they wanted."

"Half of which was true, half of which was fabrication," Mitch threw in.

Rocheleau appeared insulted. "Nothing quite so favorable to them. The ratio was more like eighty-twenty, in the Sûreté's favor."

"Get on with it," Seth ground out.

"They accepted him into the ranks," the Frenchman continued. "After several months, he told them that certain people were beginning to watch exactly what documents he copied, what areas he wandered through with no legitimate reason."

"Let's cut to the chase," Mitch interrupted again. "Your man, acting panicky, calls the Brigade. The hounds are closing in. He can't last any longer. He's going to have to run." He ground out his cigarette. "And run he does, right into the welcoming arms of the Brigade, his good friends."

Rocheleau nodded. "We used dead drops for several months; the Brigade is very distrusting, so we dared not risk direct contact. And then the leader of the Brigade—we know him only as Mercury—decided his cause needed publicity."

"Which is where the Blake woman came into the picture."

The Inspector glared at Mitch. "I was not aware that the security of this particular operation had been compromised."

Mitch snorted in disgust. "It's an old game, Inspector. I've played it myself a dozen times."

"Why didn't you tell me what was happening?" Seth demanded. "We would have cooperated."

"Ah, yes. But you see, you had no need to know."

Seth's hands flexed. "Who the hell decided that?"

The Frenchman spread his hands. "I did."

"Inspector, just who the hell do you think you are that you can play God?"

"You above all, Mr. Winter, must realize that we have to use every means at our disposal to track down the terrorists."

"Using innocent people is a lousy way to do your job."

The Inspector nodded. "I agree, but we had no choice. Our agent was firmly in place when the violence began. A blessing, as it happens, because Mercury designated our man as the middleman between Mademoiselle Blake and himself."

"And while your man ran messages for Mercury, he could carry his own. The perfect cover. Very nice, Inspector," Greg Talbott said.

"We thought so. Unfortunately, Mr. Winter disrupted all our carefully laid plans when he brought in this gentleman." Rocheleau looked at Mitch with distaste.

"Inspector," Seth said in a soft voice, "since you had a man on the inside, why the hell didn't you just arrest these people?"

Rocheleau sighed. "Unfortunately, since the bomb explosion last week, they have been in hiding. The address we had for them is now a gutted ruin." He lifted his head and met Seth's gaze. "We simply have not known where to find them."

Armand had blindfolded her. She was now inside a van, heading . . . somewhere. She had also been gagged. She was alone, blind and mute and scared out of her wits. Her only hope was that if she did whatever the Brigade asked they would release her alive. She thought of Seth and tears stung her closed eyes. It would be late afternoon before he returned to the apartment and it might be well into the evening before he realized that something was terribly wrong.

The van lurched over some obstacle—a curb, possibly—and she was thrown to the floor. Rough hands lifted her back onto the seat and she squirmed away, pushing herself into the corner.

Mitch grabbed Seth's right arm, Greg the left, when the bureau chief lunged across the desk for the Inspector's throat. The guard started forward but the Inspector waved him back.

"Please, Monsieur Winter, allow me to explain. Before communication was interrupted, our man told us that the Brigade had a member who was active in the press. From what little he was able to learn about this terrorist, and since Dateline was selected by Mercury as his media vehicle, we investigated every member of your staff. We believe that the Brigade member is Armand Pommier."

The ride was over. Cassandra was pushed and pulled out of the van and up a set of four steps. Doors opened and closed and her gag was removed, then the blindfold. She blinked against the brightness of the lamps that illuminated a run-down room with blankets hung over the windows.

A man rose from one of the three chairs in the room and bore down upon her. "Hello, Miss Blake. My name is Mercury." He had black hair and black eyes. Cassandra recognized him from the mug shots that had been televised several months ago when he was wanted for robbing a bank in Switzerland and killing the four people he had taken as hostages and used as human shields. He had disappeared inside France but Interpol had a dossier on him. His *nom de guerre* was Abu, father, and he came from the Middle East.

"We have been following Pommier for several weeks, but he has never led us to the Brigade. Either he does not know where they stay, or he has no need to go there. He will go there today, however."

"How can you be so sure?" Seth demanded, his black eyes narrowing in pure, unadulterated rage.

Rocheleau motioned the guard forward. "Because two hours ago, Pommier kidnaped Cassandra Blake."

This time it took all three men to keep Seth away from Rocheleau.

"What do you want from me?" Cassandra asked, surveying the people in the room.

The man now called Mercury smiled at her. "You are going to be our... object lesson. We could have helped one another; I offered you the opportunity to tell my story to the world. Instead, you talked to the Sûreté and hired a—" he laughed, "—security expert." He pointed to Armand. "Remove the handcuffs."

Cassandra stood quietly, offering her arms to Armand. When she was free of the handcuffs she massaged her wrists. "I repeat, what do you want from me?"

"Tomorrow morning, every paper, news service, television and radio station will receive a taped message, explaining how the world press refuses to portray us as we are—freedom fighters. We will explain how you print government lies and label us murderers, and we have no way to defend ourselves. Then we are going to strap a backpack filled with explosives on you and leave you at the UNESCO building in Les Invalides.'' He leaned close to her face. "And then, journalist, we are going to blow you up!''

Mercury spun away, as if he could not bear the sight of her. "Take her upstairs.''

One of the other men took her arm and led her up a flight of rickety stairs to the second floor. The bedroom he took her to was shabby, but the guard did throw a folded blanket at her.

"Stay here." The guard turned and walked out, locking the door behind him.

Using the blanket for a cushion, she sank to the floor and examined her cell with the aid of the braver particles of sunshine that managed to break through the peeling paint that coated the windows. There was little to see. A mattress sat in the middle of the room, the sole piece of furniture. She leaned against the wall with its torn wallpaper and waited.

Twilight settled over Paris, that enchanted time that is neither day nor night, but a mixture of both. In one of the poorer sections of the City of Light, children played in the streets and on postage-stamp lawns, making the most of the bewitching hour before they had to go in.

As always, vehicles were plentiful. Old cars, bicycles, motorcycles, panel trucks, all noisily announced their right of way and mingled their sounds with laughter and children's screeches.

In an alley behind a particularly disreputable house, a bread truck wheezed to a stop and the driver, cursing the fates that had caused the engine to die, lifted the hood and studied the maze of rubber tubing, metal and wire.

"This is the house,'' one of the men inside the truck told Inspector Rocheleau. "Pommier's car is parked one street over.''

The Inspector spoke into a small microphone. "Disable the pigeon's car.''

At the end of the alley a panel truck waited. Inside, Seth tucked a miniature receiver into his ear and listened attentively to everything that was said by the different Sûreté teams. Behind him, Mitch and Greg were readying their weapons. All three were wearing uniforms identical to those the "hit" teams would wear when they broke into the safehouse.

"All the suspect vehicles are disabled," Seth announced. "Rocheleau's calling the teams up." He picked up the Walther submachine gun he had practiced with that afternoon.

"It would be better if you stayed here," Mitch said, reiterating the statement he had made throughout the afternoon. "Right now you know just enough to be your own worst enemy."

Seth jammed the thirty-two-round magazine into the gun. "Cassandra is in there. I'm going to get her out. And if they've hurt her, if those bastards have—" He couldn't finish the thought; he had refused to listen when anyone suggested the Brigade might already have killed Cassandra. He did not so much as consider the possibility, fearing that if he did, it might become true. He wasn't sure he could survive without her. He cocked the gun. "We better get out there."

Mitch jerked his head and Greg opened one of the rear doors. Officially they were not there, but Greg had persuaded the Inspector to allow the three of them to participate in the raid. It was the least the Frenchman could do, Greg had remarked, after using an American citizen as a sacrificial lamb.

Cassandra roused herself when she heard the key turning in the lock. A strong beam of light raked the room before coming to rest on her face. Wincing, she held her hands in front of her eyes. The flashlight clicked off, leaving her in a blacker darkness now that the light had destroyed her night vision. Someone crept quietly across the floor toward her. She gasped as the flashlight was pressed into her hand.

"Keep this." She recognized the voice. This was the same man who had locked her in the bedroom earlier.

"Who—"

"There is no time. Only listen. Here is a revolver." The grip was pressed into her other hand. "I will leave the door unlocked. Go to the far corner and train the light on the door. When that is done, do not move or cry out. I will return for you if I can. If the man who comes through this door is one of the others, shoot."

He was gone. Cassandra did as she had been instructed, but instead of holding the flashlight, she propped it against the mattress so that the beam was centered on the door. Crouching in the corner, she held the heavy revolver in both hands and regretted that she was going to die before telling Seth how much she loved him.

The three Americans took their positions below the painted window at the back of the house. To reach the second floor, where they assumed Cassandra was held, they would have to traverse the kitchen and a narrow hallway to the staircase, so the owner had told the Sûreté when he was questioned about the layout. Mitch had taken possession of the miniature receiver and was listening to Rocheleau's countdown. When the Frenchman hit five, Mitch raised his left hand, fingers spread. One by one the fingers folded over his palm. When his hand became a fist, Greg jumped up, aimed the grenade launcher at the window and fired. At every first-floor window, percussion grenades shattered the glass and exploded.

The explosion nearly deafened Cassandra even though she was well removed from the impact area. Ten blasts echoed through the house, followed by a moment of stunned silence, and then she heard wood cracking, the pop of small-arms fire and, above it all, voices shouting in French.

"Cassandra Blake, stay down."

"Cassandra Blake, do not attempt to move. We will find you."

"We are the Sûreté, Cassandra Blake. Stay down."

And then a voice as familiar to her as her own overrode the din.

"Cassandra, don't move."

"Seth." She whispered his name, a talisman to keep the fear at bay. Instinct told her to run to him. Love told her to do what he ordered. She forced herself to stay in her corner.

Footsteps pounded up the stairs; the gunfire was closer now and Cassandra raised the revolver.

"You bastard, get away from that door!"

Seth's voice, sounding just outside the door. There was a long series of pops and something heavy hit the bedroom door, knocking it open. A large, masculine frame was trapped in the flashlight beam. Cassandra's finger tightened on the trigger.

"Cassandra?" Seth was blinded by the light, and for one horrible moment that seemed to last a lifetime, he thought that he was too late.

Cassandra was on her feet, crying his name, the revolver falling to the floor, and then she was in his arms, her cheeks assaulted by the scratchy clothing he wore.

Seth held on to her, knowing that his life depended on never letting her go. He kissed her hair, her cheeks, and finally her mouth. The gunfire died away, someone switched on the overhead light and she got a good look at her rescuer. His face was shaded with burnt cork for night camouflage and he was dressed completely in black. Black gloves, black sweater, black trousers, black tennis shoes. The night they'd met, she had dubbed him the Prince of Darkness. She touched his cheek and ran her hands through his black hair, smiled up into his black eyes.

"I love you, Seth."

Chapter 11

The Sûreté was finished with them. They had answered endless questions, given official statements and drunk terrible coffee. Purple shadows lay beneath Cassandra's eyes. She sat beside Seth on the leather couch in Inspector Rocheleau's office, secure within the arm Seth kept around her shoulders.

When they were finally freed, they walked hand in hand through the magnificent lobby without the slightest appreciation of its construction; they had eyes only for each other. Mitch and Greg met them on the sidewalk.

"Miss Blake, I'm Greg Talbott, with the American Embassy. May I say how glad I am that you are unharmed."

Cassandra studied him in the wavering light of the street lamps. "Thank you, Mr. Talbott. You have burnt cork on your forehead."

Mitch howled with laughter and she stared at him, amazed at the depth of emotion he was displaying.

"It's nice to see you again, Mitch. I don't suppose I'm going to learn your last name this time either."

Mitch inclined his blond head. "It would—"

"Be better not to know too much," she finished for him, then offered her hand. "Thank you, Mitch."

"All I did was count backwards from five," Mitch demurred, taking her hand in both of his and shaking it. "Seth here is the one who broke down the back door all by himself." He leaned forward and confided in a rather loud whisper, "He shouldn't do those things at his age. They could keep him in bed for a week."

Cassandra's eyes sparkled. "I sincerely hope so."

"You lucky dog," Mitch said out of the corner of his mouth as he walked past Seth. "Come on, kid. I'll give you a ride to the Embassy."

"You're taking the Mercedes," Seth protested when he saw which car they approached.

"Dynamite reporter," Mitch said to Greg. "Can't slip a thing past him." He grinned at Seth. "It was only a loaner, buddy. Buy your own."

"How are we supposed to get home?"

Mitch raised a hand while he searched his jeans pockets with the other. "Here you go." He tossed a set of keys at Seth. "Your transportation is around the corner."

Seth caught the keys in one hand while holding Cassandra against his chest. Mitch gunned the Mercedes and accelerated into the night.

They walked around the corner and found Seth's compact obediently waiting for them to arrive.

"Quite a comedown," he commented as he handed her into the car.

"I always did think this car had more character than the Mercedes," she said. When he'd slid into the car she smiled at him. "Let's go. I can hardly wait to get to the office."

He turned to stare at her. "The office?"

"Of course. Seth, we have *scooped* the competition on the story of the end of the Freedom Brigade." She leaned toward him and gave him a quick, hard kiss. "Come on, let's go. I already have the opening paragraph."

"You do realize that you could have been killed tonight?"

"I know, but that isn't important right now. What's important is the story, and if you don't get going we will lose our exclusive!"

Shaking his head at her recuperative powers, Seth drove to the Dateline office.

While she typed furiously, Seth filled Jules in on all the details and helped himself to PJ's cache of brandy. It took her less than an hour to finish the article, and Seth read it with a critical eye while she paced behind him.

"Well?" she asked when he stretched and got to his feet. "Seth, what did you think?"

He raised an eyebrow. "This is what you kept me away from our cozy bed for?"

"You don't like it." Suddenly realizing what he had just said, she blinked. "I think you just dangled a participle. Possibly more." She eyed him warily. "Are you drunk?"

"Not yet, but that might not be a bad idea. Jules, would you kindly take Ms. Blake's copy and—"

"No, Seth, I can do a rewrite," she offered, making a grab for her story. "Really, I can tighten it up—"

"Take Ms. Blake's copy," he reiterated, holding her in place with one hand while handing her story to Jules with the other. "And send it as a flash." Her struggles ceased abruptly and she just stared at him in stunned disbelief. "You, sweetheart, just may get that Pulitzer yet."

Cassandra floated on air during their ride home.

"We have to talk, Cassandra," he said when they entered the apartment. Taking her hand, he walked to the sofa, sat down and pulled her onto his lap. "You've been through a lot in the past two days, haven't you?"

"I'd say that's a fairly accurate assessment," she agreed, snuggling against him.

"In fact, since I came to Paris your life hasn't come near to approaching normal."

She pulled back slightly in order to look into his eyes. "I don't think I care for the way this conversation is going." She drew her hand over his cheek and smiled beguilingly. "We're both exhausted. Let's go to bed and talk in the morning."

Seth caught her hand, carried it back to her lap and held it there. "No, Cassandra, we're going to talk now."

The grim set of his features sent a shaft of fear through her and she swallowed convulsively. "Okay."

"Were you scared tonight?"

If this was his idea of a good question he still had a thing or two to learn about the art of making conversation. "Of course I was scared. No, I take that back; I was terrified." She brushed a wayward strand of hair out of her face. "Mercury—Abu, whatever you care to call him—told me that they were going to strap a backpack full of explosives on me and detonate it tomorrow at noon at the UNESCO building in order to show the world how unfairly they have been treated in the press." The fear she had held at bay swamped her now, making her shudder. "I would have debated his rationale, but he wasn't exactly interested in my opinion."

"Damn it, Cassandra!"

She smiled tremulously. "Nice guy, huh?"

Seth gazed at her, felt the shudder that ran through her again. She had been through so much tonight, it would be easier not to force the issue now. He could wait for a few more days, give her time to readjust to her normal life.... No, he told himself. It wouldn't be fair to either of them to wait.

"In that case, I'm glad I killed the son of a bitch," he said feelingly, unconsciously tightening his hold on her hand.

Compassion for Seth momentarily overrode her fear of where their conversation was headed. "That must have been horrible for you."

"I don't enjoy the idea of taking a life but truthfully, sweetheart, I can't regret keeping a murderer like him away from you." He cocked an eyebrow at her. "Surprised?"

She nodded. "You're not a killer."

"Ordinarily, no, but I carried a rifle for twelve months in Vietnam, and I used it. I'd kill anyone who tried to harm me or mine."

"I understand."

"Do you?" He released her hand and caught her chin in his hand. "Cassandra, do you remember what you said to me tonight in that bedroom?"

Fear descended with a heavy hand. She had pushed him too far, too fast, and he was telling her he was not prepared for the kind of commitment she was ready to make.

"Cassandra?"

She blinked away the threatening tears, forcing herself to meet his gaze just as she had forced herself to remain in that corner in the bedroom. "Yes, Seth, I remember. I said I loved you."

The crushed tone of her voice appalled him. He shouldn't have pushed tonight. Given another few weeks it was possible she would come to truly love him instead of confusing that emotion with gratitude.

"It's all right, you know," she said finally.

He frowned. "I don't understand."

"I know you don't love me—might never love me." She shrugged. "I just want *you* to know that I don't expect any kind of commitment from you, but if you would just stay—"

"Did you mean it?"

"What?"

He gave her a gentle shake. "Did you mean it when you said you loved me?"

"Of course I meant it!" Fear transmuted into anger. "I don't run around saying that to everybody!"

"Oh, sweetheart, I'm so glad. I love you so much I think I would have died if you hadn't meant it."

A slow smile curved her lips. "You love me?"

"I thought that's what I said." He rose with her in his arms and carried her into the bedroom. "But I want to show you how much I love you."

He stripped the red dress off, following its path with his hands and mouth. He worshiped her, adored her, and he whispered his love while his body communicated its own need. She cried again, this time because she was free to express her love and the joy she found with him. Heaven had to be like this. They came together in a fiery union that both seared and joined their souls.

"I love you," he said as they nestled together. "I can't even contemplate a life without you."

"You don't have to," she whispered, stroking his cheek. "Because I'll always be at your side."

Dateline News Service
Wins Pulitzer

By Kurt Leihmann
Dateline News Service

PARIS—On the list of Pulitzer Prize winners announced this week was the name of Cassandra Blake-Winter. Ms. Blake-Winter won the Pulitzer for a seven-part series detailing the birth and death of the terrorist organization known as the Freedom Brigade.

Ms. Blake-Winter has been an employee of Dateline News Service for four years and has had assignments in Dateline's London and Paris Bureaus.

When contacted by telephone at her home, Ms. Blake-Winter stated, "I am overwhelmed by the award. Winning the Pulitzer has been a dream for so long that I find it hard to believe it has really happened."

Ms. Blake-Winter is married to Seth Winter, another Pulitzer Prize winner, who until last month was the Paris bureau chief for Dateline News Service.

Mr. Winter resigned his position in order to accept a professorship at the Columbia School of Journalism. Ms. Blake-

Winter is currently on maternity leave, expecting their first child.

* * * * *

Silhouette Intimate Moments

COMING NEXT MONTH!

LIEUTENANT GABRIEL RODRIGUEZ
in
Something of Heaven

From his first appearance in Marilyn Pappano's popular *Guilt by Association*, Lieutenant Gabriel Rodriguez captured readers' hearts. Your letters poured in, asking to see this dynamic man reappear—this time as the hero of his own book. Next month, all your wishes come true in *Something of Heaven* (IM #294), Marilyn Pappano's latest romantic tour de force.

Gabriel longs to win back the love of Rachel Martinez, who once filled his arms and brought beauty to his lonely nights. Then he drove her away, unable to face the power of his feelings and the cruelty of fate. That same fate has given him a second chance with Rachel, but to take advantage of it, he will have to trust her with his darkest secret: somewhere in the world, Gabriel may have a son. Long before he knew Rachel, there was another woman, a woman who repaid his love with lies—and ran away to bear their child alone. Rachel is the only one who can find that child for him, but if he asks her, will he lose her love forever or, together, will they find *Something of Heaven*?

Next month only, read *Something of Heaven* and follow Gabriel on the road to happiness.

Silhouette Intimate Moments
Where the Romance Never Ends

IM294-1

"GIVE YOUR HEART TO SILHOUETTE" SWEEPSTAKES
OFFICIAL RULES

NO PURCHASE NECESSARY TO ENTER OR RECEIVE A PRIZE

1. To enter and join the Silhouette Reader Service, rub off the concealment device on all game tickets. This will reveal the potential value for each Sweepstakes entry number and the number of free book(s) you will receive. Accepting the free book(s) will automatically entitle you to also receive a free bonus gift. If you do not wish to take advantage of our introduction to the Silhouette Reader Service but wish to enter the Sweepstakes only, rub off the concealment device on tickets #1-3 only. To enter, return your entire sheet of tickets. Incomplete and/or inaccurate entries are not eligible for that section or section (s) of prizes. Not responsible for mutilated or unreadable entries or inadvertent printing errors. Mechanically reproduced entries are null and void.

2. Either way, your Sweepstakes numbers will be compared against the list of winning numbers generated at random by computer. In the event that all prizes are not claimed, random drawings will be made from all entries received from all presentations to award all unclaimed prizes. All cash prizes are payable in U.S. funds. This is in addition to any free, surprise or mystery gifts that might be offered. The following prizes are awarded in this sweepstakes:

(1)	*Grand Prize	$1,000,000	Annuity
(1)	First Prize	$35,000	
(1)	Second Prize	$10,000	
(3)	Third Prize	$5,000	
(10)	Fourth Prize	$1,000	
(25)	Fifth Prize	$500	
(5000)	Sixth Prize	$5	

*The Grand Prize is payable through a $1,000,000 annuity. Winner may elect to receive $25,000 a year for 40 years, totaling up to $1,000,000 without interest, or $350,000 in one cash payment. Winners selected will receive the prizes offered in the Sweepstakes promotion they receive.
Entrants may cancel the Reader Service privileges at any time without cost or obligation to buy (see details in center insert card).

3. Versions of this Sweepstakes with different graphics may be offered in other mailings or at retail outlets by Torstar Corp. and its affiliates. This promotion is being conducted under the supervision of Marden-Kane, Inc., an independent judging organization. By entering this Sweepstakes, each entrant accepts and agrees to be bound by these rules and the decisions of the judges, which shall be final and binding. Odds of winning are dependent upon the total number of entries received. Taxes, if any, are the sole responsibility of the winners. Prizes are nontransferable. All entries must be received by March 31, 1990. The drawing will take place on April 30, 1990, at the offices of Marden-Kane, Inc., Lake Success, N.Y.

4. This offer is open to residents of the U.S., Great Britain and Canada, 18 years or older, except employees of Torstar Corp., its affiliates, and subsidiaries, Marden-Kane, Inc. and all other agencies and persons connected with conducting this Sweepstakes. All federal, state and local laws apply. Void wherever prohibited or restricted by law.

5. Winners will be notified by mail and may be required to execute an affidavit of eligibility and release that must be returned within 14 days after notification. Canadian winners will be required to answer a skill-testing question. Winners consent to the use of their name, photograph and/or likeness for advertising and publicity in conjunction with this and similar promotions without additional compensation. One prize per family or household.

6. For a list of our most current major prizewinners, send a stamped, self-addressed envelope to: WINNERS LIST, c/o MARDEN-KANE, INC., P.O. BOX 701, SAYREVILLE, N.J. 08871

If Sweepstakes entry form is missing, please print your name and address on a 3" × 5" piece of plain paper and send to:

In the U.S.	In Canada
Sweepstakes Entry	Sweepstakes Entry
901 Fuhrmann Blvd.	P.O. Box 609
P.O. Box 1867	Fort Erie, Ontario
Buffalo, NY 14269-1867	L2A 5X3

LTY-S69R

COMING NEXT MONTH

#293 BORROWED ANGEL—
Heather Graham Pozzessere

When Ashley Dane witnessed a murder, she was forced to rely on Eric Hawk for protection. But danger followed him, and he wanted to free himself of Ashley—until he discovered that he could not let her go!

#294 SOMETHING OF HEAVEN—
Marilyn Pappano

Rachel Martinez had needed love and support; what she got from Gabriel Rodriguez were accusations and betrayal. Now, five years later, they are forced to work together again. Can trust—and love—be rekindled after so much time?

#295 THREAT OF EXPOSURE—
Doreen Roberts

Cade Warner's investigation of a friend's mysterious death led him to sensitive, warm and giving Eden Granger. Cade felt drawn to her, but not only did he have to protect her from the killer, he had always shied away from commitment, too. Could love conquer his fears?

#296 WISH GIVER—Mary Lynn Baxter

Cort McBride agreed to help Glynis Hamilton and their natural son on one condition: that they move in with him on his ranch. Distance and time had made them forget how drawn Cort and Glynis were to each other. But once together, long-dormant passions were awakened, leaving them both wondering how they could be quelled....

AVAILABLE THIS MONTH:

#289 TIGER DAWN Kathleen Creighton	**#291 ABOVE SUSPICION** Andrea Edwards
#290 THE PRICE OF GLORY Lynn Bartlett	**#292 LIAR'S MOON** Mary Anne Wilson

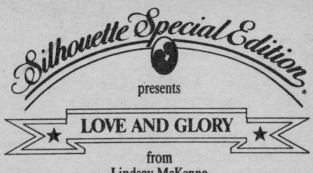